KT-496-323

Praise for *Ridley Road*

'Bloom has uncovered an episode in London's history that deserves to be better known, and her research has thrown up some appalling events ... the subject matter alone makes for a thought-provoking read'   *Independent on Sunday*

'A vivid, cinematic and exciting debut' *Red* magazine 'Book of the Month'

'A tale of love and morality set in the dark side of the Swinging Sixties'   *The Lady*

'Well-researched, convincingly evocative of an exciting era and covers events of which most people will have little awareness. It's also a timely warning against the dangers of the insidious rhetoric against people of a different race or nationality, which is rearing its ugly head once again'
    Daily Mail

'A stirring story of the darker side of the '60s' *Sunday Mirror*

'Bloom captures the vibrant '60s London scene brilliantly: the music, the clubs and the fashions ... Bloom blends the facts with the fiction to create a fast-paced story which is part-romance and part-thriller'   *Jewish Chronicle*

'The novel presents a vivid portrait of London in 1962 ... this heartening picture of ordinary, bustling life acts as a foil to the dark seam of the National Social Movement's fascist activity, whose horrors are increasingly exposed throughout the novel ... a compelling, worthwhile read, as well as a fitting homage to the bravery of the 62 Group'
    Jewish Quarterly

'*Ridley Road* is a really interesting and thought-provoking read ... there are a lot of novels set in London in this period, but *Ridley Road* felt like a story I hadn't come across before. I'll be looking out to see what Jo Bloom writes about next'

Novelicious

'The 62 Group were a real organisation, as were the two fascist groups mentioned in the novel. It's a little-known aspect of Britain's history and it brings a great deal of drama to Bloom's story, as well as social interest. These are unpleasant and shocking politics to explore, but they are handled well. At the lighter end of the social history scale, *Ridley Road* also conjures a great picture of Soho's early-Sixties jazz-and-caffeine buzz'

Emerald Street

'While the love story draws readers into the novel, it is the growing tension and drama of the political and social contexts that make this a really gripping read'

We Love This Book

'It's a tribute to Bloom's lightness of touch that her story is so absorbing'

A Life in Books

Jo Bloom has worked as a freelancer in the communications field for the past fifteen years with a focus on arts publicity and e-learning. She also contributed to the book review section of *Time Out London* for a few years. Prior to this she lived and worked in Prague and New York. She was inspired to write *Ridley Road* when she met a Jewish anti-fascist who had lived in the East End all his life and participated in numerous street battles with the fascists alongside both the 43 Group and the 62 Group. She lives in Brighton with her husband and young son.

Ridley Road

JO BLOOM

WEIDENFELD & NICOLSON

A W&N PAPERBACK

First published in Great Britain in 2014
by Weidenfeld & Nicolson
This paperback edition published in 2015
by Weidenfeld & Nicolson,
an imprint of Orion Books Ltd,
Carmelite House, 50 Victoria Embankment,
London EC4Y 0DZ

An Hachette UK Company

9 10 8

Copyright © Jo Bloom 2014

The right of Jo Bloom to be identified as the author
of this work has been asserted by her in accordance with
the Copyright, Designs and Patents Act 1988.

All rights reserved. No part of this publication may be
reproduced, stored in a retrieval system, or transmitted,
in any form or by any means, electronic, mechanical,
photocopying, recording or otherwise, without the prior
permission of the copyright owner.

All the characters in this book are fictitious, and any
resemblance to actual persons living or dead
is purely coincidental.

A CIP catalogue record for this book
is available from the British Library.

ISBN 978-1-7802-2824-2

Typeset by Deltatype Ltd, Birkenhead, Merseyside

Printed and bound in Great Britain by Clays Ltd, Elcograf S.p.A.

The Orion Publishing Group's policy is to use papers that
are natural, renewable and recyclable products and made
from wood grown in sustainable forests. The logging and
manufacturing processes are expected to conform to the
environmental regulations of the country of origin.

www.orionbooks.co.uk

This book is for the members of the
43 Group and the 62 Group
&
for those individuals who continue to fight fascism

Hackney, East London

Friday, 8 June 1962

I

Now that she had arrived, Vivien kept wanting to go home. She couldn't smile. She was quiet and distracted. The moment the landlady shut the door, she slapped the rent book on the mantelpiece and sank into the armchair by the fire, holding her forehead. For weeks all she'd dreamed of was being in London and being close to Jack again, but nerves kept taking over and changing how she felt.

She pulled off her gloves and sat for a while, smoking a cigarette and staring down at her lap until she felt better in herself. She wanted to be here. She just had to get used to it, which she would, she knew, because she'd had to get used to far worse.

She stood up, stared at her reflection in the wall mirror and reminded herself that this was her doing. Her decision to pack up and come. She nodded to acknowledge this, then, wincing at the squeak of the lino as she quickly re-pinned her hair, she slipped off her shoes and walked across the room in stockinged feet.

The landlady, Mrs Levy, had stood by the bed and talked her through the household rules but the one thing she hadn't shown Vivien was the view from the window. The mahogany dressing table was crammed tight into the bay, its dull and scratched surface scattered with numerous items a lodger might need. Folded white sheets. A hot-water bottle. A bar of lavender-scented soap.

Vivien reached over, lifted up the starchy net curtain and

looked out. A boy was riding his bicycle up and down the street. On the pavement opposite a young girl sashayed along in her red ruffled skirt like a worn-out cancan dancer and waved at the policeman strolling by. Under the only tree on the street two elderly men pushed a pricey-looking dresser into the back of a van as the afternoon sun filtered down between the leaves.

But nothing else was going on. None of the comings and goings that sometimes had Vivien and her neighbours glued to their front windows back home.

A telephone rang downstairs as she picked her suitcase off the floor and put it on the bed, then popped it open and rummaged between her nylons for the letter Jack had sent Dad.

Just holding the envelope made her feel sick again. For a moment it made her think about catching the train back to Manchester, back to everything that was familiar. And she could. She could go wherever she wanted. There was no one to keep her here, to make her stay.

2

Unpacking took no time. Four old, worn summer dresses – one skilfully patched in two places – and a few skirts, shirts and jackets to hang up in the creaky oak wardrobe. After she'd folded cardigans and underwear neatly in the chest of drawers, there was still plenty of space and she hoped she'd brought enough with her.

She'd packed and repacked three times, unsure what to take, wishing Jack could have been there to advise her. He'd only just turned twenty-four but he knew about travelling. Rimini last summer with friends; Paris the spring before. He didn't like to boast, so she had to force him to tell her about the dizzying views from the top of the Eiffel Tower or sleeping away an afternoon on white silky beaches, and when he lost himself in his memories, she liked the way his voice turned sweet like honey.

Only her blue coat remained in the case. Vivien lifted it out gently, then removed the framed picture tucked inside the sleeve. In the photo her dad was flanked by the rabbi and the cantor outside their shul. Dad was the shortest by some inches, with smooth walnut-brown hair, perfectly clipped sideburns and a beard that needed trimming.

The tumour in his stomach had not yet been discovered. He looked strong. He wasn't stooping. He wasn't using a cane. He wore his usual dark blue waistcoat and white shirt, and his eyes were cast slightly to the right as if he were trying to avoid the lens. He hated being in front of a camera. He wasn't shy, he just didn't like the fuss.

Vivien held the picture on her lap for some time, then wiped her fingerprints off the glass and propped it up on the bedside table. It was a favourite picture, and she needed him close by.

It had been nearly three months since she had found him dead in his sleep and she'd stopped pretending that the news was not real. She knew he was gone – her mind had come to terms with this – but she still thought of him all the time. She preferred to picture him before he became ill: the weight of his small pudgy hands pressing on her shoulders when he said how proud her mum would have been of her, the way he whispered Yiddish songs to himself in the kitchen when making a cup of tea. She liked to remember him sitting in his armchair, feet on the pouffe, blowing at the orange tip of his cigar in small, hurried breaths to keep it lit, and how, when he went outside to smoke on the front step, one of their neighbours would often stroll out and join him.

But at night she lost control over her thoughts. She dreamed of finding him cold in bed, the sight of the blank-faced undertaker and his son in their raincoats and polished shoes taking him away. In these dreams she ran down the street in her nightdress after the disappearing car, then stood, hands pressed against her cheeks, whispering into the chilly morning, 'Who will I tell about my life? Who will care?'

She snipped the air with her new scissors, a parting gift from Leo, and decided they would sit nicely between her perfume spritz and the glass jar of hairpins on the dressing table. Dearest Leo. Never bought her so much as a sticky bun in four years, then gave her these and threw her a surprise shindig at the salon. Cashed up early one afternoon, changed into a fresh shirt and ushered in her regular clients for home-made Victoria sponge and a glass of Babycham.

For a while she'd glided around, clutching warm hands and breathing in eau de cologne, but the more the salon had filled, the less she had believed she was actually leaving. She'd had to stand alone by the hood driers for a few minutes and drink it all in. A couple of dozen women in their best frocks. Yellow balloons tied to the backs of the salon chairs. Her best friend Stella topping up everyone's glass. All of this for her.

Dad had never respected Leo's stinginess but he'd have shaken his hand for making such an effort, and she recalled the strong wave of longing for Dad and Jack that had caught her off balance at the party. She was still swallowing it down when Leo had grabbed her and fastened her to his side. Clapping his hands, he asked for quiet to make a toast.

'I didn't want Vivien to go,' he'd started off saying. He brushed his thin blond moustache with the side of his finger. 'I refused to make it easy for her.'

A round of amused laughter set everyone off but Leo was serious. He'd given Vivien the cold shoulder for two days after she told him she was off to London, then strode in and offered her double wages and every other Tuesday off. She was backcombing Mrs Humphrey at the time, and when she calmly met his stare in the mirror, his lips had parted and he had sighed. He knew whatever he offered would not be enough. She'd learned all she could from him.

Since her apprenticeship had finished two years earlier, just after her eighteenth birthday, it had been only her, Leo and a junior tending to the needs of the local women, many of whom were much older than Vivien, and came for a weekly wash and set and the chance to be pampered. Occasionally one of them might accept Vivien's suggestion for an alternative colour or a new style with a little flourish, a little more panache, but usually the idea of change appalled them and they batted her away. They felt more confident leaving the salon looking exactly the same each time.

So she listened to them. She put their hair in rollers, then brushed it out and sprayed it solid. She did it expertly and willingly; she put her best self into every task. But when the ladies patted her cheek gratefully and stuck a tip in her hand, her smile always felt mechanical. A bit false. They didn't know she had spent the entire appointment imagining herself in a fancy London salon, where her reputation meant clients asked for her by name and embraced her style suggestions. Where her boss would enter her for international competitions, convinced she would win. Where it was not uncommon for her clients to fill the pages of a fashion magazine.

This was pure fantasy, of course. A way of passing time as the days ran dully into each other. The truth was she'd happily settle for a job where her clients were a little younger and less predictable, and where every now and again she was afforded the chance to transform someone and amaze them with their reflection.

These thoughts never frightened her. She was good enough. She just needed the chance to prove it.

Day was disappearing. As the last arrows of lemony-pink sunlight coloured the room, Vivien lit a cigarette and looked around.

Nothing could be done about the oppressive wallpaper, purple with yellow and white daisies, and the heavy greenish curtains, but the uninspiring watercolour of a rabbit sitting near a warren would soon be hidden under her bed. Rabbits were something of an unappealing theme in the house. She'd already noticed several porcelain rabbits on display downstairs and the yellow crochet bunny hanging from a nail above the toilet cistern.

But she was glad of the bits of furniture, the overstuffed armchair and little Ercol coffee table in particular. It was easy to picture Jack sprawled out by the fire, long legs crossed at the ankles, scribbling away in his notebook – the idea of it made her smile gently to herself. There was something right about this room, as if it was already a natural extension of her. Best of all, it was only two streets away from Mary Drake's boarding house where Dad had lodged when he used to visit London. Vivien had telephoned Mary weeks ago but learned that she too had recently died and her son was selling the house. Undeterred, Vivien still made her way to Hackney, trailing up and down the main streets with her suitcase until she came across Mrs Levy's neat card stuck in a tobacconist's window.

She moved the fireguard carefully, conscious of every noise. Her presence in the house mustn't disturb Mrs Levy or set her on edge – this place was such a find, Mrs Levy could have her pick of decent lodgers. Vivien couldn't say the same about the guest house near Euston station which she'd randomly chosen on the night she arrived. She had barely slept, lying wide-eyed and wary on the hard bed with her side lamp on, staring at the scrappy handwritten warnings on the wall about noise levels and NO GUESTS and heavily underlined reminders about not wasting water, while a Spanish couple in the next room argued in between making love, and the man above her stamped around like he had concrete in his shoes.

She stubbed out her cigarette and stared again at the chair where Jack would sit. She missed him tonight. He was often in her head, like he was watching her while she went about her day, but sometimes he took over completely and made it hard for her to think about anything else. Sometimes he made it hard for her to breathe.

She had felt like that the first time they met in her front

room, four months ago, when Dad was still here. She'd glimpsed the back of him on the settee first, but then he had turned, smiled, and said, 'I'm Jack,' before Dad had had a chance to introduce them. 'Jack Fox.'

'Pleasure,' she'd said, flushing a little, loosening her grey scarf away from her neck.

She had immediately registered his good looks. Reddish-brown hair. Long body and broad shoulders. Eyes as dark as treacle, dominating a lovely lean face. He was by far the most appealing man she'd seen in a long time.

'I thought you were out tonight,' said Dad.

'I was.' She put her handbag down on the piano seat. 'Stella's got a migraine.'

'Another one? She told me she'd been in bed all day Wednesday. Poor cow,' he said affectionately. 'And with three kiddies.' He shook his head.

Vivien had nodded sympathetically. Stella and Vivien, born a day apart on the same hospital ward twenty years ago, had always been close, even after Stella got married on her seventeenth birthday and had three children in quick succession. 'I offered to look after them, but her mum's over there.'

Catching Jack's gaze on her, she had flushed slightly, and her body felt unsteady and faint, as if his presence had leaked into every corner of the room and sucked up all the air. Turning away to unbutton her jacket while Jack told Dad about his auntie's terrible nausea-inducing migraines, Vivien wondered where he was from. Dad often invited people back from the shul, visitors who heated up soup in the kitchen or hogged the bathroom for hours. Strangers with rucksacks and fascinating life stories but no money, nowhere else to go.

But not him, she thought, stealing another look at Jack. Not this one with his impeccably cut suit, clean fingernails and short, tidy hair – nothing like the local boys, bulging in their cheap trousers, hair plastered solid behind their ears. This one had somewhere to be.

'Jack's come on the train from London,' said Dad. 'He needs to pick my brains for a book he's writing.' For the past fifteen years Dad had taught history at the local school, but he was better known for his political articles and columns that made their way into journals and newspapers.

'Have you been to Manchester before?' she asked Jack.

He shook his head. 'But I plan to have a good look around.'

When he mentioned an interesting article he'd read on the architects of the new CIS Tower, she had soaked up his deep polished voice. His eyes had moved easily between her and Dad; he appeared relaxed and comfortable. He was neither under-confident nor did he act like he had to show off and prove himself, unlike Tommy, her last boyfriend, who liked to dominate every conversation.

'How long are you here for?' she asked.

Jack glanced at Dad. 'Not sure. A few days.'

Dad was hunched over, rubbing his side, wincing.

'Shall I run you a bath?' she asked him.

'I'll go up in a minute. Thanks, love. I'm not quite the force of nature I used to be,' he explained to Jack. 'This afternoon I dozed off in the after-school Hebrew classes I run at the shul. I woke to find the classroom empty except for two boys sticking bits of apple peel in my beard.'

The instant Jack threw back his head and roared along with Dad, Vivien wanted him for herself. She wanted to hear him laugh as he lifted her up and held her against him.

'We'll see each other tomorrow, yes?'

'Yes, sir.'

'Call me Phil, please. Vivien will walk you round to the

guest house,' he said, adding to Vivien, 'I've booked Jack
into Denise's.'

Jack looked sideways at Vivien. 'If it's not putting you
out.'

When he smiled, she had to turn away.

'Not at all,' she had said stiffly and got up, her heart
beating that little bit faster.

She could still remember how strong and low the moon
was that night as it cast their shadows along the pavement.
She had wanted to look away and glance at Jack but she
wasn't brave enough.

'It's a quiet street at night,' he said. 'I like that. You can
walk and think.'

She'd never been to London but she guessed it would
be bursting with life. When she thought of the city, she
imagined the lights never fading, the din of the streets
never letting up. Cars and bikes everywhere, trains zigzag-
ging beneath the ground as thousands of people scuttled
through the city's arteries, always in a hurry, always trying
to beat time.

'Where are you from in London?' she asked.

'Whitechapel, in the east. But we moved to Golders
Green in the suburbs last summer when some of my mum's
cousins and other families from the shul moved out there.'
He shrugged. 'I like it just fine. I'm not there much.'

'I want to work in London one day,' she announced after
a pause.

'You should. It's quite the city.'

'In a hair salon,' she said dreamily. Noticing him staring
at her, she straightened up. 'I'm good enough.'

'I bet you are.'

She stopped walking and frowned. 'You're laughing at
me.'

'No.' Jack shook his head. 'I wouldn't do that. I mean it. I bet you're good at everything you turn your hand to.'

She held her chin up and looked ahead. 'Well, I don't know about that.'

Jack placed his hand on her sleeve. 'Really,' he said quietly. 'I wouldn't laugh at you,' and when he removed his hand, she wanted him to put it back.

'I'm not good at sewing,' she said. 'I've not got the patience for it.'

'I don't blame you. It looks fiddly. What would you rather do?'

'Anything else.'

'Like?'

'Dancing. I'm mad on dancing.'

'I bet you're good at that.'

'I'm not bad. Do you dance?'

'Nope.' He didn't look too sad about it. 'It's not for me. Born too big and clumsy.' He moved his arms and legs around as if he could hear music playing. 'See? I look like a big bird trying to take flight.'

'You might be right,' she giggled.

After their laughter died away, they walked on for a bit without talking.

'I really do want to go to London one day ...' she said. 'And when I've got more experience under my belt, I might even try to get a job at Vidal Sassoon's.'

'Really?' Jack looked impressed.

'Dad knows Vidal. He hasn't seen him in ten years but he said he'd try and pull a few strings for me.'

'I hope it happens. That would be something.'

'What are you writing about, if you don't mind me asking?'

A light came on behind curtains in an upstairs room. They both glanced up. 'Post-war stuff ...' Jack faltered.

'Politics.' He smiled apologetically at her. 'Probably sounds very dull to you.'

She shook her head. 'Not at all.'

'Your dad's pretty ill, isn't he?' said Jack unexpectedly.

She chewed her bottom lip and nodded.

'He wanted to meet me in London. He'd planned to go to one of Mosley's meetings.'

She nodded again. 'He's been talking about it for ages, since Mosley started appearing in public again. But it was too much for him ...' her voice trailed off.

'It's better that he rests. Looks after himself.'

He was kind and she liked that. She tried to smile. 'Is it? He feels useless. I can see it in his face.'

She stared at the pavement again. Do not cry, she told herself, heat stinging her eyes. Do not cry in front of him.

She looked up and, seeing Denise's house ahead, slowed her last few steps, willing Jack to ask her something else. More than anything she wanted to delay knocking, convinced that Denise's youngest, Ruth, one of the pushiest girls on the street, would come to the door with her milk-white chest squeezed into a low-cut top, ready to pounce on Jack.

But Jack didn't seem to notice her standing in the hallway, rearranging her long blonde hair over her shoulders like a cape. Instead he ran his hand over his jaw and didn't take his eyes off Vivien.

'I'm never good at this bit,' he said quietly.

'At what?'

He rubbed his jaw even harder, then stretched his arms out nervously as he spoke. 'Do you have time to show me the sights this weekend?'

Jack had stayed for nine days, six days longer than intended, and they met up every day. They took buses around the city, ambled down streets she'd never been down before and sat in coffee bars for hours, talking. She taught him dominoes. He taught her chess. He took her to see *Jules et Jim* at the pictures and didn't make her feel foolish because it was the first French film she'd seen. She made him come dancing with her and Stella, and didn't mind when he spent most of the night leaning against the bar, staring at her. She liked looking over at him, feeling he belonged to her.

They told each other things they had never told anyone else. She said that she felt ashamed for not remembering much about Mum. How for years after Mum's death she would occasionally wake in the night to the sound of Dad's muffled sobs, but didn't know if she should go to him. And, in an embarrassed voice, she admitted that she had always been troubled by her flat chest and non-existent hips, and couldn't bear how easily her fair, papery skin bruised.

In turn, Jack told her that he was a twin but his brother had died five days after he was born. He had once watched his school friends taunt a girl in a wheelchair until she broke down and cried, but he hadn't intervened or stopped them. It took him a while to admit that he did love his dad, but loving his mum came far more easily.

Soon she could list the countries he'd visited. She knew the towns where he'd stayed and how he'd filled his time and why Italy was his favourite country. He loved modern jazz and the writings of Jack Kerouac, but he would never have been one of those beatniks. He took his tea milky and with three sugars but liked his coffee bitter and black. The summer after he turned eighteen he had contracted polio but swiftly recovered. He was a keen long-distance runner. His skin was smooth and clear except for a cluster of three birthmarks on his clavicle, and if he didn't shave every day a fleck or two of grey showed up in his auburn stubble. He hadn't cried in six years.

Yet, regardless of the truths they'd learned about each other, they had still not kissed. Twice he had bobbed his face close to hers, leaned in and stared longingly at her lips; so sure it was about to happen, Vivien's stomach had clenched. But both times he had recoiled with a brusque shake of his head as if he were chastising himself, and she had been left red-faced and wanting.

In its absence she had spent hours imagining what his kiss would be like. She would be at work and suddenly remember the weight of his arm pressing against hers at the pictures, or the feel of his hand cupping the small of her back as he guided her through a busy street, and desire would force its way into every bit of her. Her knees would weaken. She would feel warm and slightly sick. And she would inevitably forget what she was doing.

On the sixth day, under a bridge by the canal, he had turned his face to her, then turned it away again, muttering to himself. But this time he had swung back, held her against the wall and kissed her furiously in the echoing darkness. Afterwards, he buried his face in her hair and they held each other, laughing quietly. He pressed his hands on her shoulders, then lifted up her hair and massaged the back of her neck with his long, strong fingers. 'This means something,' he had said. And when he kissed her nape, a spot where no one else's lips had ever been before, she knew he was really saying, this means love.

'Take me back to London with you,' she'd whispered to him two days later. Rushing out the words she'd practised in her head, she couldn't believe she'd been brave enough to say them aloud. They had just left the pub and were standing on the pavement while he searched his pockets for a lighter. She'd ringed her arms around him and pressed her head into the firm, reassuring slope of his back. She knew he was leaving soon. She had felt a slight shift in him and noticed a blank, faraway expression which suggested that he was already somewhere else.

He turned around. 'I can't.'

'I know.' She nodded nervously, immediately regretting her words. 'Anyway,' she added, 'I have to stay and look after Dad.'

'I promise I'll come back for you.'

Her breath caught in her throat. 'When?'

'I can't say ... soon.'

She felt he wanted to say something else, yet nothing came. Not a word. The next day he had packed his belongings and left.

In the days after Jack left she had wept often because she missed him, yet she was also sure he would return. She believed he'd meant every word he'd said to her and that one day soon he would say those words again.

It was only three weeks later when, holding a cup of tea, she had knocked on Dad's bedroom door and called out to him. As she opened the door, she fully expected him to rise up and greet her good-naturedly, as he did every morning, but he did not stir. She called him again, more forcefully this time, but as she put the cup down on his bedside table a bad feeling had tightened in her chest. She clutched him through the sheets and shook him repeatedly, then stared at his empty, colourless face and still eyes.

His death had changed everything. It mattered far less what she was feeling about Jack; she didn't seem to care about anything. She stopped going to work, drew the curtains and sat for hours on end in the front room. If the doorbell rang, she rarely answered it, but when she did, she quickly drove visitors away with her silence.

Then, one Saturday a month or so later, she was lying on Dad's bedroom floor rooting through boxes of his photographs and got stuck staring at one of him and Mum outside the house just after they'd bought it. Mum was not much older than Vivien was now, and her smile was broad and thrilled. The photo said it all: they were ready to get on and live. That was what they would want for her too: to hold tight to each day, squeeze the most out of every single one.

Holding the photo above her face, she thought how easy it would be to picture herself and Jack embracing in the doorway of their new house. She sat up quickly, as if assaulted by the idea – but suddenly it seemed so obvious. She would have to rebuild her life, and since she could do that anywhere, why not London? Yes, Jack was there, but it wasn't just about him. It was about taking a chance; living somewhere new, finding a job and learning things about herself which would remain undiscovered if she squandered her days at home. In London, she felt, true change was possible.

So here she was.

She got up and reached into the drawer of the bedside table for the letter she'd brought with her. A couple of days after she made up her mind to leave, she and Stella had begun sorting through Dad's belongings. The letter from Jack to Dad, discovered between the pages of a television hire purchase agreement when she'd cleared out his desk, was the briefest of notes – four short sentences – and all Jack had done was thank Dad for his hospitality and wish him well. But scrawled in the top right-hand corner was an address. In Bow, east London.

From the room below came a whoop of canned laughter as Mrs Levy turned on the television. Vivien held the envelope and wondered, yet again, if she should have written first. Let Jack know she planned to come to London. She had tried a couple of times, but the words never sounded right and her tears kept smudging the ink when she explained about Dad. Besides, she didn't want Jack to think he was the sole reason for her coming. It was important that he knew she was doing this for herself too, to vanish into something new.

Thoughts of leaving home came rushing back. Her and Stella crushing each other on the station platform, attempting, but failing, to leave the other's side.

'I'm going to miss you like crazy,' Vivien kept saying.

'Not half as much as I'll miss you.' Stella had smoothed down Vivien's hair and rolled out her bottom lip. 'My days will be spent wiping the boys' runny noses and you'll be gallivanting around London.'

'Oh, it won't be like that!' said Vivien. 'When have you ever seen me gallivant? Will you write? Tell me everything that's going on?'

'Will I? Jesus, you'll be sick to death of me,' said Stella through her tears. 'I want to hear that you're dressing the hair of the rich and famous. And that Jack will make an honest woman of you.'

'Well, we'll see about that. You won't forget to check on things, will you? In case I've forgotten something?'

Vivien kept running over everything in her mind. The windows and doors had been locked, a notice pinned to the letter box guiding callers to Stella's house. A plumber had fixed the leaky pipe in the bathroom. Mrs Harper at the corner shop had cancelled Vivien's account and even made a point of coming around the counter to embrace her.

'Don't worry about a thing.' Stella had grabbed Vivien's hands and they had swung their arms back and forth, like they used to do in the school playground. 'You'd better get a move on.' Looking towards the train, Stella had lifted her arms away and tried to keep smiling. 'Go on. Be the best you can be, Vivien Epstein. Be bloody brilliant.'

3

Mrs Levy only took one lodger in at a time, and they were expected to use the kitchen and make their own meals except on Friday night. Then, she always invited them to eat the Shabbos meal with her, unless she was visiting her children or one of her four sisters. Mrs Levy was delighted that Vivien had arrived on a Friday as it gave them a chance to get acquainted, but as Vivien knocked on the closed kitchen door she wished the tradition didn't exist. She would have preferred to mooch around her room, read a magazine or write a postcard to Stella.

'Evening, Mrs Levy.'

'Oh, call me Nettie, dear. Come in. Sit yourself down.'

Vivien was touched by the effort Nettie had taken with her appearance. She had taken off her housecoat and was wearing a yellow cotton dress that fell to her knees and was pinched at the waist, her nut-brown curls teased into a stiff sphere. The distinct wrinkles around her eyes and mouth and her rounded back suggested she was in her mid- to late fifties, but she was still light on her feet and moved nimbly around the kitchen.

'Make yourself at home.' Pickle, her ginger and white cat, leaped from her arms. 'I'll put the kettle on.'

It was a pleasant, spacious kitchen, full of light. The piles of crockery and rows of drinking glasses on the green-painted shelves gleamed in the last rays of sun coming in through the window. The Shabbos candles stood nearby, waiting to be lit. Nettie reached into the walk-in pantry for a carton of eggs, then frowned at the washing machine, which was spinning to a furious finish.

'My son-in-law bought this for me last month.' She shook her head. 'Still can't get used to it. The first time it took longer than doing it by hand because I sat and watched an entire wash go round.'

As Vivien pulled out a chair from the table, she heard children in the next-door garden squealing, catch me, bet you can't, dare you, scaredy cat. The smoke from the chip pan had misted up the side window, so she rubbed a hole in the steam with the palm of her hand and looked through. Over the top of the low wall she could make out two small girls in identical pink blouses and ruffled skirts tearing after each other.

She didn't want to feel homesick but it came fast and sudden. All those evenings at the kitchen table, painting her nails or ironing Dad's shirts, listening to next door's crazy terrier bark every time someone passed by. Thursday nights at Stella's, three doors down, playing Helen Shapiro records and drinking cheap white wine. Holding Stella's hand on the dance floor at the Belle Vue, giggling at the boys who dared to try and break in between them. The tightness in her chest made her feel as if she wanted it all back, but she didn't. They were just memories now.

After the children had been shouted into the house next door, she reached across the table and unfolded a copy of the *Jewish Chronicle*, where a series of photos dominated the front page.

'It's an absolute disgrace.' Nettie stood opposite her, pointing a potato peeler at the two headlines, FINES FOR JEWISH MEN IN STREET CLASHES and MOSLEY AND JORDAN BATTLE FOR SUPPORTERS.

Her jowly face, which was still pretty, looked furious.

'The bloody Jew baiters are back again, every Sunday. And not just Mosley's lot this time, neither. Archie would be spitting feathers if he were here.'

Vivien stared at one of the photos. A crush of men and police surrounded a platform on which a couple of figures stood beneath a KEEP BRITAIN WHITE placard.

'If my dad were still around,' she whispered, 'he'd have been up at the front with them.'

If the tumour hadn't hollowed him out, she added silently. If he hadn't needed to nap most afternoons and had been able to get through a day without the pain doubling him up. If he'd been half as strong as he'd been when he was fighting them on the streets after the war.

'Archie was the same. He was never afraid.' Nettie moved a bag of knitting off the table. 'Bet he and your mum couldn't stand to see you go. I was in a terrible state when my Lorraine got married. She only went two streets away.'

Vivien cleared her throat and stared to the side of Nettie's face. 'Dad passed eleven weeks ago. Mum died when I was five.'

Nettie's gasp was so shocked, Vivien wished she'd lied. So used to hearing the words inside her head, she had forgotten how they sounded out loud.

'Eleven weeks ago! I'm so sorry.' Nettie fiddled with the enamelled brooch on her dress collar. 'That's just terrible. And you say you don't have any brothers or sisters?'

'No.'

'No other family?'

Vivien shook her head. No other living relatives.

'You poor thing.' Nettie's voice wobbled. 'I can't imagine.'

Nettie's brimming eyes made Vivien feel awful. She had to stop telling people. Her loss always became theirs, and, reflected back like this, it was painful for everyone.

She reached for the teapot and concentrated on the sound of the tea pouring into her cup while Nettie gripped the top of a chair so hard Vivien could see the whites of her knuckles. 'I couldn't bear Clive or Lorraine to be left on their own so young.'

'I manage fine.' Vivien reached over and lightly touched Nettie's wrist. 'Really.'

Still shaking her head, Nettie wiped her eyes with her apron. 'Fried egg with your chips?'

'Lovely. Thank you.'

Nettie cracked two eggs into a frying pan and glanced over her shoulder.

'Well, at least you've got a job to get you settled. Which hair salon did you say you'll be working in?'

Vivien turned to look out of the window again. 'Oh, one in Soho.'

This was a lie. There was a salon in Soho which she would visit on Monday morning, but she didn't know if there was a job for her yet. But a small lie would do no harm. Besides, she still had a bit of money left over from Dad's savings, which would cover the first month's rent, by the end of which she would definitely have a job.

After tea Vivien crept quietly up the stairs and lingered on the landing outside her bedroom, looking at all the framed pictures on the wall. There was Nettie, seated in front of her husband in his military garb. Nettie and her husband holding the knife over an impressive three-tiered wedding cake. A young Nettie, with long wavy hair, wearing a swimsuit, her slender legs curled beneath her. But most of the pictures were of their two children, at different ages, striking a variety of poses, and newer pictures of Nettie and her grandchildren, her husband noticeably absent.

Surrounded by all these photos, Vivien felt her shoulders loosen. She was less afraid now. This place was a proper

home – people had come and gone and been loved here –
and by the time Vivien shut her door again, something big
had shifted inside her. She wanted to stay.

4

Vivien spent the next couple of days roaming around her new neighbourhood, getting a feel for the place. And although she'd promised herself she must find a job before seeking Jack out, she couldn't resist a practice run. She took the bus to the high street close to the address on his letter, stood marvelling at the prospect of seeing him, then crossed the street and took another bus straight back to Hackney.

By the time the weekend was over, it had started to sink in that she was in London for more than a passing visit. She also slept very well in her new lodgings, so by Monday she was ready to pick her way down Oxford Street in the dazzle of the early-morning sun. Most people were heading to work and she felt their impatience with her for being out of time with their hurried walk. A few suited men clipped her sides. A girl in a tight pencil skirt and strappy heels asked her to move along. It made her feel tense, so she was glad to turn off into Poland Street, where it was quiet and shaded and people did not keep crowding her path.

Halfway down, the bus conductor's directions to Dean Street were already forgotten; someone else would have to guide her to Oscar's, the hair salon where Leo had told her to mention his name. But in a way she loved being lost, happy to be ambling along the wonderfully shabby Soho streets, past the waitress polishing spoons and singing Italian through the window of a trattoria, and the blonde woman with the old face and young voice calling out goodbye and looking mournfully at the handsome boy in the pink shirt as he drove off on his Vespa. She loved walking past the open doors of the Greek, French and Italian restaurants, where unfamiliar, exotic cooking smells might come at her and make her feel like she was in another country.

The unexpectedness of it all delighted her. Some of the buildings may have been bare and run-down, in need of a lick of paint, but the shops and people more than made up for that. Manchester was also busy and colourful, but here she barely knew where to look first – so much was happening all at once. Housewives jabbering about the price of oranges. Schoolboys giggling at pictures of semi-nudes in the window of a dirty bookshop. Girls with impressive beehives, wearing ski pants and bright dresses and flat pointed shoes. Barrow boys. Office clerks. Men in dapper suits talking earnestly about theatre and film. It was the sort of place that excited her; ordinary yet intoxicating.

Soon she suspected that Dean Street was long behind her. About to turn back, she heard a snatch of music and quickly walked towards it, rounding the corner into Carnaby Street, where she realised the rhythmic sounds were coming from one of the men's clothing shops nestled between the tailors and tobacconists. Each shop burst with exuberance. Garments hung around the doorways, young male shop assistants strutted around inside, kitted out as stylishly as the clothes they were selling. No wonder there were mostly boys on the pavement around her, in the dark mohair suits that Jack favoured, or pastel shirts and trousers and boxy jackets that skimmed their waists.

Nothing could have prepared her for such flamboyance, and Vivien took everything in with a childish delight until she caught sight of herself in a strip of mirrored glass outside a second-hand bookshop, and her life, her uncertainties, came rushing back.

She did not fit in with the young people hurrying past. Her chignon was neat but dull, her wool suit frumpy, her low-heeled shoes far too sensible. She had dressed conservatively, imagining Dad standing behind her, jingling the change in his pocket and throwing out his exacting opinion on what suited her best. But she looked years behind everyone else. She would need to make changes, and fast.

She was walking on, liberated by the idea that she could now dress just to please herself, when she noticed a young nervy lad leaning against a wall, clothes rumpled, jacket short in the sleeves, looking just as out of place as she did. Immediately she knew he was straight off the train from somewhere else. He smoked awkwardly as if he'd just taken the habit up, and he had done nothing to shape his mess of hair.

'Hello,' she said, surprising herself. And when he said hello straight back, she could tell that if she hadn't carried on walking, he'd have said anything that came into his head just to keep talking to her and pretend that he was someone too.

She took directions from a newspaper seller and began to make her way back to Dean Street. But she still made detours, went down streets that interested her, looping around until her feet ached. Soho was like a mysterious party she had gatecrashed. She didn't want to miss a thing.

At first Stevie had enjoyed amusing the girls in Oscar's, but now he was getting restless. He got up, marched over to the reception desk and rapped his knuckles on the top of the till. When Barb swivelled around on her stool, he pointed at himself. 'Hello?'

'Mrs Sawyer, excuse me just a moment.' Barb pressed the telephone receiver against her breast. 'What?'

Stevie shrugged and pointed to his wet hair. 'I'm still waiting.'

'Two minutes.'

'I've already waited ten.'

'So another two won't kill you.'

'I've got things to do.'

Barb's eyes narrowed. 'Yeah, yeah, Mr Big Shot.'

'That's me, baby,' he said.

They both pulled faces at each other before Barb carried on her conversation. The woman beside him having a perm might have raised her eyebrows at the exchange but Stevie never stood on ceremony with Barb. They'd been next-door neighbours for as long as he could remember and they treated each other like family.

He wandered back to his chair and sat down. Now what? He was bored. Lydia had already given him a cup of tea and a copy of *NME* to flick through. Deirdre had spent ages complaining to him about her boyfriend's tight-fistedness, and now Barb had disappeared. He was just about ready to pull on his suede jacket and walk out, but pride wouldn't get him a free haircut.

The week before he'd lost his job at HMV on Oxford Street for oversleeping two days in a row, then he had to pay his mum this week's board. So he was broke. The fact was he needed Barb more than she needed him, which was why he was in a ladies' hair salon in Soho and not horsing around with Tony, the Greek barber he usually went to in Dalston.

He was about to stand up again when a girl stopped on the pavement outside and stared at the pink and black Oscar's sign. She appeared to be straightening her shoulders and taking a couple of steadying breaths before heading inside.

Stevie's chair was far enough from reception that he could watch her without being noticed. The girl didn't shut the door properly the first time, so she gave it another quick shove, then edged towards the desk, her face set in a nervous grin. Her hands kept fluttering towards her glossy dark hair or fiddling with her drab jacket and skirt. She looked concerned, as if she had guessed that not everything was right with her appearance, but from where he sat, she wasn't a lost cause. She had lovely doe eyes, a sweet intelligent face and smashing legs beneath her skirt. There was something about her that made you want to look, look again and keep looking.

He followed her eyes as she glanced around. It was early on a Monday morning but already there was an air of frenzy about the place. Her eyes were huge with surprise, as if she had not expected to witness so much activity through the fug of hairspray and bluish cigarette smoke. Her gaze drifted to the blown-up photos of models on the back wall, towards the elegant oval mirrors in front of each client and across the row of new top-of-the-line driers, before finally coming to rest on Maeve, who, flanked by a junior, Lydia, was teasing the last curls of a client's already intricate updo into place.

The girl's expression was still curious when Marcia walked over and greeted her. She put out a hand for Marcia to shake, but as Stevie stood up to see if she was wearing a wedding ring, Barb appeared behind him. She pushed her black-rimmed glasses up her nose and gave his head a little swipe. 'Sit up straight.'

She forced his shoulders down and clamped her hands against his temples. As she combed through his damp hair and parted it into sections, Marcia tapped her on the shoulder.

'Someone to see you, Barb.'

Stevie glanced up at the mirror. All he could make out was the girl standing close by before Barb tipped his head forward.

'What can I do for you?'

'I can see you're busy, Miss Wiseman. I'll come back.'

'I'm always busy. How can I help?'

'My name's Vivien Epstein. I've been working with Leo Miller in Manchester.'

'Leo Miller!' Barb laughed. 'That old dog. I haven't heard his name in a while. How is he?'

'He's in good health, Miss Wiseman,' she said.

'Good. And what can I do for you?'

'I need a job. Leo said to look you up.'

'Did he now?'

'He said you do the hiring. And Leo,' her voice faltered but only slightly. 'Leo says I'm terrific with colour and a very good cutter.'

'Is that right?' Barb handed Vivien a pair of scissors and pointed at Stevie. 'Show me.'

'Well, I don't usually cut men's hair.' She took the scissors hesitantly. 'Just my dad's.'

'Don't worry,' said Barb. 'Stevie's not paying.'

As Barb ran through how he liked it, Stevie began to protest, but Barb told him to be quiet. When she ignored his stern look he silently fumed. She knew how he felt about his hair. She made more jokes about it than anyone else. 'Careful with those crown jewels, Stevie,' she'd called out of her bedroom window at the weekend after she spotted him on the street spruced up for a night out. Stevie knew he was fanatical about his thick sandy hair, that the wave at the front had to be perfectly held and the sides slicked back, but there was a lot riding on it. He supposed he was pretty good-looking – his eyes were leafy green, and his grandma often told him he had nice even teeth – but he wasn't stand-out crazy handsome like his cousin Gerry, who only had to walk into a coffee bar to have women teetering over, trying to find ways to make him want them.

Vivien gathered up tufts of hair and nodded to herself a couple of times. He couldn't accuse her of taking the job lightly. Her focus was intense. She tapered his hair at the back, then snipped away at the sides, the tip of her tongue poking out between her teeth. When she worked her way round to the front, Stevie was finally able to make out that she wasn't wearing a ring.

At first Barb watched her closely but soon she relaxed. She got distracted by a spot on the mirror and asked Marcia to bring a splash of white vinegar and a cloth, then took a phone call and welcomed a regular client at the door. By the time she returned, Vivien had buttered up her fingers with Brylcreem and groomed Stevie's hair into the exact style he'd hoped for.

'Very nice,' said Barb. 'You know what you're doing.'

'Best cut I've had here,' said Stevie, smirking.

Barb ignored him. 'Let's say a month's trial and see how we get on.'

'Oh, thank you. You won't regret it.'

'Be here eight thirty on Thursday. Marcia will show you the ropes. We'll work out the money then.'

'Thank you, Miss Wiseman.'

'Everyone calls me Barb.'

'Thank you, Barb.'

'Stop thanking me. You did well.'

Barb shook Vivien's hand and walked off as Stevie stood up and admired himself in the mirror. 'Great job.'

Vivien smiled. 'Glad you like it.'

'What brings you to the city?'

'A change.'

'Where are you staying?' he asked.

'Off Hackney Road.'

'Hackney? We're neighbours then. I'm in Dalston. Amhurst Road. Other end to the shul.' He brushed loose

31

hair off the shoulders of his V-neck top and smiled, thinking of his mum. Given her colouring and her surname, he
was certain Vivien was Jewish, like him, but it never did
any harm to discreetly double-check.

He swung the door wide open and bowed from the
waist, expecting her to giggle at him like the other girls
did, but instead she scuttled through, holding herself away
from him. He knew he'd embarrassed her and then he was
embarrassed for himself.

'Where are you off to?' he asked.

'To get the number six.'

'I'll walk some of the way with you. I need to get to
D'Arblay Street.'

'All right. Thanks.'

'I'd get the bus back to Hackney with you but I have an
audition.' Stevie waited for her to ask him about it. 'I play
the drums,' he said after a pause.

'That sounds fun.'

'Yeah. I've got a really good feeling about this band.'

As they walked side by side down Old Compton Street,
he carried on the conversation. He was enjoying it, even
if he was talking too fast about how hard it was to find a
band he fitted with. She wasn't saying much at all, though,
and it made him nervous, which made him talk even faster.

A little way down Wardour Street, someone belted out
his name, and when he turned and spotted Frankie Green,
he groaned inwardly. Frankie had lived in the next street
but one for years until his dad, big in men's ties, had got
rich. Now they lived in Finchley, and Frankie ran two
of his father's shops. His fiancée, Pauline, was a plump,
broad-shouldered typist who Stevie had taken on two dates
before she dumped him for Frankie. That, combined with
Stevie's ambition to be a professional musician, meant he
was a great source of amusement for Frankie.

But Frankie was a berk and everyone knew it – except him. Now Stevie had to stand next to a friendly, fresh, unusual girl he'd quite like to know better, and humour Frankie in the hope that he would avoid being humiliated.

Frankie sauntered towards them. A snappy dresser like his dad, he was wearing a buttoned-down white shirt, an Italian suit and one of those pork-pie hats that Stevie didn't really like but everyone else seemed to think was cool.

'Stevie,' he said, hands deep in his pockets.

Stevie murmured hello.

'Aren't you going to introduce us?'

'Vivien, Frankie Green.'

'Pleasure's all mine.' Frankie peered at Stevie over his sunglasses. 'Still a Billy fan, I see.'

Stevie felt his shoulders slump. He knew what was coming. He was about to be seriously mocked for the heinous crime of not caring enough about modern jazz to spend his weekends queuing up outside Ronnie Scott's to see some hip American jazz saxophonist like Zoot Sims. And because rock 'n' roll was his first love, and probably always would be, and because he did think of Billy Fury when he shaped his hair, he was now about to be stamped on in front of the girl he was trying to impress.

'Billy Fury?' Vivien asked him.

Stevie gulped. 'Yeah.'

'Oh, he's terrific. What a showman! My best friend Stella and I love him. Such charisma.' And when she turned her warm gaze on both him and Frankie, Stevie couldn't tell whether she'd said this innocently, because she meant it, or if she had guessed he was about to be teased. Either way he didn't care. She was lovely.

'I've got to go. I have an audition,' he said coolly to Frankie. 'Say hi to Pauline.'

He smiled at Vivien to suggest they set off, and they

walked away. Although he wasn't sure she caught every word, and at times she looked a little vacant as if pre-occupied with something else, he felt so relaxed and so good about himself, he just babbled on about his love for Billy Fury and how he'd seen him in *Play it Cool* three times already.

As they approached D'Arblay Street, a delivery boy holding a wooden crate on his shoulder pushed them so close together Stevie could see the rusty-coloured flecks in her irises and the freckle above her upper lip.

He pointed towards the pub on the corner. 'That's me.'

'Thanks for walking with me,' she said. 'And good luck with your audition.'

Her voice was light and pleasant; it hadn't changed, but she didn't seem to be inviting anything further from him. She might even have moved her slight body away from his. For a moment he felt a faint dismay, but then, watching her back as she crossed the road, he told himself it was fine. He could wait.

5

On Wednesday, the day before she was due to start at Oscar's, Vivien repeated the bus journey from Hackney to the high street in Bow. As the bus rolled gently further east, her nerves grew and by the time she got off she was shaking. She continued to shake as the neighbourhood women outside the haberdashery read the address on Jack's letter and talked over each other, advising Vivien on which way to go. They mentioned the launderette and the infants' school where their kids had gone, and, as she went around the corner, they shrieked with laughter at long-held memories of the teachers and headmaster.

She wasn't entirely sure she'd taken it all in. At best her sense of direction was weak, and she could easily get lost today, distracted by the voice in her head which wouldn't die away. It must have started up as she slept because she woke before daylight with an ache behind both eyes, convinced that Jack would not be pleased to see her.

As she got up and drank a glass of water, the voice had reminded her that the letter she had found was for Dad, not her. There might be a good reason why, apart from the one postcard to say he was back in London, Jack had not written directly to her in nearly three months. Things could have changed. He might have met another girl in the buffet car on the train coming back or at the stationer's while he purchased a new ribbon for his typewriter. They might already be going steady.

These were all distinct possibilities but Vivien couldn't turn back, not after she'd promised herself that once she had a job and a place to stay, she would try to find him. Although, it was true, she hadn't expected to feel quite so rattled. Since leaving the house she had swayed between gentle, bearable states of excitement or nerves, but now she was in close proximity to where he was living, she felt horribly nauseous and her legs seemed to be unable to support her.

When a car horn blasted close by, she yelped; she had stepped into the road without thinking. She leaped back, cowering on the pavement as the driver swivelled in his seat and raised an angry fist at her. Nodding at the retreating car, she tried to pull herself together. If she didn't watch it, she would get herself killed. She didn't know what was in Jack's head, and until she did, she was better off not trying to second-guess him.

Now she looked around, she realised how grey and uninviting the area was. There wasn't a tree or flower in sight, save for stringy weeds pushing up through the cracks in the pavement, and she had to sidestep a pile of bricks and a broken pram. All the terraced houses were squeezed together haphazardly, and the sky squatted low and heavy on the roofs, making the narrow streets look even more cramped. It surprised her that Jack would choose to live around here, especially since several houses advertising bed and breakfast had NO COLOUREDS, NO IRISH, NO DOGS signs propped up in the front window, which she took to mean that Jews wouldn't be welcome either.

She remembered to take a sharp turn left, then right at the launderette some way down the street, but arriving at the address on the letter she was startled by the grubbiness of the house and wondered if she'd made a mistake. One of the windows was broken and hadn't been replaced. The front step was unpolished and cracked. She couldn't imagine any of her neighbours back home letting their houses get into such a state.

Her hands went to her hair, pushing it away from her damp neck, then down the front of her blue flowery sundress with the stiff sugared underskirt. It was years old but one of Jack's favourites. She knocked, blood pulsing through her veins, then stepped back onto the pavement and waited.

The door opened. 'Yes?' A severe-looking woman with coarse black hair tightened the cord on her dressing gown and tried to silence a barking dog.

'Hello, I'm looking for Jack Fox.'

'Who?'

'Jack Fox.'

The woman yanked on the dog's collar until it sank down quietly. 'He's not here.'

'When will he be back?'

'Oh, he's long gone.'

Vivien's heart shrank. 'Long gone?'

'He only took the room for a few weeks.'

'Did he say where he was going?'

'No, love.'

It took Vivien a few seconds to think of what to say next. 'Thank you,' she mumbled. 'Sorry to bother you.'

The letter crumpled in her hand as she listened to the dog barking behind the shut door. She considered the hours spent grieving for Jack and then Dad, grieving for everything she'd had and then lost. She was shaking still, completely unsure of herself and waiting for something else to happen. But the door remained shut. There was nothing more.

She couldn't just leave. She had to insist the woman think harder about whether Jack had mentioned anything helpful. A pub where he took an early-evening drink. A café where he liked to read the newspaper over a fry-up.

She knocked again.

When the woman reappeared, Vivien's voice quivered. 'I really need to find him.' She ignored the woman's raised eyebrows. 'Are you sure you can't remember anything? Like where he was going next? Or—'

'Look, if they pay and they're no trouble, I don't ask questions.'

'But ...'

As the woman slammed the door shut, the only thing left for Vivien to do was burst into tears.

She was lost. Her head was hurting and she couldn't remember the way back to the high street. She stumbled up wrong roads, then back down them again. Every now and again she'd stop and steady herself, trying to rearrange her thoughts. Soho and Oscar's and her love for London suddenly didn't mean very much. Jack wasn't here. He was gone.

She had just begun to weep again, openly and noisily, when an old man walking his dog passed by. He cocked his head in her direction and pushed his cap up his forehead as if to afford himself a better look. Vivien covered her face with her hands and turned away, momentarily embarrassed to see herself through his eyes, a hysterical girl weeping through the cracks between her fingers while the world moved around her. She suddenly felt so utterly alone and scared. She had fooled herself into believing Jack was not the main reason she had come to London, but now she realised just how much he mattered to her. Without him, this sprawling city felt alien. She took her hands away and looked up. The man was still staring at her, transfixed, and she had an urge to share with him just how unfairly life had treated her these past few months. First Dad, now Jack. Then, as if thinking about Dad jolted her into seeing things differently, her sorrow flipped to anger.

'Vivien Epstein, don't you dare compare Dad's death to this,' she whispered aloud. 'This isn't the same. Nothing like it.'

It just felt similar, that was all. It just all felt like one big crushing loss.

An hour and a half later she stood under the shade of a butcher's awning in Dalston, examining herself in her compact mirror. Her red eyes needed a little fixing and her cheeks were tight from the tears. She'd have preferred not to have to think of her appearance at all and be on her way home, but she'd telephoned Sid Klein the night before and promised she would drop by. She couldn't disappoint him. He was one of Dad's oldest friends, the best man at his wedding, and he'd sounded delighted to hear from her.

A thud behind her made her jump. Through the window she saw the butcher bring his cleaver down on a set of ribs as his customers, mostly girls her age, held on to prams and children's hands while bantering with him over which cut of meat his arm muscles resembled the most.

Their cries of amusement put Vivien in a lighter frame of mind. Watching them, she told herself not to feel injured by Jack. He hadn't really done anything wrong. She'd chosen to find him and announce she was building a life for herself close by. He hadn't written to her, begging her to come. He'd made it plain that he would come back for her, and if she took it upon herself to tread the streets looking for him, clutching a letter that was not even addressed to her, then she must shoulder the disappointment. She only had herself to blame.

*

The door to Sid Klein's pawnbroker's didn't open easily. Convinced it was stuck, Vivien realised she was pushing against a wave of people waiting to be served. The shop smelled of cheap perfume and ale. An old man with a droopy eye clutched a tatty violin case to his chest. A woman was emptying a bag of gold jewellery onto the counter and repeating how valuable her wedding ring and necklace were. Another was holding a clock and showing the girl behind the counter how it worked.

She smiled at the striking redhead behind the cash register. 'Excuse me. My name is Vivien Epstein. Mr Klein is expecting me.'

'I'll let him know, dear.'

Vivien took off her gloves and braced herself. She wasn't comfortable seeing people who knew Dad because she felt so unpredictable in their company. Sometimes she wept uncontrollably, sometimes she was dry-eyed and numb, and she could never tell in advance which way she'd go.

A few minutes passed before a door at the back of the shop opened and a heavyset man with a dour face and grey-brown hair took off his glasses, screwed up his eyes and peered out. When he saw her, he winked and waved her over.

'Vivien, darling.' Sid lifted the top of the counter and ushered her through the hatch. 'What a pleasure,' he said, and kissed her forehead.

'I'm sorry. I didn't give you much notice.'

'What are you sorry for? You're Phil's daughter.'

He guided her down a hallway littered with boxes of knick-knacks and files.

'Hungry? You want a little something to nosh on? I can send one of the girls out.'

As she shook her head and said thank you, he stared sideways at her. 'Aren't you the spit of your mother! Same

40

big brown eyes. She was a real knockout, let me tell you.'

Sid's office smelled of stale woody cigar smoke. He waved her into the chair on the other side of his desk, then cleared away stacks of files until all that stood between them was a leather-edged desk blotter, a red telephone and a table lamp.

'What's that?'

He jabbed his finger at her chest, and as she glanced down, he playfully pinched her nose. She smiled but only out of respect. This had been Sid's favourite trick when she was a kid, but she was twenty now and would have preferred him not to do it any more.

He sat down in his tilting chair and swung one leg over the other.

'Your dad had a good turnout, didn't he?'

Vivien fixed her eyes on the desk fan whirling on a heap of newspapers in the corner of the room. She didn't want to discuss this. She had deliberately never dwelt on the funeral or the shiva, and by putting them out of her mind, her recollection had been dulled. Now it was difficult to remember who had turned up or what she might have said or felt, but it was easier this way.

'I thought he had a bit longer in him.' Sid sighed. 'Just shows you. Neither of us was good at keeping in touch.' He shook his head. 'I should have tried harder.'

'He was very fond of you.'

'Well, we went back a long way.'

On the other side of the wall a toilet was flushing. A tap was turned on and the sound of running water made Vivien realise how dry her throat was. It was all too much. She stared at the floor and took a few moments to compose herself, then released the clasp on her handbag and fished around inside.

'I found a pile of these in a shoebox in Dad's wardrobe.

Photos of the 43 Group. You're in so many of them I thought you might like a few.'

Sid took the paper bag from her. He slipped on his reading glasses, pulled out the photos, then placed each one carefully on the desk like a set of playing cards.

'Good God,' he said. 'These take me back.' He was close to tears.

She supposed he was remembering when he and Dad first met, just after the war, during the early days of the 43 Group, when the scores of men and women, mostly ex-servicemen, who had united to run fascists off the streets had turned into thousands.

Sid shook his head for what seemed like ages, then held up a group photo. 'This was our first meeting. March, 1946. Didn't have a clue what to call ourselves. We only ended up naming it the 43 Group because that's how many of us turned up.

'And this,' he said, tapping another photo, 'was taken at a coffee house we loved in Hampstead, where we used to meet to plan our next move. They did bloody marvellous doughnuts. That's me waving at the back.' He turned the photo over and read aloud: 'June, 1946. Four hundred members. Best week yet. Turned over seven meetings. No arrests.'

Sid glanced at her. 'The Group had a lot to thank your dad for. What he did went beyond the call of duty.'

'He had to do it,' Vivien said matter-of-factly. 'You know he couldn't get over not going to war.'

Born with one leg an inch shorter than the other, the army had refused him, and he would often get choked up telling her of the shame he felt, staying at home while so many of his friends went off and defended their country.

Sid batted the air with one hand. 'Always with the guilt. Phil more than made up for it.'

He held up another photo in front of her. 'That's me and

my brother Freddie, God rest his soul. Passed away three months ago. Another one gone before his time.'

He put down the photo, took off his glasses and rubbed both baggy eyes with the heels of his palms. 'Now he had balls. Still went to meetings at Ridley Road, right up to the end.'

A tingling rose up through her chest as she leaned forward to let Sid light her cigarette. One night, over a tea of sardines on toast, Dad had asked Jack if he was familiar with a particular tobacconist in Ridley Road. Jack had sat back in his chair for a while, trying to locate it in his mind. Impressed by how many shops he could reel off by name, she'd assumed he was a regular visitor to the popular street market.

She thought back to the headline in the *Jewish Chronicle*. 'Is Ridley where some men were just fined for fighting?'

Sid nodded. 'It can get nasty. Some of the younger lads fight hard. But who can blame them? Jordan's lot have painted swastikas on three shuls in the past fortnight.'

'Jordan?' she said. 'He's the person Mosley's up against, isn't he? Those men were protesting against him.'

'Yep. Colin Jordan. He was kicked out of the BNP for being too extreme so he started the National Socialist Movement. Now let me tell you, he's someone to worry about.' Sid blew out his cheeks and stacked the photos together. 'It's terrible out there again. We need to get organised.'

'That's what Dad would say.'

'He'd be right.'

Vivien drew on her cigarette. An excited chatter was mounting in her head. She felt there was a good chance Jack went down to Ridley to protest. After all, he wrote about post-war politics, and he too had been furious about the revival of fascism that had taken place over the past few years. His face would tense at the merest mention of it and there had been nothing neutral about his expression in the silence that usually followed. He would look deep in thought and quite serious. But it wasn't just what he had said. He had backbone. He wouldn't look to fight but he'd care about defending others. Now she felt a little shaky, a little elated. She should have thought of it before. Jack was like Dad. He would want to get involved.

'Thank you, dear. I shall treasure these.' Sid opened a desk drawer and pulled out a half-smoked cigar and ash-tray. 'Now, I know you've found lodgings but I still think you should stay with us.'

'I like it where I am.'

'A girl your age shouldn't be on her own. Your dad would go barmy if he knew.'

'I'm fine,' she said. 'Sid, do you know a man called Jack Fox?'

Sid made a noise in his throat, then tilted back in his chair and puffed on his cigar, obscuring his face in a plume of smoke. 'Never heard of him. Why?'

'He came to interview Dad in Manchester. He was interested in what Dad did after the war. I know he's in London. Well, I think he is. But I don't know any more than that.'

Sid shrugged. 'Can't help you, I'm afraid.'

He talked a little more about how busy pawnbroking was these days, because everyone had something to get rid of and wanted to make a few bob. When it was time for Vivien to go, he made his way round to her side of the table, cigar in hand.

'Come over soon. Elaine would love to see you. So would the boys.'

Funny to hear Barry and Danny being called boys when they were at least three or four years older than her.

44

'I will.' She stood up and ringed her handbag over her arm.

'No one can ever replace your old man but I'm here if you need me.'

Ridley Road was near Sid's office, so Vivien decided to walk over, buy a pad of writing paper and have a wander. When she got there she found there was far more to the market than she had expected: something for everyone, even if she didn't know it yet. No, she didn't need a tea cosy or a second-hand pair of National Health glasses, a puppy or a pound of the ripest plums.

She walked slowly through the market, stopping only to buy the writing pad and to look at the man in the bagel shop stirring the vat of dough with a long wooden spoon. On the pavement outside ELLENBY HOSIERY & LINGERIE and D. GLASS, BUTCHERS she tried to work out why the signs seemed familiar, then realised that glimpses of the shopfronts had appeared in the *Jewish Chronicle* photos behind the men chucking stones at Jordan as he was led onto a platform.

The smell of warm bread rose from a bakery chimney, filling the sky with a doughy sweetness and reminding her that she had passed on breakfast and not yet eaten today. She bought a cinnamon twist and an Eccles cake, then sat out of the glare of the sun on the warm ledge in front of the bakery.

With an Eccles cake in one hand, she wrote to Stella. Stella would have received the postcard with her new address, but now Vivien wanted someone to share her news about the job. She described each of the girls and wrote how the manager, Barb Wiseman, reminded her of their old school friend Lillian, who also wore large heavy-rimmed glasses and had a ring to her voice that made everything sound important. But she quickly got to the bit she knew Stella would be dying to read – the news that she hadn't found Jack because he wasn't living at the address on the letter. She didn't explain any further because she didn't want to start crying again but she said she was fine and loving London. She underlined the words 'fine' and 'loving' twice because otherwise Stella might think she was putting up a front. And in a way, she wasn't. The idea of returning to Ridley Road on Sunday had buoyed her.

She carried on walking but wasn't in any rush. She was enjoying herself now. The sounds and smells of the market made her happy. Hot tomato soup and fried onions. Cries of 'Mind ya backs' and the rumble of handcarts. Elderly women bargaining over mops and buckets. Teddy boys throwing chips at the pigeons. A man walking through, shouting, 'The End is Nigh'. It was a feast for her senses, making it hard to imagine that the street could be stripped of this vibrant, raucous market and crammed with thousands of demonstrators.

Vivien pictured Dad climbing off the bus every weekend full of fight, striding down this street, pushing towards the platform. Knowing he wanted to give everything of himself but remembering his wife and young daughter at home and silently saying a prayer that today's protest wouldn't turn out to be too messy, that no bones would be broken. Then she thought of Jack and his friends turning up to meetings. Breaking through the police ring protecting Jordan, rushing after his car and banging on the windows or the bonnet, anything to let Jordan know that the Jews weren't afraid. They couldn't be driven out of sight.

It was warm but she shivered. The more she thought of it, the less she wanted to go to a meeting, but she couldn't let fear stop her. She would come back. She would come back every Sunday if it meant she might see Jack again.

*

Barry Klein should have left the office half an hour ago. He was always late home these days, so he couldn't blame his wife for cursing *The Times* and wishing he still worked for the *Hackney Gazette*. All day Sandra looked forward to six o'clock, when she could hand over their children and sit down quietly with a gin and lemon and a cigarette.

Barry's editor George was pacing, reading Barry's copy about Colin Jordan, but Barry didn't like George any better just because his expression suggested an appreciation of Barry's work.

'Good stuff,' said George. 'But use fewer funny names next time.'

'Funny names?'

'Feingold. Brownstein. Baum.' George flung the article at Barry's typewriter and walked away. Barry thought of all the decent Jewish people he'd interviewed for the article and he'd have liked to tell George to stop being a bigot, but it wasn't a battle worth fighting. Instead he clipped two pens to his suit inside pocket and picked up the ringing telephone.

'Newsroom.'

'It's me.'

Barry straightened up. His dad never called him at work. 'Everything all right?'

'Vivien Epstein paid me a visit,' said Sid.

'Vivien? Phil's daughter?'

'Yeah. She's down from Manchester.'

'Why?'

'She's looking for Jack.'

6

Maeve. Chrissie. Lydia. Marcia. Deirdre. The next morning, Vivien's first day at Oscar's, the girls huddled around her in the back room, passing around Gauloises cigarettes and iced buns, and saying in a chorus of sing-song voices, 'Ask away, Vivien. Anything you need to know. Don't be shy.'

She had a good feeling about all of them. She had expected them to be London-haughty and full of themselves, but they were plain-speaking and down to earth, except for their hair, which was beautifully styled and made each of them stand out.

'Here's your tea, Viv.' Lydia, one of the juniors, was a plain, friendly girl with a lot of bounce who until six months ago had been a telephone operator at the Park Lane Hotel. She was tall but not awkward about it. She seemed happy with herself. 'I can call you Viv, can't I?'

Vivien nodded, impressed by the neatness of Lydia's French pleat.

'I know I will cos my sister's called Viv.'

'He's got some bloody front,' said Maeve loudly. 'Already parading around with that tart.'

Maeve, a senior stylist like Chrissie, stared into the long wall mirror and poked a finger at her elaborately back-combed red bob. 'I never liked him. He's got beady eyes and thin lips.'

Maeve, as Vivien quickly discovered, was a straight talker. She'd already told Vivien her lipstick was too dark against her milky skin and teased the postman about his big feet.

'Chrissie's boyfriend went off with a cloakroom girl at the Flamingo Club,' Marcia whispered to Vivien behind her mug.

Vivien couldn't understand why anyone would choose to leave Chrissie. With her faded blue eyes and curtain of thick pale hair, some of which was drawn away from her face in a loose knot, she had a lovely dreamy quality.

'My skirt's too tight,' said Deirdre.

'Maybe you're pregnant,' said Maeve.

'Course I'm not! What a thing to say.' Deirdre sat in the corner with her shoes slipped off, resting her brown beehive against the back of the chair. By all accounts she was one of the oldest there, but her chubby face and baby-ish voice made her appear younger. 'Jesus. That's all I need.' She pulled at her skirt waistband. 'Dave hates me plump.'

Maeve stopped poking and turned to Vivien. 'We're off to La Crème after work. It's a coffee bar around the corner. The house band's playing tonight. Will you come?'

Vivien nodded. 'Yes, please.' Although she was not yet earning, she carried a small amount of money in her purse for emergencies. She was reluctant to spend it on going out, but even more reluctant to hide away on her own again like she'd done every evening since she got to London.

Marcia put down her tea and pinched the corners of her mouth. 'Right, Vivien, let's show you what's what.'

She began her short tour of the salon. Vivien followed and pretended to listen in a serious way but she had started working with Leo a week before her sixteenth birthday; she knew the drill.

Marcia wiggled her hips as she walked. She moved briskly and with purpose. Brushes and sprays got rearranged en route. Chairs were pushed into place. After fifteen minutes of non-stop talking, she gave Vivien a blue overall and her own pad for writing out bills.

'Barb said to break you in gently. So get yourself acquainted with how we do things. Don't be scared to ask questions.' Marcia smiled. 'We don't bite.'

All morning Vivien helped out where she could. She swept up hair and cleaned brushes. She collected towels and gowns and tidied the roller trays. She mixed up tints and filled small bottles with beer, which the salon sometimes used as setting lotion. And just after lunch she was rewarded with a client who hadn't booked an appointment.

Ivy Wimpole, a blank-eyed elfin girl with bitten-down fingernails and black knee-high boots, wanted blonde streaks. As Vivien gently pulled her hair through the holes in the rubber cap, Ivy didn't encourage conversation or look up from her magazine. It was only later that Marcia told her that Ivy was a regular from a strip club off Wardour Street, a detail that Vivien knew would make it into her next letter to Stella.

Mostly Vivien hung about the other stylists and gleaned what she could. She was excited. They were the best she had met and she could tell straight away that Chrissie was exceptional. She listened intently to her client's requests, and if they handed her a photo of a film star whose hair they wanted to copy, she would study it carefully. Then she'd always go her own way. If the client protested, which they often did, sometimes covering their heads with their hands, she would offer up her hazy smile and tell them not to worry. She would make them look gorgeous. And it worked every time. They bristled and pouted but always settled down and believed her vision for them.

Maeve was skilled in a different way. Vivien stood behind her for some time, drawn into her precise, delicate method of snaking and pinning up strands of a client's hair so it resembled a beautiful tapestry. As she watched, Marcia came up behind her with a mug of tea and whispered, 'Isn't she terrific? We poached her from Mr Teasy-Weasy.'

Raymond 'Teasy-Weasy' Bessone! Vivien could hardly wait to quiz Maeve about working with such a legend. When she caught him on television she was always mesmerised by his fake French accent and theatrical flair. Full of admiration for the deft way he handled his models' hair, she understood that his artistic work was something unique.

'How are you, Vivien?'

Vivien was folding clean gowns when Barb came up behind her.

'Fine, thank you, Barb. Everyone's been very welcoming.'

Barb's shoulder-length blonde hair was simply set and sprayed and her make-up was discreet. Vivien also noted her stylish but unshowy cream dress and simple red-beaded necklace. It was impressive that for a manager of a popular salon, Barb appeared to be uninterested in drawing attention to herself.

'Vivien's going to fit in fine, Barb.' Maeve plucked grey hairs from a brush. 'She's already done a couple of sets and she did a smashing job on Ivy Wimpole's streaks. Ivy said she's only going to use her from now on.'

'Good girl,' said Barb. 'If you have any questions just give me a shout.'

'How did you get on, Barb?' asked Maeve. 'See anything you like?'

Barb sighed. 'Only what I couldn't afford.'

'Barb's getting married in August,' Maeve said to Vivien. 'She's on the hunt for bridesmaids' dresses.'

'Miss Dent!' Barb suddenly exclaimed. 'What a divine coat!'

A girl in dark sunglasses had come through the door

with a white coat hung over her shoulders like a cloak, emphasising her jutting breasts. A black cigarette with a gold tip hung between her fingers.

The moment Barb walked away, Maeve moved in closer to Vivien. 'She's in films. We get a lot of actresses in here,' she said, then lowered her voice and added, 'I try to make a fuss about the wedding because Barb's had terrible trouble. Don't say nothing, but last month her dad left her mum to go and live with another woman. Went out for milk, and bam! Never came back.'

As Maeve raised both eyebrows and pulled the last of the grey hairs from the brush, Vivien wished she hadn't been told this. It was stifling to carry around other people's secrets and she didn't want to have to watch what she said or did, which usually happened when you knew something you shouldn't.

The sun warmed the back of Stevie's neck as he walked through Brewer Street market, but that didn't bother him. His cotton shirt was airy, his denim jacket was hooked comfortably over his shoulder. He had dressed exactly right, and this small victory flooded him with pleasure. What a good day this was! None of the usual doubts were crowding his mind. He felt clear and strong, as if he was finally going places. He flirted with the grandmas shovelling carrots and cabbages into shopping bags and greeted almost all of the stallholders by name. On Frith Street he pretend-tangoed with Mrs Choy, who was sweeping the pavement in front of Choys, his favourite Chinese restaurant, then chatted with the two old Irish fellers playing dominoes outside the pub.

In the café on the corner of Charing Cross Road he looked around for the Marvels, a band from Sheffield he'd played with the night before. Yesterday morning the manager of

Le Noir, who knew Stevie from afternoons spent browsing in HMV, had telephoned him about the gig. The Marvels were headlining that night but were a drummer down after a bout of food poisoning. The manager admitted the band couldn't find anyone else at such short notice and he knew Stevie was a drummer. That phone call had been Stevie's one slice of luck these past few days.

'Afternoon, Stevo.' The old Italian behind the counter wiped his hands on his white apron. 'Cuppa?'

'Cheers, Mr C.'

Stevie saw the band playing cards at a table near the back so he made his way over.

'Stevie boy! Park yourself.' Jim reached out and shook Stevie's hand. 'A bloody good night, wasn't it?'

Stevie returned his grin. 'I loved every minute of it.'

It was a miracle to hear Jim, the raw-boned shouty guitarist, being so pleasant. He hadn't been the day before, but then, in hindsight, Stevie might have been a touch too confident at first. It hadn't translated to his playing. He'd loved hearing the band perform – their sound was fantastic – but when the long afternoon of rehearsals began, he'd sat nervously behind his kit and made so many mistakes Jim had shouted at him to stop and huddled the others into a corner. Stevie had wiped his face with the bottom of his T-shirt while they rolled their cigarettes and whispered furtively. He had prayed for their compassion, and his prayer must have been heard because they didn't replace him, the gig went ahead and he'd killed it. His trembling hands did what he wanted them to do and the crowd had gone barmy. He felt like a star.

Stevie pulled up a chair and listened to their stories about clip joints and saucy girls. There was an enviable hint of sex and booze coming off them, and he wished they'd told him they were hitting the town after the gig.

He rubbed his hands together. 'What time tonight?'

Everyone fell quiet.

'About tonight,' said Jim.

Stevie drew in his breath.

'Pete's right as rain this morning,' said Jim.

Stevie exhaled and stared at Jim chewing down his chips. That was fast, he thought. His first break in ages snatched away from him before he'd even had time to take any real pleasure in it. Now it felt like a crack had formed down his middle and his good humour was seeping through it.

'OK,' he said. 'Glad he's feeling better.'

'That's my boy,' said Jim.

Stevie forced a smile, then took a sip of tea. He was no one's boy. There were a few awkward seconds, a throat-clearing cough, but then they just carried on talking about nothing much. Stevie joined in but his heart wasn't in it, so after a while he threw down some change and said his goodbyes.

On the street he let himself feel the disappointment that he chose not to show in front of them. 'It's just a gig,' he whispered to himself furiously. 'It's just one of those things.'

He would have screamed if he'd been at home. He knew his mum was right when she told him he was too old to throw tantrums and kick doors, but he couldn't always control himself. He still got angry when he was disappointed, and sometimes he became so caught up in it he would say and do things he didn't mean. The sort of things that upset other people and were impossible to take back.

The sky was darkening, the shops had shut up. Stevie pressed his forehead against the front window of a burger bar on Old Compton Street. He was still hungry, but unless he wanted his evening to end here, a bag of chips was all he could afford. Now he was on the lookout for people he knew, keen for some company to take the edge off his mood. A drink or two. A leisurely game of pool. *Anything*. He just couldn't bear to head home yet. The idea of trying to watch television while his mum talked him through every show and his dad snoozed depressed the hell out of him.

He walked around for a while, drifting in and out of pubs and coffee bars, but he didn't recognise anyone and eventually he grew bored of looking. But on his way to get the bus, he spotted Maeve and Vivien at the top of the queue making its way inside La Crème. He called their names and ran over but they didn't hear, and he was left queuing on the pavement behind a knot of other people.

Inside it was already hot and the air was scratchy with smoke. Johnny Kidd & The Pirates 'Shakin' All Over' came on the jukebox and Stevie stopped next to it, briefly closing his eyes and letting the music pour over him. This was one of his favourite tunes. It always filled him with joy, and it made him feel as if good things might still happen to him tonight.

The upstairs was so narrow, everyone was locked tightly together. As he pushed his way through, he said hello to the musician he knew who went everywhere with a guitar strapped to her back, and shook the hand of a friend who washed dishes at a greasy spoon two doors down. The tiny girl with the bird-like features working the coffee machine caught his eye and waved, then carried on sliding small cups onto saucers.

He raised himself up on the balls of his feet and scanned the rest of the room until his eyes landed on the girls sitting on stools by the kitchen door. He called out and clicked his fingers but they didn't notice. They were in a world of their own. Marcia was dipping her finger into the bowl of brown sugar and licking off the granules. Deirdre was puffing up Maeve's hair at the back with a comb. Chrissie was dancing alone with her eyes shut, twirling her hands gracefully around her body. But when he arrived in front of them, they all came together and seemed happy to see him. Chrissie tried to pull him into her dance, and Maeve hung her arm around his neck and mocked him like he was her kid brother, because she'd just turned twenty-one and it wasn't his birthday until the following week. But tonight he didn't care. He just wanted Vivien to turn round and notice him.

She was a couple of feet away by the wall, bent over slightly, gazing at all the photos of the musicians who'd played in the basement over the years. Her suit had been replaced by a simple pink dress with pink cloth buttons, and when she bent even lower, he caught a glimpse of nylons as her skirt rode up. Her shoes were flat, blue and pointed, identical to Lydia's, and he wondered if Lydia, who knew most of the local shop owners personally, had taken her shopping in her lunch break. Vivien already looked more like one of the girls.

As she squeezed into the gaps between people, hands clasped lightly behind her back, he had the feeling he could stare at her doing small, ordinary things all night, and never get bored. He walked over to her.

'Hello.'

He'd bellowed to be heard over the record but it ended just at that moment. Vivien spun round, wide-eyed, her palm pressed against her chest.

'Sorry,' he said. 'I didn't mean to make you jump.'

'It's all right. I was miles away.' She smiled. 'How was your audition?'

'Great,' he said, delighted that she'd remembered. 'I ended up playing with the band last night. It was a killer gig but it was just a one-off. They don't need me again.'

'That's a shame.'

'Well, that's the music business.' He shrugged and tried to appear indifferent, but her penetrating look made him think she could tell he was pretending to be something he wasn't.

'We had a few actresses in today,' she said, dropping her voice and looking sweetly excited, as if she was letting him in on a secret.

'You had a good first day, then?'

'It was great.' She threw her arms open and looked around, grinning. 'I keep pinching myself. I can't believe I'm here.'

Watching her take a cigarette from the packet he offered, Stevie wondered how he could get to know her better. If he knew her better he could brush away the strand of hair from her lip. He could ask her what her middle name was. He could drape his arm around her waist and call her sweetheart.

A muted drum roll and the clatter of a cymbal interrupted his thoughts. The band must be limbering up. Before he could suggest going downstairs, Vivien looked over his shoulder and smiled. He turned. Maeve was beckoning to her.

'I should get back to them,' she said nicely.

'Sure.'

He stood aside but then he wanted to call her back. He'd done nothing to impress her. Everything he'd wanted to say had stayed inside him, and he felt a pang of despondency similar to the way he'd felt the last time he'd watched her walk away.

'I'll come downstairs too,' he called out, but he was talking to her back because she and Maeve were already heading down the dodgy staircase. He waited while others moved ahead of him, but then went downstairs too. At the bottom, when he pushed open the door to the cellar, a blast of heat and music and sweat hit him in the face.

Twice that month Stevie had seen the resident band play, and although he didn't mind their jazzy beat, it didn't set him on fire. But tonight he wasn't there for the entertainment. He elbowed his way through the crowd until he was behind Vivien, and when he touched her shoulder, she gave him a quick bland smile, then turned away. Her eyes were fixed on the band, pounding away on the tiny makeshift stage, which wasn't much more than planks of wood secured over milk crates.

'I'm twenty-one next week,' he said loudly as Maeve took Vivien's hand and attempted to drag her even closer to the front. 'Will you come to my party on Saturday with the others?'

He was grateful that she nodded before slipping away. At least he had that to go on. He lit a cigarette, watching her eyes dart around nervously when Maeve started dancing. She appeared to be studying all the girls around her as if she were sizing herself up against them. He edged forward, wanting to go to her and make her feel better, but then she began to dance and her self-consciousness immediately vanished. She flung her arms above her head and twisted around, moving perfectly to the music, like she knew exactly what she was doing. She looked happy. Glowing.

He was transfixed. He barely moved except when he was bumped around by others. He stopped hearing the music. He stopped caring that he wasn't the one up on stage behind the drums. He only had eyes for her, and he wondered if this was what they called love.

7

The next day Vivien's sore feet rubbed against her shoes. She was relieved to be walking down her street, knowing she could soon soak in the bath and go to bed. It was the first time she'd been dancing since Dad died and it felt new to her, like her body had forgotten how to do it.

Nearly there, she thought, reassured by the thought of chicken pie, which Nettie had informed her that morning she would be cooking for their Friday night dinner. But as she drew closer to the house, she recognised the woman crouched down on the pavement.

'Nettie?' She squatted next to her. 'What's the matter?'

Nettie looked up at her with confused eyes. She was clutching an apple so hard, her nails had dug into the peel. 'I dropped my shopping.'

Vivien picked up three onions from the gutter and put them in Nettie's bag while Nettie rose unsteadily and looked around her. She was ashen-faced and wobbly, holding on to the gate as if her legs were about to give way.

'I think that's everything.'

'I've had a bit of a shock,' said Nettie.

'What happened?'

'I bumped into a friend in Tesco on Mare Street. He told me hooligans had got into the cemetery where Archie's buried. They've painted graffiti all over the place.'

'Oh no,' said Vivien, horrified.

Nettie's eyes were watery. 'They painted swastikas on

some of the graves and kicked over some headstones. What … what if … Archie's …?'

Her voice shrank to no more than a whimper, and although she was still talking Vivien couldn't understand a word.

'Is the cemetery nearby?' she asked.

'Lauriston Road. A bit of a walk.'

'Let's go and make sure everything is OK.'

Nettie shook her head. 'I'll go tomorrow.'

'Let's go now,' said Vivien. 'Otherwise you won't sleep. We'll just put your shopping indoors.'

They didn't talk about what they might find but it hung over them during their quiet twenty-minute walk. A neighbour bumping a pram along stopped to say hello and ask Nettie how she was, but Nettie waved her away and claimed she didn't have time to chat.

At the cemetery entrance KEEP BRITAIN WHITE was painted on a wall. Neither of them commented as they passed it, but Vivien held Nettie's hand a little tighter. There was a stillness everywhere, except for the gentle rhythmic shushing of the trees and the sound of a man scrubbing FUCK OFF YIDS from a wooden bench.

Vivien stared at the graffiti. The writing looked so childish and messy, as if it had been a struggle even to get these few simple words right.

The man faced them, his brush dripping with foam. 'Who would do something like this?' he said.

Nettie shook her head.

He turned away, scrubbing at the paint so hard the water flew in all directions. After asking him if he needed any help and getting no response, they left him alone and carried on walking. Then Nettie stopped and grabbed Vivien's arm.

'Oh, thank God.' She clapped both hands over her mouth. 'They've left him in peace.'

Vivien stood a few feet away while Nettie moved closer to Archie's grave and knelt down to talk to him. She looked around at the rows of headstones and thought of her last visit to the cemetery where Dad was buried and the tidy rows of snowdrops and daffodils she'd planted on his grave.

The memory of it made her long for him. She thought of him telling her about his students as she trimmed his hair and beard. How fresh and talkative he was from the instant he woke up. The pleasure he took in every meal she cooked for him. The pleasure he took in her. Vivien felt choked up. She closed her eyes, took a deep breath and tilted her face to the sky.

The next evening, after a busy Saturday in the salon, the girls trooped down the street towards Stevie's small plain house in Dalston, where he was holding his twenty-first-birthday party.

The other girls were glammed up and feverish with excitement about the prospect of meeting new men, but Vivien found it difficult to join in. She regretted agreeing to come. She liked Stevie and usually she loved parties, but she felt quiet and was already exhausted at the thought of strangers cajoling her story out of her. All she could hope for was a stream of great music so she would have the excuse of dancing without appearing to be either rude or disinterested.

A home-made HAPPY BIRTHDAY banner was draped over the front door. Laughter and exuberant voices rushed through the open window; music stopped and started. As they went inside, Vivien braced herself to be greeted by dozens of intimidating musician types, but instead the front room was only three-quarters full, and there were just as many elderly relatives as guests around her own age.

Stevie shot out towards them in a blue suit, arms open wide. 'Don't you all look a million dollars.'

Chrissie crinkled her nose and batted him away. 'Someone's been drinking.'

'That'll be me.' Stevie rearranged his narrow tie. 'Hello, Vivien,' he said, glancing at her.

'Happy birthday, Stevie,' she said and noticed with alarm that the girls had already left her side, scattering across the room.

'How are you?'

'Fine, thank you,' she said.

'You had a good time at La Crème the other night, didn't you?'

'I did.'

'You're a cracking dancer.'

'Oh, thank you. The music was great.' She smiled and looked around, hoping one of the girls would catch her eye.

'What's your poison?'

'White wine, please.'

'You got it.'

As she waited for her drink, a woman introduced herself as Stevie's auntie, then shouted in her face every last detail of the mystery illness she'd just recovered from. Nausea and the shakes. Stomach rash. Diarrhoea. She would have talked on except Stevie's dad Howie put on a record by Georgie Fame and the Blue Flames and ordered everyone to stop nattering and dance.

Vivien had just taken out a cigarette and lighter when Stevie reappeared. He whipped the lighter from her hand and held the flame up to her cigarette. As she took a puff, he lowered his face towards her, his boozy breath warm on her cheeks.

'You look great in that dress.'

Vivien stared at the ground and took a gulp of her drink, scared of what he might say next.

'I mean it,' he added.

62

'Oh this,' she said. 'It's very old.'

'Have you had your hair cut?' He stepped back and squinted at her.

She puffed on her cigarette and willed him to stop studying her. 'Just a trim.'

'Suits you.'

She wanted to be friendly – she liked him – but she didn't want him to notice her clothes or the way she danced or if her hair had been cut. She didn't want him to single her out. He was good company and she liked his look and the way he carried himself, but he wasn't Jack. He would never have Jack's shine.

'I love this song.' She swayed around a little. The year before she'd bought a copy of Helen Shapiro's 'Walkin' Back to Happiness' and spent several happy evenings darting, wet and loosely towelled, between the bath and the record player in her bedroom.

'Yeah? She's playing live soon. I bet you'd love to see her, right?'

Sensing an invitation was on its way, she was relieved when Barb's appearance cut short their conversation and Stevie was called away to welcome a distant cousin.

'You've not met my fiancé Alan, have you?' Barb said.

Alan shook Vivien's hand enthusiastically. He looked a few years older than Barb, with a mouth of overcrowded yellowing teeth, but his greeting was warm and effusive, his smile broad, and Vivien liked the way his arm was permanently crooked around Barb's waist.

'Congratulations,' said Vivien. 'Not long now?'

'Nope.' Alan looked sideways and kissed Barb's cheek. 'Can't wait. Barb said you've come down from Manchester. Finding your feet OK?'

'Oh yes. I've got smashing lodgings and –' she sneaked a quick look at Barb '– I couldn't have found a better job.'

'Best boss in London, right?' Barb raised her glass.

'Absolutely,' said Vivien, smiling as they clinked glasses. 'How did you get that?' Alan's left eye was terribly bruised and puffy. 'It looks painful.'

'Fighting,' said Barb.

'That's not how it sounds,' he said to Vivien.

'He protests at those bloody fascist meetings in Ridley Road every Sunday,' said Barb. 'Against my wishes, let me add. Most weeks he comes back with a different injury.'

'Don't start, Barb.'

'I'm not starting! I worry. Tell Vivien how you got the eye. Go on. Tell her about the hiding you got last week.'

'That's awful. You poor thing,' said Vivien, thinking about Jack.

Alan sighed. 'There was a lot of aggro, but it's not as bad as Barb's making out.'

'Please.' Barb moved angrily out of Alan's grasp. 'You don't know shit from sugar.' She turned to Vivien. 'He was in bed for two days. Couldn't even open up the shop.'

'Do you go to meetings often?' asked Vivien.

'As often as I can.'

'Have you ever come across a man called Jack Fox?'

Alan frowned and thought for a moment. 'Don't think so. But there's always a big turnout. Faces I don't know.'

Vivien nodded and tried to conceal her disappointment. 'I'm going tomorrow. I want to see what it's all about.'

'Those meetings are no place for a young girl,' said Barb. 'Tell her, Alan.'

'Barb's right. It can get rough.'

'I'll be careful.' Vivien watched them exchange a glance.

'Well, at least go with Alan,' Barb said. 'He'll keep an eye on you.'

Alan nodded. 'I'd be happy to.'

'Oh, I'd like that,' said Vivien. 'Thank you.'

'But I won't be down Ridley tomorrow.' He took a huge mouthful of ale and used the back of his hand to wipe the froth off his upper lip. 'Jordan has hired Trafalgar Square for his first proper National Socialist Movement rally. It'll be a circus. Television and the papers will be all over it. A load of us are going together. You can get the bus up west with me.'

Vivien left the party an hour or so later. She'd had a good dance around with Stevie and the girls, she'd even had her glass refilled a couple of times, but she couldn't muster up any more enthusiasm. She wanted an early night, to dream of Jack until morning. Everything else seemed like a waste of time. She shut Stevie's front door, then heard it click open and recognised, without turning around, the voice calling her name.

'Where are you going?' Stevie stood in the doorway.

'I'm a bit done in,' she said.

'But it's early.' He moved from foot to foot. 'The party's just getting going.'

'Have a wonderful evening, Stevie,' she said firmly. 'And happy birthday again.'

'I'm really pleased you were here tonight.'

His words came out in a rush, like he'd been storing them up. She smiled, panicked. She shouldn't have danced so close to him. She should have kept her distance and said something to make him realise she wasn't interested.

'Well, thank you for asking me. It was nice of you.'

Standing in the dim shaft of light, she could make out the hope in his smile and realised he was probably working up the courage to ask her out. Her cheeks flamed red. She wanted to run away, or for the ground to swallow her up. But then his smile faded, his mouth shut and he stepped back.

He's changed his mind, she thought, relieved. He'd read her mood.

'I should go,' she said and gestured vaguely behind her.

'Yeah. Sure.'

'Night-night, Stevie. It really was a lovely party,' she said in an over-friendly voice, waving as she walked away.

8

At one o'clock the following day Vivien and seven men stood together outside a bookshop on Charing Cross Road, preparing to walk down to Trafalgar Square.

On the bus ride over the men had fooled about and teased each other, but now most of them seemed uneasy and tense. Alan was the worst. He took small sips from his bottle of Pepsi and talked fast about anything that came into his head.

Only Davy, a wiry, balding cabbie from Dalston with a Star of David hanging on a chain outside his shirt, didn't seem scared of what was coming. When Alan turned to greet the last of his friends, Davy opened up his bag and whispered to Vivien to take a look. She peered in and saw a long brown sock, which on closer inspection seemed to be filled with sand. Davy wound the end of it around his hand and hit the sock against the side of the bag so it gave a menacing *thwack*.

'I don't trust anyone.' He closed the bag. 'Especially the police. They're in bed with those bastards.'

'Davy, be quiet.' Alan turned around. 'You'll frighten Vivien.'

'Should I be frightened?' she asked Alan. She didn't like the way her voice quivered but she was only here as an onlooker. She was here to find Jack.

'No,' Alan said firmly. 'You'll be with me. Nothing will happen to you.'

It was early afternoon, the hottest day of the summer so far, and Vivien was plucking her skirt away from her waist when a circular was pressed into her palm.

She met the flinty eyes of the boy passing out the leaflets and smiled, then read the headline KEEP BRITAIN WHITE. Immediately she wanted to let the leaflet drop but she held on to it, frozen. There were people all around them and someone might be watching. She couldn't be sure whose side anyone was on.

When someone let out a long whistle and shouted at everyone to get going, Alan clutched her arm. 'Stay close. Barb'll gut me if I let you out of my sight.'

They were several minutes away on foot from Trafalgar Square and the atmosphere on the streets was still calm. People were buying tickets for the pictures. Groups of tourists were holding up maps and pointing in all directions, and through the window of a tea shop Vivien could make out an elderly couple choosing cream cakes from a trolley. It was like any other Sunday in the city.

From where she stood nothing much seemed to be happening in the square either, but as they drew closer she steeled herself. Hordes of people were walking between the traffic, bringing it to a standstill. Drivers were sounding their horns and leaning out of windows to shout at those walking in front of their cars. When they got to the top of the square, Vivien looked down and gasped. There must have been a thousand people at least already gathered in the square's grey and concrete vastness. She could have wept with disappointment. What chance did she have of picking Jack out in this crowd? The day already felt doomed.

'All right, Vivien?' asked Alan.

'I didn't realise Jordan had so many supporters.'

'Oh no, they're not supporters. Most of them are here to protest.'

Her eyes swept across the square. 'That's a lot of people in one place.'

'Yeah. It's a big day for Jordan.' Alan raised his voice as someone tested the tannoy. 'We'll have to make sure it doesn't work out for him.'

They began walking down the steps towards Nelson's Column, where a platform had been erected on the plinth with two large placards set behind it painted with BRITAIN AWAKE and FREE BRITAIN FROM JEWISH CONTROL. A banner with NATIONAL SOCIALIST MOVEMENT hung in front of the plinth, the four bronze lions at the base shining in the sun.

Vivien was relieved when Alan shouted to the others to stop where they were. As far as she was concerned they had gone far enough already, and she didn't want to press on into the crowd any further. They could clearly see what was happening on the plinth, feel the tension rising off the crowds near the front, but she felt safe where they stood. Police were lined up nearby, and the steady flow of water from the fountain, a short distance in front of her, felt cooling somehow.

Alan passed Vivien a lit cigarette. As she smoked, she looked around for Jack. Twice she thought she'd seen him, only to crane forward and realise it wasn't him. But, glancing at everyone, it was becoming clearer which side people were on. There were Jews wearing yellow stars and communists waving red flags, and a few young people holding up CND placards.

Next to them a man in a long blue robe with hair like golden stalks of corn was yelling that the concentration camps had never existed, and two teenage boys with photos of Hitler pinned to their leather jackets shouted, 'Heil Hitler!' and, 'Jew bastards!' As soon as this happened, Alan darted in front of Davy. He gripped Davy's upper arms and

69

she couldn't hear what he whispered into his ear, but Davy stood back and turned his face away from the boys.

A chill ran through her. She wasn't sure what she'd expected to find but she'd never been so close to this sort of hatred. She'd read about the meetings, and her dad had told her about his experiences, but this was something entirely different. What was worse, she realised, was seeing all the well-groomed, ordinary-looking women. The sort who'd baked her pies and given her motherly advice after Dad's funeral, except these women had swastikas pinned to their blouses or flowery summer dresses.

A roar ripped through the crowd. Several men in brown shirts and heavy army boots were climbing onto the plinth. People pushed forward and the line of police moved with them.

It was beginning.

The first speaker was tall and tubby with a grating voice that got lost under a storm of abuse. He screamed into the microphone that Jewish people were the assassins of Europe, and when he shrieked, 'Heil Hitler!', a wave of people surged forward.

Vivien held her breath, not sure what to do. Men were already trying to climb the plinth, lasso the party placards and pull them down. Others, like Alan and Davy, were shouting and swearing. She wanted to clap her hands over her ears and crouch down. This was far more terrifying than she'd expected. She wanted to turn around and leave. Forget she'd ever come to London. Transport herself back to Manchester, where she could lie on her bed and feel safe.

Now coins and fruit were flying through the air, aimed at the man who had just stridden onto the platform and informed the crowd that he was Colin Jordan.

He took the microphone and shouted into it, 'More ...

people every day … opening their eyes and … seeing Hitler was right … Our real enemies … were not Hitler and the National Socialists of Germany, but world Jewry … In this country …'

Crammed into a brown uniform, chunks of hair falling across his forehead, it was a comfort to discover that Jordan wasn't remotely the impressive figure she had thought he would be. She could scarcely make out what he was saying. His voice did not carry well; he sounded weak, and he lacked presence.

As she strained to hear, and wondered how much shoving she could stand, she saw a boy climb the fountain and stand on the surround.

'I'll be back,' she said to Alan.

'Vivien!' He pulled on her arm. 'What the hell are you doing?'

She shook his hand away. 'I'm going to climb that fountain.'

'What?'

Before he could pull her back, she'd squeezed in through the crowd and headed towards the fountain.

'This Jewish government of Britain is … the disregard of real British interests at every turn … this Coloured Invasion …'

She hoisted herself up and found her balance. Now at least she could breathe and move without fear of being squashed or pushed. She scanned the crowds for Jack, and as she did, she was shocked at the number of people near the front who were fighting with men in brown shirts.

Jordan's talk was crumbling. He was flailing around, repeating what he'd already said and ducking the objects flying through the air. The hostility was escalating.

Jordan shouted into his microphone, 'Hitler was right—'

The crowd booed and clapped.

'Our real enemy is the Jew—'

Now people were going crazy. Vivien's hand leaped to her mouth. A female protester holding up a star was being dragged along by two policemen. Her handbag was torn from her and tossed into the air. Davy punched someone in the face, pulled back his fist and punched the same person again.

Her eyes went back and forth for what seemed like ages. Things were getting more dangerous by the minute: scores of police were now embroiled in the fighting, pulling people apart, waving truncheons.

Defeated, Jordan was led off the plinth and forced into the back of an old army-style truck, but the sight of him getting away seemed to whip the crowd into an even greater frenzy. They were trying to get to the vehicle and overturn it while a long line of Jordan's men in brown shirts opposed them. With their arms hooked around each other they pushed back against the unruly crowd while the police tried to intervene and break things up.

She should go. This was happening too close to her. As sirens sounded nearby, she wanted to insist that Alan take her home, but at the same time she could not stop looking, drawn to the unfolding drama. She glanced again at the men around the plinth, and then her eyes fell on one man jumping down from the back of the truck.

It was Jack.

She could tell by his narrow face and strong jaw, the broad slant of his shoulders. Nothing about him had faded from her mind. Her mouth dried. Her heart pounded in her chest. For a brief moment she was overcome with bliss.

'Jack,' she screamed. 'Jack Fox.'

'Get down, miss.' A policeman stood in front of her.

'Jack!'

The policeman tapped her shin twice, but she refused

to take her eyes off Jack and kept calling his name even though she knew he couldn't hear her. She thought about climbing down and running to him, but she would only get trampled if she went into the crowd now.

'If you don't get down, Vivien, they'll nick you.' Alan was standing by the fountain, tugging hard at her skirt. 'Are you listening to me?'

She ignored him. Instead she called Jack's name so many times and so violently she thought she might be sick. She held her stomach, coughed, then steeled herself for more, and as she did so Jack turned his face in her direction, and everything else between them became as faint as a watermark.

He was all she could see. She waved frantically, blew him kisses and waited for him to smile or wave or do something to acknowledge her. But he didn't.

At first he just stared in her direction, open-mouthed. Then, as it dawned on her he wasn't waving back, he turned his whole body to face her, raised his arm into the air and executed a perfect Nazi salute.

The din of the crowd sounded very far away as if she was underwater. Her eyes blurred. 'Jack,' she said under her breath. A man next to Jack, whose arm was also raised in the air, said something to him, and they both turned and pushed hard at the police.

'Miss, get down right now, or you're nicked!'

Alan found them all spaces on the top deck of the bus. He steered Vivien into the seat next to him by the window and she sank into it, detaching herself from everything around her. She felt as if she was dreaming. As the bus moved off, Alan put his arm around her shoulder and gave it a gentle squeeze. He was being very kind. On the walk over he'd already asked her who Jack was, but her body was shaking and she couldn't speak. He'd simply squeezed her hand and didn't ask again.

Davy was pacing up and down. He ignored the stares of the other passengers and banged his fist against every rail, shouting abuse about Jordan.

'Davy, sit down and behave. You're upsetting people,' said Alan. Then he spoke quietly in Vivien's ear, 'You look done in. Did it scare you?'

'A little.'

'We'll go to the pub.' He patted her arm. 'Get a stiff drink into you.'

Vivien looked through the window at the blur of London. She looked at every tree and every building, waiting for something that made sense to her. Eventually, she tried using only her eyes and not letting in any thoughts at all, because every single one was destroying her inside.

9

She'd intended to leave the pub after one drink, but Alan strong-armed her into taking another and another after that. She found it difficult to say no to anything at all. She just sat very still and accepted everything. When Alan put the third glass of brandy in front of her, she raised it to her lips and took a swallow. The brandy burned the back of her throat and made her splutter. She pushed the glass away and with her eyes lightly shut, she leaned back in her chair, half listening to an old man share his stories about scrapping with fascists in Cable Street in the mid-1930s.

'Vivien.'

Opening her eyes, she saw Stevie leaning towards her holding a pint of Guinness.

As she struggled to sit up properly, a rush of blood came to her head, making her dizzy. 'What are you doing here?' she asked.

'It's my local. I live next door to Barb, remember? I'm meeting my brother here in a bit.' He frowned at her. 'You look pale. Are you OK?' He set his glass down on the table, pulled up a stool and sat opposite her.

'I think so.'

'How was the rally?'

'Horrible.'

'I bet.'

He raised her glass to his nose and sniffed. 'Brandy.' He wrinkled his nose. 'Can't stand the stuff.'

'Me neither.'

Stevie's eyes were on her as he ran his hands over the sides of his hair and straightened his shirt.

'You'll be all right in a bit,' he said. 'Barb said Alan used to come home shell-shocked the first few times he went to meetings.'

His head was tilted to one side and his eyes were soaking up her discomfort. His concern was sweet and Vivien appreciated it, but she could not make conversation. She did not lift her eyes from her glass. In the silence he tapped his beer mat against the table. He jiggled around in his seat. He exhaled noisily. And then, as if he could no longer hold himself back, he began talking in a whoosh. The records he'd been listening to that afternoon. The sick stray dog he'd found on the street. His mum's extraordinary roast potatoes which he would soon devour with a lick of home-made gravy. He was still talking when she stood up, smoothed down her dress and announced she needed the loo.

In the cubicle she crouched against the locked door and wept, only stopping when a woman banged on the door and told her to hurry up.

At the sink she held on to the edge, splashed cold water on her face and rubbed away smudges of kohl from her eyes. She still felt ghastly, like she might vomit or faint. She needed to go home.

What she didn't need was to pull back the door and come face to face with Stevie, leaning against the wall opposite. He looked up and moved towards her.

'You've been crying.' His voice was solemn. 'Did I say something wrong?'

'No. Not at all.'

'You shot out of your seat.'

'Not because of you. Look, I just need to go home.'

'I'll walk you.'

She shook her head.

'Please let me.'

'Stevie, I can't ...'

When he reached out to her, she tried to raise her arm in protest but all the strength had gone out of her. She let her arms fall; her bag dropped to the floor, and she burst into tears again.

As she pressed her head into his shoulder, he muttered her name and stroked her back. She said sorry but he couldn't have heard. Her voice was hidden in his shirt. Her lips were trembling. Her eyes were sore. Eventually she stopped crying and drew back a little, and the cold air rushed pleasantly at her, but as soon as she lifted her head, he put both hands on her cheeks, brought his lips down onto hers and kissed her. She let him for a moment, then pulled away and shook her head.

'Sorry,' he said. 'I didn't mean—'

'No. It's my fault. I'm sorry.' She avoided his eyes and bent down to pick up her handbag. She glanced up at him, planning to explain herself, but when she saw his tender, confused expression, she stepped back clumsily, mumbling *sorry sorry sorry*, and ran off through the pub and out into the street.

The next day Barry Klein hurried down Whitechapel Road. The recently appointed news editor had insisted on shaking hands with each of the reporters at the end of the editorial meeting and enquiring about what they were working on. Now Barry was late. But as he crossed the road in front of Bloom's restaurant, he forgot about everything except being famished and whether he could still order something to eat now that it was mid-afternoon.

He'd just opened the door when someone called out to

him. He turned to find an old school friend, Lloyd Rabin, already at his side, clutching his upper arm a little too hard, just as he had done in the playground when he regularly found a reason to seek Barry out in the breaks and pick on him.

'Long time no see.' Lloyd clapped him on the back. 'I hear you're at *The Times* now. Little Barry, who'd have thought,' he said, widening his eyes in disbelief.

'Lloyd. You well?' said Barry coolly.

'Can't complain, thank God.'

Of course there would be no complaints. Barry knew the business of selling tortoiseshell combs and sunglasses was highly lucrative. Lloyd already owned a three-bedroom detached house in Edgware and drove a black Renault.

They went inside. Except for the ten men seated around the long table in the far corner and the two women rooting through their purses at a table some distance away, there was none of the typical lunchtime bustle. Most of the wait-ers could be heard laughing on the other side of the kitchen doors. Every other table had been cleared.

Sid sat in the middle next to Barry's older brother Danny, who, after being sacked from a series of jobs – which ap-parently was never his fault – was now being trained up to work alongside his father in the pawnbroker's.

Sid greeted the two newcomers and gestured for Barry to take the chair across from him.

Barry was familiar with all of the men and he grasped each of the hands that were offered to him. Most of them were Sid's age and had served with him in the war. Barry didn't have to say his name; he was Sid's son, and they each made it their business to know about him and his life because Sid commanded more respect than most. Everyone Sid had invited had turned up because if he asked them to come, then he had something worth saying.

Barry was taking off his jacket when he noticed Sol Grant, another of Lloyd's friends from school, at the end of the table.

'So you're at *The Times*,' Sol called out with a smirk. 'You always were a clever sod.'

'I don't know about that,' said Barry, smiling.

But Sol's attention was already elsewhere. He'd swivelled around to stare at one of the women, who was smoothing down her tight skirt. 'Will you look at those pins,' he said to no one in particular.

Barry sighed and handed his menu back to the sinewy, olive-skinned waiter, who was trying to hurry him up by saying yes several times in a clipped voice. 'Egg and onion and a side of rye bread, please.'

Sid raised his hands. 'Let's get the ball rolling.' He leaned forward in his chair, then looked up and down the table. 'Some of you know we've had plans to get organised since Jordan broke away from the BNP. And if you were at the rally in Trafalgar Square yesterday, you can see why.' He glanced around the table. 'We're not dealing with the likes of Mosley now. No one can dub Jordan a kosher fascist. He's Arnold Leese's heir.'

As Barry wiped a handkerchief over his brow, everyone shifted uncomfortably in their seats. Even now, six years after his death, the hard-nosed, uncompromising fascist Arnold Leese's name was not one anyone wanted to hear.

'There may be other anti-fascist groups springing up, but as far as I'm concerned they're all small change. None of them are doing enough,' said Sid. 'We need to get organised again. Deal with it properly, on the street, like we did after the war.'

'Too fucking right,' shouted Danny.

'Some people think we should keep our heads down and say nothing,' continued Sid. 'Not draw attention to

79

ourselves. Well, you're here today because you know that doesn't work. We've got to get out there and fight back. Take direct action.'

Everyone clapped and there was a muttering of 'hear, hear'.

'But we've got to do it properly. Go at it from all sides.'

'How?' asked Jeremy.

If Barry had seen Jeremy Hadden walk down the street in his Savile Row suit with his chiselled face and silvery hair, he'd have assumed the man was a suave advertising executive with his mind on the next Martini, not an out-standing, courageous soldier who'd fought with the Jewish Brigade during the war.

'We've got to stop those bastards meeting in public,' said Sol. 'Take over street spots and get into the halls. Like the 43 Group did.'

'I agree,' said Sid. 'But we need men for that. We need to start recruiting.'

'That won't be a problem,' said Jeremy smoothly. He and the other ex-servicemen had done this on a much larger scale for the 43 Group; they were used to leading. 'Word is out that you're getting organised. The response is already good. We'll have the numbers.'

'Some men will need training,' said Sid.

'I know a guy who boxes,' said Sol. 'He'll teach them how to take care of themselves.'

'Get on to it,' said Sid.

'We also need to start our own newspaper, like *On Guard*, and get it onto the streets,' said Barry. 'Oppose some of the fascist propaganda out there. And we have to find out who's printing that horse shit and get them shut down. It won't be easy. Some of it will be printed in private houses.'

Everyone clapped, another round of 'hear, hear', but

when two waiters hovered around them, Sid asked everyone to stop talking. As Sid tucked a napkin into the neck
of his shirt, he put his hand gently on Danny's forearm
and said something quietly that made them both laugh.
Barry let his eyes linger on them before looking away. He
was sure they never intended to make him feel excluded.
He grabbed his plate from a waiter and took several bites
of bread before he realised what a pig he was making of
himself and slowed down.

'Chicken soup?'

'Here,' said Sid.

At the same time as the waiter hurriedly put down the
shallow bowl of soup, he attempted to take Sid's side plate
with one pickled gherkin still remaining.

Sid briefly clamped his wrist mid-air. 'I haven't finished
with that.'

Once he'd walked away, Sid lowered his head and dipped
pieces of challah into his soup as he spoke. With his robust,
passionate talk, he had no trouble firing up the men, and
they grew determined about what lay ahead.

'What do we call ourselves?' asked Sol.

'It's 1962,' said Jeremy after a lengthy pause. 'What about
the 62 Group?'

10

The linoleum was cold and raw under her bare feet. Goose bumps prickled her arms. Vivien reached for her cardigan hanging over the fireguard and tugged it around her, wondering if the weather had taken a turn. It might have done. Anything could have changed in the three days she'd spent in bed, a sheet pulled up to her chin.

She lit another cigarette and dropped into the armchair, dangling her legs over the side, watching the smoke curl into shafts of dusty light. Soon she must do something. Draw the curtains. Open a window. Get rid of the bitter, depressing smell that hung about the place.

And she had promised herself that today was the day. Today she would change her bed linen and air the room. Today she would get on with her life. She couldn't lie in bed for ever, sleeping, or sort of sleeping, dwelling on Jack.

The afternoon stretched emptily before her; Barb believed she was sick so work was not a problem. She could sit on the bench by the pond in the park and throw bread to the ducks. Go swimming. See a film. She sighed and rubbed her itchy, bloodshot eyes. She knew she had to go somewhere, position herself in the world again, but images of Jack at the rally made it hard. They kept dragging her back into the darkness. Kept her inside that awful space, thinking again and again about his salute and the swastika on his shirt pocket. What the hell was he playing at? And why?

When the cigarette had burned down to the filter, she crushed it out in the ashtray and stood up. The room swayed a little, and she might have fallen had she not put her hands on her waist and steadied herself. Jack used to do that, she thought. He liked to put both hands on her waist, squeeze hard and whisper sweet, silly things so close to her face that his breath tickled her skin. No, she thought, shaking her head hard. No more bloody tears. Not for him, anyway. They were wasted on him.

At the sink she ran a damp cloth over her body and brushed her hair until it crackled and the ends jumped. Only then did she dare glance at herself in the mirror. Her skin was too pale, almost waxy – nothing a spot of rouge wouldn't fix – but her eyes had lost their shine. They were cold and dull and reflected nothing back.

She sighed and opened her wardrobe, flicking through hangers, indifferent to everything, old or new. In the end she put on the first blouse and skirt to slip into her hands and had just done up the zip when a short knock at the door startled her.

'It's just me,' shouted Nettie and pushed her way in. 'I heard you up and about. I thought you might be hungry.' She held up a tray, then put it on the edge of the coffee table.

'That's very kind of you.' Vivien sat down in the armchair again. It was the first time she'd spoken aloud that day, and her tongue felt thick in her mouth.

'It's just chicken soup.'

'It smells delicious.'

'I heard crying,' said Nettie. 'You must miss him.'

A moment lapsed before Vivien realised Nettie was talking about her dad. She pressed the cold round of the spoon against her palm and nodded. She did miss him. She thought of how strong he was. He didn't give up after Mum

83

died. He hadn't acted like life had short-changed him. He understood that grief was part of living. He soldiered on, got through.

He was such a wonderful man, and it was terrible that Jack had taken him for an idiot. She tore off a strip of bread, dunking it in the soup as her sorrow turned to anger in her chest on Dad's behalf.

'I think I'll go into work after this,' she said to Nettie.

'Really?' Nettie said on her way out. 'You still look a little peaky.'

'This is helping,' Vivien called as Nettie shut the door.

I'll be fine, she thought determinedly. She would surprise herself. She would need less love than she thought.

The girls at Oscar's crowded around her, a web of concern. They accepted her story of nausea and shakes and offered her tea and sympathy. They didn't seem to notice her pale voice, how lying always made her fold into herself.

Except Barb. She wasn't so easy to fool.

'You still don't look well.' She pushed her glasses up her forehead. 'Are you sure you should be here?'

'I feel much better.' Vivien turned away from Barb's steady gaze and fanned her face. 'It's like a sauna in here,' she said in an attempt to change the conversation. The sun was pushing against the window, mingling with the doughy heat from the driers.

Barb leaned in and pressed her mouth up close to Vivien's ear. 'Alan mentioned you'd had an upset at the rally.' She pulled back and rubbed Vivien's upper arm. 'Something to do with a boy?'

'Something like that.' Colour burst across Vivien's face. Please, she thought. Please don't make me think about it.

'Your job's safe, if that's what you're worried about.'

'I'm fine, Barb. I'm here to work.'

'OK.' Barb's face softened. 'But remember –' her voice fell to a whisper '– nothing shocks me.'

Vivien nodded. 'Thank you, Barb.'

Barb lifted up her arms, then dropped them back down, as if the idea of a hug was best left in her mind. I wouldn't want to embarrass her, Vivien could see her thinking, I wouldn't want to get carried away.

Vivien smiled bravely. She could have done with a hug. She wouldn't have minded a clumsy embrace where arms didn't go where they should and laughter was false and uncomfortable.

Barb's voice grew large again. 'I know what Vivien needs!' She clapped her hands. 'A trip to Madame Floris.'

'Who?' asked Vivien.

'Oh my God!' Lydia snorted excitedly. 'Viv don't know Madame Floris!'

'You're in for a treat,' said Chrissie.

Everyone came at Barb with cries of shortbread and almond pastries, Bakewell tarts and strudel, and after she'd scrawled down their orders, she ushered Vivien outside.

By the door a girl with parched blonde curls was searching for her keys.

'Afternoon, Veronique,' Barb said. Vivien had never met her, but she'd seen the sign VERONIQUE. FRENCH MODEL. FIRST FLOOR above the bell, and heard her loud, blunt voice and men's laughter in the pause between customers, or at the end of the day when the girls were quietly sweeping hair from the floor or washing around the sinks.

Veronique smiled vaguely, then opened the door to her flat and slammed it behind her.

'Charming,' said Barb as she linked arms with Vivien. 'You wouldn't believe the money she makes. And with a face that could turn milk sour.'

'I know you're busy. Please don't feel you need to look after me,' said Vivien as they set off. 'I'm fine.'

'Darling, I look after everyone.' Barb blew a kiss to the young newspaper seller on the corner. 'You're one of mine now.'

Vivien didn't need to worry about talking; Barb did it all for her. Madame Floris's thirty-seven types of bread. The best stallholder to buy hairpins from in the market. Alan taking her to Café de Paris for her birthday. Turning into Brewer Street, where shoppers crowded Vivien's path and the stink of fresh fish made her nauseous, Barb had to shout over the rumble of barrels being rolled alongside them towards a pub as she told Vivien about a pair of green shoes she'd seen.

In front of a chocolatier, the first of Madame Floris's shops, they smacked their lips over pineapple in kirsch, the towers of round dark chocolates on silver trays and slabs of nougat and fudge atop cascades of lavender silk. They slowed down when a client of Barb's wearing thick pancake make-up and heavy false lashes greeted Barb from the step outside a strip joint, then hurried on towards Madame Floris's bakery further down the street, where another lavish window display was drawing in the tourists.

Inside, they waited in the short queue, trying to guess the smells that hung over them and made them hungry. The comforting aroma of hot white bread, barely out of the oven. Warm sticky raisins and candied peel. Cooked cheese. A spice, maybe cinnamon or nutmeg.

Eventually, against the gasp of the coffee machine, they placed their orders with the waitress behind the counter who focused her attention entirely on Barb.

'She's a trained actress,' said Barb on their way out. 'Desperate to get into showbiz. She told me all about it the last time I was here. I couldn't get a word in edgeways.

You'll find, my dear, that a lot of people in Soho think their story is far more interesting than everyone else's.' She rolled her eyes at Vivien. 'And she knows that I'm friends with Madame Floris. She's making my wedding cake.'

'What an honour,' exclaimed Vivien. 'You are lucky.'

'Am I?' said Barb. 'Sometimes I wonder if getting married is worth all the fuss.'

'Really? I'd love to be getting married,' said Vivien, then flushed from the jaw up.

'No boyfriend?'

Vivien shook her head.

'It won't take you long. Mark my words.' Barb sighed. 'But don't be in a hurry. Sometimes I think Alan and I should live together. Scrap the wedding. We're spending all this time and money on it, and for what?' Her voice, as velvety as malt, had turned sour. 'For him to wake up one day and decide he's had his fill of me.'

She quickened her pace. Her step was light, but from the angry clench of her jaw Vivien realised she was talking about her dad's departure.

'Alan adores you,' she said breathlessly, trying to keep up. 'Anyone can see that.'

'Now, maybe. But things change.'

'I can't imagine anything changing Alan's feelings for you, and—' Vivien stopped suddenly, the pastries sliding around inside the box she'd been carrying so carefully. Her breath flew out of her. Across the road, up a ladder, a man was running a wet shammy over the delicatessen's sign. A man she was sure was Jack.

His auburn hair caught the glint of the sun. His strong torso was pressed against the ladder rungs, and his trousers were rolled up, revealing muscled calves and bony ankles.

She was poised, about to bolt across the street, when he swivelled round and shouted out something to a prostitute in a neighbouring building sitting by her window in a skimpy nightie, calling out to passing trade.

His voice was coarse, his face was fleshy.

What was she thinking?

It wasn't Jack. Of course it wasn't. It was never going to be.

She took Barb's arm, forcing out a smile, forcing Jack away.

In the back room she put on her overall and slowly did up the buttons, shocked at how much weight she'd lost. She must start eating properly again, more than just a mouthful of apple strudel or a bowl of soup. She had to look after herself and not disappear back into the life she'd led in the days following Dad's death, when stews and casseroles and plates of cold cuts from visitors went untouched in the fridge and she grew thin and weak.

Not today though. She'd pulled herself out of bed and into work. That was enough of an achievement for one day.

Thirty minutes later she put her client – a French girl who worked at Les Enfants Terribles, a popular espresso bar a few doors away – under the drier. As Vivien looked up, Barb beckoned her over to reception.

'I'm sorry. I forgot about this.' She passed Vivien an envelope. 'Marcia put it in the bottom of the till. It was on the mat yesterday when I got in.'

Vivien stared at her full name penned in neat unfamiliar capitals. She couldn't imagine who would write to her. No one, except Stella, even knew where to find her.

She dragged a fingernail across the envelope and pulled out a single sheet of thin blue paper, which she unfolded. Then she froze.

Jack will meet you at the Arnot Guest House,

Auderely Square, Camberwell, London SE1 on Friday at 6 p.m. Tell no one.
  Yours,
  Barry Klein

Vivien sleepwalked through the next few hours. She did whatever was asked of her, she did everything she was paid to do, but she was no more present in her job than she had been that morning, lying in her bed.

On her knees unpacking bottles of perming lotion or making frequent unnecessary trips to the loo, she would find herself staring into space, bewildered. Jack knew where she was. Barry Klein knew Jack. The connections shocked her; they kept taking her by surprise, shifting her off balance.

Jack will meet you.

There was that, too. Words that made her want to scream. She hadn't even been asked nicely. She'd been instructed. Assuming, she supposed, that she would just turn up tomorrow. Is that how Jack remembered her? As a pushover? Someone who always did what she was told?

No one had ever made her feel this angry. Surely he must realise what she was going through? That she felt winded every time the whole ugly business of the rally came into her mind? That he'd stained every glorious, life-affirming memory she held of them together in Manchester?

She held her head in her hands.

None of it made any sense.

She touched the letter in her overall pocket. She felt like tearing it into shreds but she knew she wouldn't. She needed the address, after all.

The next day Stevie hovered on the corner where Dean Street met Old Compton Street, holding the wet ends of the chrysanthemum stems away from his fresh blue shirt.

89

It was Friday. By his watch he still had ten minutes before the girls finished up for the day, so he was caught off guard when Vivien emerged from the salon alone and set off so fast she almost disappeared from sight. When he did catch up with her, he almost wished he hadn't. From her heavy, dramatic eye make-up and the sparkly pins set into her chignon, he knew she was off to meet another man.

'Vivien!' He put his hand on her arm to slow her down. 'Glad I caught you.'

'Oh. Stevie, hi.' Her face was turned sideways but her body was twisted forward. She was itching to keep moving. 'Good to see you, but I …'

'I was worried about you. Barb said you were off work.'

'Yes. A tummy upset. I'm much better now.'

'Oh, glad you're over it. Here. These are for you.' He pushed the flowers clumsily in her direction, trying to ignore how reluctant she was to take them.

'Thank you.' With her face lowered to smell the flowers, her voice came out muffled. Eventually she looked up at him. 'I'm really sorry about collapsing on you like that in the pub.'

Her words surprised him. 'I didn't mind.'

'I do. I was upset but I shouldn't have involved you.'

'I like you involving me,' he said with a flirtatious smile that he immediately realised was misplaced. He knew this because she was shaking her head slowly at him, her hesitant smile full of pity. All she wanted was to find a decent way of letting him down.

He should leave. He should say good night and go right now. Lick his wounds somewhere private. Instead he ploughed on, reaching into his jacket pocket for the tickets to Helen Shapiro's concert at the Palladium.

'I got us these. You said you loved Helen Shapiro.'

She stared at the tickets. 'I can't go,' she said softly.

'Stevie, if I've given you the wrong impression, I'm sorry. I like you but I can't ... I really am sorry.'

Her voice didn't falter. Her huge eyes didn't leave his. He slapped the tickets against his palm and nodded pleasantly, trying to quell his rising misery, hoping his expression wouldn't give him away. He mustn't get angry. It wasn't her fault that he liked her, that she was the last thing in his mind at night and the first in the morning.

He stared at the ground as thoughts came to him of Marcia pinching his cheeks, and Lydia jokily asking if he needed to pay for his coffee with his pocket money. He could already hear them cackling when Vivien told them what a fool he'd made of himself.

'Stevie.' He looked up. 'I'm sorry to leave things like this,' she said, 'but I need to go. Otherwise I'll be late.'

'Where are you going?'

'Across town.' She gestured vaguely behind her.

'Who are you meeting?'

'No one you know.'

'A bloke?'

'Stevie, please ...'

'Just tell me who he is.' His voice was rising. 'What's the big deal?'

'It's none of your business, Stevie,' she said sharply, 'where I go or who I see.' Her voice was so hard, she might as well have slapped him.

'You're right. I'm sorry.'

She sighed, reached over and touched his arm. 'See you soon, yes? And thank you again for the flowers. They really are smashing.'

He should have left it at that. Held that lovely sweet smile of hers in his mind and watched her disappear down the street in her shiny red kitten heels, swinging her hand-bag by her side. He should have let her go graciously, then kicked a lamp post or the rubbish bin. Not kept pace with her, rabbiting on about bumping into Helen Shapiro outside the draper's on Homerton Row last year and cadging her autograph.

He didn't know how to stop. It was as if he was in a dream and had convinced himself that by keeping the conversation going, the invisible wire between them would remain; she would slow down and embrace him, tell him that she'd got it wrong, he was enough of a man for her. Instead, she stopped abruptly outside the Stockpot and turned on him.

'Stevie, please! Enough. Stop this.'

The dream was over. The wire was cut. People parting around them were glancing over, intrigued by the pretty girl shouting at the boy with the crimson face. He wanted to cry.

'I'm sorry,' he said. 'Really sorry.'

She nodded, and said all right, no harm done, and when she walked away his chest ached so hard he was frightened for himself.

II

The bronze nameplate announcing THE ARNOT GUEST HOUSE was so discreetly placed Vivien walked the length of the street and back before she noticed it in the alcove by the door, out of the glare of the evening sun.

She stood on the bottom step for a few minutes, looking up at the house, regretting her wool jacket – not nearly flimsy enough for such a warm evening – and unsure of whether she even wanted to go inside. She wasn't sure of anything any more.

When a figure inside walked by the ground-floor bay window, she realised she might be seen loitering and worked up the courage to ring the bell. Almost as soon as she had, the door was opened by a woman wearing a smart twinset whose eye-glasses rested in her wiry greying hair. She smiled as she pushed the doormat into place with the toe of her shoe.

'Hello,' said Vivien. 'I'm here to meet Jack Fox.'

'Of course.' The woman had a rich, comforting voice. 'Do come in.'

This was no ordinary house. The well-polished door handles were brass, the staircase was wide and sweeping with sturdy banisters. The red patterned carpet was lush under Vivien's feet and a smell of wood polish mingled with the woman's lemony perfume. And so many paintings and framed photographs hung on the walls, Vivien's eyes couldn't settle on anything for long. A watercolour of a swimming pool set oddly beneath a snow-topped mountain and an old map of the Persian Empire caught her eye as she passed.

The airy room Vivien was shown into contained a couple of well-stuffed armchairs and a settee in blue velvet, with piles of sheet music scattered across the top of a piano in the corner. Two walls were given over entirely to shelves crammed with books. On both sides of the long glass doors leading to the garden were bright orange drapes that collapsed in great swirls on the floor. The room exuded the same confidence as the hallway; the owners knew what they liked and could afford it.

'You must enjoy reading,' Vivien blurted out, then blushed.

'We do.' The woman laughed girlishly. 'Make yourself comfortable. I'll let Jack know you're here.'

Vivien smiled. 'Thank you.'

She laid the flowers Stevie had given her on a coffee table near the piano, took off her gloves and sat in one of the armchairs with her back to the door. The room was quiet and still except for a wasp hovering over a vase of long-stemmed pink roses and the chime of a clock in the hallway. She kept her gaze fixed on the garden and tried not to think about anything other than the greenness of the lawn and the two sparrows perched on the feeder.

'Hello, Vivien.'

She stood up and turned. There he was, lean and sad-looking, his intense eyes searching her face and making her belong to him all over again.

After he'd shut the door, Jack came over to face her. 'I heard about your dad. I'm so sorry.'

'Barry told you.'

He nodded. 'It must have been a terrible shock.'

'Yes.' She stood stiffly, chin out, shoulders back, only moving her handbag, which she tapped gently against her thigh so the metal clasp made a light thudding sound.

'I did want to write,' he said.

'So what stopped you?'

Jack looked startled and took a backward step, but he didn't respond.

When he motioned for her to sit down, she headed for the opposite end of the settee from him, next to the piano. The lid was up and she stared at each key, running her eyes up and down them as if she was watching someone play. Anything to take her mind off his gaze, which was fixed on her.

Neither of them said a word. The room was speckled with evening sun, so she removed her jacket and hung it over the arm of the settee, then smoothed her hands over her skirt. In the silence she could still feel his eyes on her.

'For God's sake, Jack,' she snapped eventually. 'You can't drag me here and then not say anything.'

He leaned forward, elbows on his thighs, and stared between his feet. 'I know.'

'Well?'

'I wanted to write to you so many times. I was desperate to explain.'

'But you didn't.'

'I couldn't.'

'I'm not surprised,' she said. 'After what I saw.'

'I'm not what you think I am.'

She stared at him, waiting for more.

He looked up at her. 'Can I trust you?'

'What?'

'I need to know I can trust you.'

'Can you trust me?' she said incredulously.

He opened his mouth and closed it again, then stood up

and paced back and forth in front of the bookshelves, frowning as if he was trying to get things straight in his head. All she could do was watch and wait until he was ready to speak.

'I don't know where to start,' he said finally. 'And it's going to sound crazy, so I'm just going to tell you in whatever way it comes out.' He cleared his throat. 'I told you I was writing a book but really I'm a journalist. That's my trade. It's how I met Barry. We both worked at the *Hackney Gazette*. I left to go to *The Times* and he joined a year later.'

'What's that got to do with being a fascist?'

'I'm *not* a fascist,' he said. 'I'd been writing about politics for a while. When I started writing about fascist organisations an old contact told me that Colin Jordan was breaking away from the BNP to start his own party, the National Socialist Movement. And he'd made a deal to take Spearhead, the BNP's paramilitary wing, with him.'

'I've never heard of Spearhead,' said Vivien.

'You wouldn't have. It's like a private army. They keep it hush-hush.'

Jack walked over to Vivien and handed her a folded piece of paper from his back pocket. A deep cut was scored into a knuckle and a grubby, fraying bandage was wrapped around his left wrist. She stopped herself from asking him about the wounds, but wherever they had come from, he did not look nearly as fresh as he had in Manchester. His eyes seemed tired.

'This is the leaflet Jordan produced about Spearhead for party members.'

Vivien unfolded the circular. On the front was an ink drawing of a man in a Nazi uniform with his arm raised in salute. 'The Spearhead man,' she read, 'steps forward and marches on in the spirit of Hitler's storm troopers of the 1930s ...'

On the back page was a grainy photograph of Hitler and beneath him a childlike drawing of a boot and an advertisement for an agency in Germany that sold top-quality jackboots.

'I don't understand any of this.' Angrily she tossed the paper onto the coffee table.

'I'm trying to explain,' he said in a quiet voice. 'I'd wanted to get into Spearhead for a while. I had an agreement with my editor to write a series of front-page exposés but I could never get close enough when it was with the BNP. The BNP was too big. I had a much better chance when the National Socialist Movement started up because new fascist organisations are always desperate for members. So I decided to join.' Jack tapped two cigarettes out of the packet, lit them and handed her one.

'I quit *The Times*, moved into a bedsit across town and started hanging around their street meetings. Then I wrote to the party from my new address. I said I was convinced by everything Jordan was saying about Jews and immigrants. One of Jordan's lackeys wrote back and invited me to come and meet him.

'It took a few months but I'm a member now. They trust me. I distribute their rag on the streets and run errands for the big shots in the party. I'm pretty sure they've got plans for me.' He hesitated. 'You understand what I'm telling you, don't you?'

'No.' She shook her head, a little embarrassed. 'Not really.'

'I'm not a fascist,' he said slowly. 'I'm an infiltrator.'

Vivien opened and closed her mouth. She had been holding the hem of her skirt in a fist, and when she unclenched her fingers she saw how crushed the soft pink fabric was.

'Vivien? Are you all right?'

Jack edged towards her, but she turned away.

'I don't believe you.' She wouldn't look at him. 'You're lying.'

He shook his head. 'I'm not.'

'I think …' She couldn't go on. She stood up and went over to the piano, arms crossed over her chest, determined to gather the right words. But the words wouldn't come.

'Vivien,' he called softly. 'Do you imagine that Phil—'

She gasped. 'Shut up!' Her voice went thin with anger. 'Just shut up! Don't you dare mention Dad's name. You knew how sick he was. And you still took advantage of him. I don't know why you did it but I will never forgive you for that. It's just despicable and I hate—'

Jack strode over. 'Vivien, you have to listen to me.' He seized her shoulders and shook them gently as he spoke. 'I never lied to him. I wouldn't do that.'

'You did!' she shouted. 'I was there.'

'Vivien, he knew everything. Sid Klein set up my visit to Manchester. Your dad was helping me.'

She stared at him, then pushed him away. 'Helping you?'

'Yes.'

'How could he do that?'

'When Jordan branched out on his own Sid started talking about setting up an organisation like the 43 Group. He wanted me to be involved and thought Phil could help.'

'But why him? Why Dad?'

'Because he was an infiltrator too.'

'No he wasn't!' she exclaimed. 'That's absolute rot.'

Jack nodded. 'He spent six months with Mosley's Union Movement.'

'No.' She shook her head. 'You're wrong.'

'I'm not, Vivien,' he said softly. 'When he stopped he became a handler and took charge of other infiltrators. He was preparing me for all sorts of things.'

'Like what?'

'Like ... like he arranged a new birth certificate for me so I could operate under a new name.'

'You're not Jack Fox?'

'I am Jack. Fox isn't my real surname.'

'What is it?'

He paused. 'Morris.'

She dropped heavily onto the settee and stared at the carpet. Everything was jumbled up in her head. As he sat down next to her, Vivien clutched the arm of the settee to check that she was in a place that was still real.

'Vivien? Are you OK?'

'I think so.'

'It's a shock.'

She nodded slowly. 'I can't believe I didn't know that about Dad.'

'Only a few people did. He didn't talk about it.' Jack edged closer until their knees touched. 'He asked me not to tell you what I was up to. He knew that we were getting close and he wanted me to wait until my work was over. I guess he couldn't have known you would come looking for me. Well, now you know why I left in a hurry. Why I acted the way I did at the rally. I had to scare you off.' He shook his head. 'I still can't believe you spotted me. But I knew I had to see you. So I asked Barry to set it up.'

'Why Barry?'

'Because the 62 Group became official after the rally and I operate under their rules now. Barry helps Sid run things. They had to agree that I could meet you. I'm sorry, Vivien,' he said. 'I've put you through hell.'

'I thought I'd fallen for ... I don't know what.' Her voice grew soft, the anger falling away. 'But I haven't. You're not.'

She got up and then stood in front of the long doors which led to the garden, with her arms wrapped around her waist.

'It's a lot to take in,' she said.

'I know.'

'It sounds so dangerous. Is it?'

She heard him move, then felt him close by. 'No,' he said. 'I'm doing well.'

She sighed. What did that even mean? 'Are we allowed to go outside? I need some air.'

'Sure.' He reached around her and opened the door. 'Charlotte, the woman you met, is an old friend of Sid. She said to come and go as we please.'

To the right of the doors the lawn rolled gently downhill towards an oak tree, where a swing hung between two strong branches. Vivien sat down on it, facing a small summer house whose creamy-yellow paint had been worn away by harsh winters. Several deck chairs, a set of golf clubs and a garden parasol could be glimpsed through the window. Holding on to the rope, she pushed herself off the ground and started swinging. She looked up. The sky was so blue and sharp today, with only a light stack of woolly clouds above her.

Beyond the tall trees she could hear the scrape of cutlery against china. One child was shouting at a bumble bee to leave her alone, another was laughing and splashing about in a paddling pool. Vivien imagined contented families eating supper outside, appreciating the bright, still evening. She caught Jack's eye but still did not speak. She kept swinging until suddenly he came over and clutched the rope, forcing her to an abrupt stop.

'You do believe me now, don't you?' he asked.

'I think so.' She nodded. 'I feel a bit dazed by it all.'

'I know,' he said gravely and ran his thumb down the side of her face. 'I hated not telling you. I wrote a hundred letters I never sent, and in every one I told you how sorry I was for leaving without an explanation. How ... well, how much I thought of you. But I was already caught between two worlds. Then I heard that Phil had died ...' He touched her cheek again. 'What you must have gone through. Alone.' He shook his head. 'I couldn't stop thinking about it. I kept seeing your lovely big eyes and I was this close –' he gestured with his finger and thumb '– to jumping on a train to Manchester. But what then? Stay a while. Lie about what I'm up to? Confuse you with yet another disappearing act? I began to convince myself that I'd let you down so badly you'd probably want to have nothing more to do with me any—'

'Jack,' she interrupted, a finger pressed to her lips. 'Ssssh.' She slipped off the swing and stood in front of him, then laced her hands in his and caught his kisses all over her mouth and face and neck.

'I'm so sorry, Vivien,' he whispered into her hair.

She kissed his forehead. 'I know.'

They clung to each other for some time as if scared to break apart. Then they slipped down. The grass was their blanket. He lay on his back looking through the gaps in between the branches and running his hand up and down her side. She was huddled close to him, her hand under his loosened shirt, her fingers pressed into the heat of his skin.

A quiet joy sat between them. She did not need to ask how he was. She could feel it inside her as vividly as she could feel his chest rising and falling against the palm of her hand. They were together now. She had never felt so happy and she had to stop herself declaring it aloud.

Jack groaned. He was stiff. He took her hand off his chest and edged himself onto his side while she rolled onto her back. Propped up on his elbow, he picked a blade of grass and trailed it under her chin.

'You look stunning,' he said.

'I do?'

'Yep. London agrees with you.'

'Oh, it does, Jack!' She sat up. 'I just love it.'

She crossed her legs and faced him. She took the daisy he gave her and twirled it against the palm of her hand as she told him that, although it had only been a few weeks, she loved seeing the Oscar's sign in the distance, knowing it was her place of work. She loved all the girls but especially Barb and Chrissie, although Maeve was a real card and Deirdre funny when she could be bothered to speak. She loved her small list of clients from the shops, theatres and strip shows around Soho. She loved rubbing in a bit of olive oil and sunbathing in Soho Square during her lunch break, or walking around Foyles on Charing Cross Road, marvelling at all the books and making a mental note of all those she intended to read and discuss with Jack. She loved *Breathless*, the French film she had seen last week with Chrissie, and spotting actresses in coffee bars poring over scripts and talking up their acting jobs. She loved Nettie for all the midweek teas she kept cooking for Vivien, even though it was not part of their arrangement.

She loved much more but already she was talking like a maniac and she fell back onto the grass, laughing.

'I needn't have worried about you.' Jack squeezed her hand as they watched an aeroplane move above them. 'You've done brilliantly on your own. Your dad would be proud.'

She smiled. 'I like to think so.'

'Oh, I almost forgot.' He sat up and squeezed his hand into his trouser pocket, then brought out a folded-up envelope. He tore across the end and tipped a pair of pink earrings into her palm.

'I saw these in a shop a while back. You always wear such pretty earrings.'

Vivien held up one of the studs and turned it in front of

her face. No one had ever bought her earrings. No one had ever bought her jewellery. Come to think of it, she wasn't sure anyone had ever noticed she wore earrings before. She twirled the pink-coloured stone between her fingers.

'Thank you. It's the perfect gift.' She carefully dropped them back in the envelope, then blurted out suddenly, 'Jack, don't go back to them. Please.'

'I have to.' His eyes were fixed beyond her.

'Do you?'

'Vivien,' he whispered, 'don't ask me to choose.'

'I'm not,' she said reluctantly. 'But what if someone finds out?'

'They won't. I'm careful.'

'But you look tired.'

'Well, I am pretty tired.'

'I'm here now,' she said, and stroked his face. 'I'll look after you.'

'No, sweetheart.' He held her hands in his. 'We can't see each other again until this is over.'

'Why not?'

'I can't risk putting you in danger.'

'I don't care, Jack.'

'Well, I do. And so do Sid and Barry. It took me ages to twist their arms about meeting you. They only agreed because it was a one-off.'

'So this is it?' She held his gaze. 'For how long?'

'I don't know. Maybe a couple of months. It's hard to say. I shouldn't even have met you today.'

'Can't we meet somewhere else? Another town? We could talk on the phone.'

'I don't know.'

'All right, Jack. I won't go on about it.'

'You're a terrific girl, Vivien.' He squeezed her hand. 'You really are.'

'You're pretty special yourself.'

'Listen, darling.' He bent a finger under her chin and turned her face towards his. 'You can't tell anyone about me. Not Nettie or Barb or Stella. Not a single person.'

'All right.'

'I'm not kidding,' he said. 'No one can know.'

At the bus stop Jack told her to wait. He took off the long silver chain he wore around his neck and dropped it in her palm.

'Why are you giving this to me?' She looked scared.

'Just because.' He smiled sheepishly. He felt foolish now, but he'd wanted to give her something of himself.

She clasped her hand tightly around it. 'I don't need anything to remember you by.'

'Good.'

'I'll look after it for you.'

'Thank you for coming,' he whispered.

He waited on the pavement while she stepped onto the bus and the other passengers shuffled aside for her. She was still in his sight, yet already he was starting to feel flat. All he had to look forward to was another evening in his bedsit. He already missed hearing her laugh or chattering on about the salon girls, about what this one said or that one did, as if he knew them intimately. He wanted to be back in the garden with her while he talked himself empty, said more than he had in months, because he was terribly lonely but hadn't really known it until tonight.

As the bus slithered into the slow rumble of evening traffic he panicked about losing sight of her and ran along the kerb beside it. He ran fast to keep up, his free hand stretched out towards her. He liked the way she pushed a man aside to move into a window seat, dangling his silver chain in one hand and waving, her nose squashed against the glass. Then he realised two other people on the bus were also watching him: a young man eating an apple and a West Indian woman.

What was he thinking, dropping his guard like this?

He lowered his head, pulled his jacket collar up over his jaw and thrust his hands into his pockets. One last quick glance over his shoulder told him the bus had gone. He wondered whether Vivien was still pressed flat against the window, or whether she understood that he had to disappear, that it was his job to slip quietly through each day. Unnoticed, anonymous, invisible.

In the square opposite the Arnot Guest House Stevie had hung back behind a large bush, chewing his thumbnail. He shouldn't have come, but he hadn't been able to tear himself away. When lights came on in the second- and top-floor rooms he made himself crazy by believing that Vivien was inside one of the rooms undressing. Running through everything in his mind that she could possibly be enjoying with another man, he clutched the railings so hard his fingers grew sore.

As daylight began to fade he became just another shape. When Vivien eventually emerged, her hair was loose and her jacket undone, and a man towered over her. But they didn't hold hands and weren't pressed together the way lovers should be and Stevie felt good. He began to cheer up, thinking he might have got it all wrong.

But then, as he followed them towards the bus stop, he caught a glimpse of Vivien's profile and saw how happy she was as the man with the sharp cheekbones lowered his face towards hers.

Stevie slumped against a postbox, winded, as if someone had punched him in the stomach.

12

On Monday Jack was the only one working late. The other workers on the factory floor had gone as soon as the bell rang, quick to get a rise out of each other as they breezed around the machinery and through the door. He'd ducked into the gents and stayed crouched in the only cubicle until he was sure they were halfway down the street. He didn't need them to know he was staying late again. He'd only been working there a few weeks and they were still keen on knowing his business. Fresh meat, the women called him, and hung around him like flies.

Then he set to work. A couple of hours passed. Day turned to evening. Still folding the last of the circulars and packing them into a cardboard box, he glanced through the open window at the small shabby houses opposite. Sharp slices of light behind curtains. Shadows of children moving, playing, the occasional flicker of a television. The grimy smell of burned meat wafted towards him, then accusations, the slam of a front door. As he taped up the box, there was more noise – a woman shouting, the stagger of high heels on the pavement. He glanced out again and saw the backs of two girls, one of them tall and drooping, waving her arm around as if the air was fighting her.

'Come on, lovely,' the other girl called out, pulling her up the street by the wrist. 'Let's get you home. Tuck you up.'

Her sweet voice made him strain towards the window,

but only the tips of their shadows remained in sight. The scene reminded him of Vivien, propping up Stella on the night of her birthday. Drunk, sad, tearful Stella insisting to him and Vivien that she wasn't unhappy, she was just tired. Tired of mothering three boys under five. Tired of life squeezing her dry. And Vivien, sitting next to her on the kerb, stroking her blonde curls and telling her what a great job she was doing. Telling her how much she was loved.

This memory of Vivien fell on him suddenly and he let it sit for a moment; her patience and warmth and the sheen of the smile she gave to everyone, even strangers in the street. Then he remembered there was work to be done and he killed the memory and carried on taping up the box. He finished that, then put it next to the other one.

He rubbed a cloth at the quicks of his fingernails, trying to remove what muck he could. Every night he had to go home and soak his hands in hot soapy water. The press he worked on turned out university course prospectuses and desk calendars ten hours a day and was an old and filthy bit of machinery. There was grease all over it.

About to grab his jacket and leave, he heard whispering, then clattering on the steel staircase that led down from the boss's office. Out of the corner of his eye he saw the secretary, a watery-eyed blonde, tuck her blouse into her skirt.

Jack hid himself behind some boxes as she walked past. It had been the same every time he'd worked late printing out fliers and posters for the party. Neither of them made eye contact, an arrangement which suited him fine, since she was as nice as pie to him during working hours. He didn't care if she fooled around with the boss, Doug, who would emerge at the top of the stairs any minute now, shaking himself back into his trousers and trying not to look too pleased with himself.

He was still wiping his nails when Doug appeared behind him. Tall and spare, he and Jack were a good head taller than the other men in the factory.

'Just finished.' Jack pointed to the boxes.

'That was fast.'

'I said you'd be happy with my work.'

'You did.' Doug nodded. 'I can see why Jordan's got plans for you.'

Jack handed him a leaflet advertising the official launch of the National Socialist Movement in St Pancras Town Hall. 'They came out nice.'

Doug barely looked the page over before he handed it back. 'Tell Jordan we may have to slow things down for a few weeks,' he said.

'Can I tell him why?'

'A print shop in Kilburn got smashed up by some yids the other night. I know the owner. He did a lot of Mosley's printing. He was there when they broke in, and they gave him a really good hiding.'

'We're careful,' said Jack. 'No one else here knows what I do after hours.'

'Keep it that way. Jordan may be an old friend but I've got a good business here.'

They each carried a box of leaflets through the factory to the main door. Doug pulled it open and Jack stepped out onto the pavement. Turning his head to the left, it dawned on him that the lights he was seeing weren't car headlamps. Rows of people were walking along holding lit candles.

'What's going on?'

Doug peered out. 'Must be another torchlight parade. Mosley's held quite a few lately.'

'I should get over there and hand these out.' Jack took the other box from Doug. 'Convert some of his supporters.'

'That's the spirit.' Doug reached up to fasten the bolt at

the top of the door. 'No wonder you're going places with initiative like that.'

The next morning Jack's heart sank a little, as it did with every trip to the NSM party headquarters. Based in Jordan's ramshackle three-storey Victorian house in Hammersmith, it was one of the most depressing places he'd ever been. He would never get used to going there.

He pushed aside the straggle of ivy and rang the bell as a drip of water hit him. Looking up, he saw the hopper was jammed with leaves so that water was spilling over the side. Jordan must be taking a shower. As he moved back, he heard footsteps. Ralph Forster, Jordan's main lieutenant, opened the door holding a blue china cup and saucer in one hand. Sunlight flooded the dark hallway and made him blink in surprise.

'Jack.' A retired history professor with a thin voice, an even thinner comb-over and a fondness for cheap grey suits, Ralph lacked presence. He wasn't someone Jack would ordinarily take seriously.

'Afternoon, sir.' Jack steeled himself as he went inside. Everywhere in the house smelled rotten, like something was festering under the floorboards. He lowered himself to the floor and put down the two boxes he'd carried in. 'Launch fliers,' he said when Ralph raised his eyebrows.

'Ah, good. Colin was asking where those were.'

'I'm on the rota to hand out the newspaper later but I thought I'd come early,' said Jack. 'You said some needed packing up.'

Ralph nodded. 'Friends of Colin in Coventry and Manchester plan to distribute them for us. The details are on the mantelpiece.'

As he spoke they walked into the living room, where at midday the curtains were still drawn. Bundles of the latest issue of the *National Socialist* were stacked up on the floor and sofa. It fell to Jack and the other foot soldiers to get rid of the party newspaper each month, yet every time he walked out with a pile under his arm he had to brace himself to be seen with them in public. Five issues had been produced but the first was by far the worst: beneath the masthead was Hitler's portrait and the caption HIS SPIRIT LIVES ON.

Jack took off his trilby and put it on the arm of the sofa. 'I'll get on with it,' he said.

'Thank you, Jack.'

Ralph took a sip from his cup and watched Jack for a few seconds before making his way up the narrow staircase to the second floor of the house, where he and Jordan had neighbouring offices. Standing by the doorway, Jack heard Ralph knock and say something to Jordan, their voices mingling, then the door shut and there was silence.

As Jack took off his jacket and rolled his shirtsleeves back to the elbow, he glanced at the framed photo of two dozen party members on the walnut dresser, next to the broken telephone and the bust of Hitler.

The photo had been taken on 20 April, Hitler's birthday, the day the NSM went public. Jack was in the middle of the front row, standing between a stout man with slumped shoulders and an iced cake which had been decorated with a swastika cut out of marzipan. Like all the other men in the photo, Jack was performing the Nazi salute, the greeting the party insisted on.

He could remember biting down on the inside of his cheek while joking with everyone around him, conscious that if the party was going to take him seriously, he had to be seen to be happy and proud to be part of the celebration. Yet every time he saw the photo he wanted to run, and he had to remind himself why he was here and that this time in his life would pass.

He flicked on the light switch. As he turned back into the room, he stepped on an empty can of cat food by the door, then realised what the smell was. 'Jesus. Cat piss.'

He screwed up his nose in disgust and kicked the can to one side.

After boxing up newspapers for a while, Jack sat down on the sofa, smoked a cigarette and drank a glass of water. Behind the drawn curtains one of the windows was open, and he enjoyed watching the curtain blow gently in and out. His sleep had been so erratic the past few weeks, his body quickly drooped and it was an effort to stay awake. When he heard a noise, he opened his eyes and rubbed them, then raised his arms above his head and stretched. As he sat forward, he heard, then saw a football bounce down the stairs and into the room, landing near his feet. With the ball resting on the palm of his hand, he got up and walked over to the door.

'Looking for something?'

'Jack!' Henry ran down the rest of the stairs and grabbed the ball back.

Ralph's only son was fair-skinned, narrow-faced and had tight brown curls. Today, like most days, he was wearing a buttoned-up blue shirt beneath a crisp grey waistcoat, knee-high socks and lace-ups. Jack thought it was a shame that whoever dressed the boy always wanted him to look like a little grown-up instead of a ten-year-old child.

'Do you like football?' asked Henry.

When Jack nodded, Henry's face lit up. His mother had fallen sick with pneumonia a few months earlier and still hadn't fully recovered. She was too tired to leave her bedroom for any length of time, and although Henry's sister had gone to stay with relatives in Somerset for the summer, Henry hadn't wanted to leave his mother for that long. This meant he spent too much time moping around the house, constantly announcing he was bored and lonely and looking for activities to get involved in. He was a much sunnier kid around other people.

'Will you play with me?'

'I can't right now,' said Jack. 'I'm busy.'

Henry peered around him into the room. 'What are you doing?'

'Packing up newspapers.' Jack pointed at the boxes.

'I can help. I'm good at packing.'

'I bet you are. But I think I should do it myself.' Jack squeezed Henry's shoulder. 'There's a lot of counting involved.'

'I could play down here,' said Henry excitedly. 'Near you.'

'Great idea.' Henry often hung around asking Jack lots of good questions, such as why do people blink, or how many bones are there in a human hand, or where do numbers come from. Jack might not know the answers, but he was fond of hearing Henry's innocent, probing voice and it was always a good escape from whatever else he was doing.

Henry kicked the football up and down the hallway, shouting out a commentary and goal tally while Jack counted newspapers and either wrapped them in brown paper or folded them into boxes. Several party members came in and out of the house, stopping to greet Jack and comment on Henry's nifty footwork – one man even engaged him in a short game before disappearing up the stairs to see Ralph.

Jack had nearly finished when he heard glass smashing in the street. He quickly stood up from where he was kneeling. 'Henry?'

There was no answer so he headed into the hall, where he

saw the front door was ajar. He heard a flurry of footsteps coming up the path then the door was pushed open and Henry threw the football inside. He looked frightened.

'I broke the neighbour's car mirror.' His bottom lip wobbled. 'I didn't mean to. Daddy's going to be really angry.'

Henry shook his head and kicked his foot against the step as if he couldn't believe his own bad luck. Ralph had forbidden him to play in the street.

'Come inside,' said Jack.

Henry didn't move.

'Come on.' Henry slipped in under Jack's arm. 'Wait for me in the front room.'

Jack pulled the door to and walked to the neighbour's house holding the shards of broken mirror. The woman, wearing a light blue wool suit, who answered the door was a similar age to his mum, but her smile withered when he said he was from next door.

She crossed her arms over her chest and took a step back. None of the neighbours liked Jordan. A couple of times Jack had seen them approach him or Ralph as they made their way into the house, angry at all the comings and goings and quick to remind them that this was a quiet, respectable neighbourhood.

When Jack displayed the glass in his hand and explained that her mirror had been broken, her lips tightened.

'It was my fault,' he lied. 'I got carried away. Obviously I'll pay for the damage.'

'Fine. Please speak to my husband when he's home.' She closed the door a little. 'I trust that's all?'

Henry was sitting on the bottom stair with his head in his hands, scuffing the grey threadbare rug with his foot.

'Is she going to tell Daddy?' He glanced up as Jack crouched in front of him.

'No. I said it was my fault.'

Henry appeared confused before breaking into a half-smile. 'She doesn't know it was me?'

Jack shook his head, then reached behind Henry's ears and fiddled with the ends of his wire-rimmed glasses so they jumped up and down on the bridge of his nose.

'Hey, your glasses are crazy,' said Jack in a silly voice. 'They've got a mind of their own.'

'Who doesn't know it was you?'

Jack heard Ralph before he saw him standing at the top of the stairs, legs planted wide, hands knitted behind his back. He detected the coldness in Ralph's voice and froze for a moment before deciding to come clean.

'Henry kicked the ball outside and smashed the neighbour's car mirror. I went to see her and took the blame.'

'Henry? Is this true?'

Henry nodded.

'What do you have to say for yourself?'

'I'm sorry, Daddy. I shouldn't have been playing in the street.'

'We'll discuss this later. Go and gather your things. The taxi will be here in a few minutes to take you home. Thank you, Jack. Relations with the neighbours are awkward at best.'

As Ralph walked away, Jack winked at Henry. 'See you later, alligator.'

Henry smiled, then headed up the stairs with his ball tucked under his arm and his hand trailing on the banister, repeating lightly under his breath, 'In a while, crocodile.'

Jack was shrugging back into his jacket when Ralph came down the stairs with Iris, Jordan's niece. Iris had an English degree from Oxford and wrote most of the editorial for the *National Socialist*. She was erudite, full of witty anecdotes about her professors, and the first time they had a conversation Jack had to remind himself not to enjoy it.

'All done,' he announced.

'Jolly good,' said Ralph.

'I'm off to get a bite to eat.'

'May I have a quick word first?'

'Of course,' said Jack.

'Damn,' said Iris. 'Left my sunglasses on your desk.'

As she disappeared up the stairs, the sight of her shapely legs beneath her skirt made Jack think of Vivien.

Ralph walked on ahead of him into the living room. He stood with the fireplace behind him and gestured for Jack to shut the door.

'We're pleased with you, Jack.' Ralph brought out a silver case from his blazer pocket and offered Jack a cigarette, then took out one for himself and tapped it on the back of his hand. 'We could do with more men like you.'

Jack prayed his fingers wouldn't tremble as he lit his cigarette. It was the first time Ralph had offered him one, and the gesture was strange but reassuring.

'It's my pleasure to serve the party,' he said.

'And I appreciate your interest in Henry.'

'He's a terrific kid.'

'Quite. And jolly lucky to have you looking out for him.'

Jack nodded but didn't know how to reply to the unexpected compliment.

'Jack, we want to step up your involvement. We need men we can trust.'

'Of course.'

'There's a few things that we need help with,' said Ralph. 'Colin's very careful about who he asks.'

'Understandably.'

Ralph crushed his cigarette out in a saucer on the

mantelpiece and called out, 'Come in,' when someone knocked at the door.

'Ah, Mickey, excellent timing,' he said, gesturing at the man peering round the door. Mickey, one of Ralph's most trusted men, had been with the party since the start and had worked for Jordan at the BNP. 'I've been telling Jack that Colin wants him to be more involved in his plans. I was about to explain that you'll both be following some new instructions.'

Mickey nodded and ran a hand over his shaved head while Jack smiled through clenched teeth. Mickey was the last person he wanted to be paired with. Everyone felt edgy around him. A head shorter than Jack, with a wide creamy face and thick neck, Jack had seen men twice Mickey's size make way for him on the pavement.

'Incidentally, Jack, do you have a clean driving licence?'

'Yes, sir.'

'And you have your own car?'

'I do.'

'Good. We're running a training camp for our Spearhead members next week. Might need you both to run a few things down there.'

'Yes, sir.'

'We'll speak again soon,' said Ralph, adding, 'Congratulations,' and patting Jack's shoulder on his way out.

It had just gone four when Jack finished cramming bundles of the *National Socialist* into the boot of Mickey's Rover.

'Let's get some grub first,' said Mickey. 'I'm starving.'

Jack wouldn't have set foot in the café Mickey had parked outside. It looked bleak. The building was blackened in patches as if it had only just survived a fire, and several letters were missing from the name above the door.

Inside it was just as bad. The door handle was sticky and

there were splashes of tea on the grubby floor. Next to the window a mucky-looking teenage girl sat with her suitcase at her feet, sniffing and crying. At another table a woman with mussed-up red hair and a tired face was listening to a man three times her age tell her about his holiday in Margate while he ran his hand up and down her thigh.

Mickey pointed at a table and they sat down. As he brushed away the spilled sugar with his hand, Jack thought back to the state of the house. He was surrounded by grime.

Mickey snapped his fingers at the lad behind the counter. 'Ready when you are.'

The boy slouched over.

'What d'you want?' Mickey asked Jack.

'Black coffee.'

'I'll have tea.'

The boy nodded. 'Anything to eat?'

'Bacon and eggs,' said Mickey.

'A sausage sandwich,' said Jack.

Mickey thumbed through the pages of a local newspaper he'd grabbed from another table and they sat in silence until their food came. He poured lots of sugar into his tea and kept pinching his eyes open and yawning in Jack's face. When the plate was put in front of him, he rubbed his hands together.

'I need this after the night I had.'

Jack raised an eyebrow. 'Big night?'

'Hard night.' Mickey smirked and cut through the bacon.

'You got a bird?' asked Jack.

'Yeah. She's nice. Works in a shoe shop. Hey!'

A skinny dog with short dirty-looking hair was sitting on its hind legs, eyeing up Mickey's food. Still holding his fork mid-air, Mickey went stiff. He turned to the old man who'd just sat down in the corner and shouted at him to get rid of his mutt.

'No dogs,' said the boy, leaning over the counter. 'Hey, old fella. No dogs.'

The old man kept nodding in Mickey's direction as he headed towards the door. Jack thought he might just take his dog outside but he didn't come back.

'I don't get along with dogs,' said Mickey.

'No?'

Mickey shook his head. 'I'm a cat person.'

Jack was about to say he couldn't stand cats but he thought better of it.

'Someone's happy with you,' said Mickey.

'Sorry?'

'Colin. Being asked to step up.'

Jack nodded. 'It's nice to be noticed.'

'Doesn't surprise me. Colin's good like that.' Mickey pushed a chunk of bread into the egg yolk, then folded it into his mouth.

'Like what?'

'Clocks what people do for him,' said Mickey, his mouth full. 'Rewards loyalty.'

'Yeah, he does,' said Jack, adding casually, 'Is that why you went with Colin when he left the BNP?'

'I didn't know him personally then. I just like the way he thinks. He's proud to be called a Nazi. He doesn't hide what he believes in.'

'You're right.' Jack nodded. 'You know where you are with him.'

'Exactly.' Mickey pushed his plate away and wiped drops of fat from his chin with the side of his hand. 'That did the trick.'

Jack glanced around. No one else was sitting anywhere near them. 'So what's Colin got planned for us?' he asked in a discreet voice.

Mickey shook some change from his pocket onto the

table. 'No idea.' He thumped his chest and belched loudly. 'Come on. Those papers aren't going to hand themselves out.'

Jack stretched out in the passenger seat, but a couple of minutes after setting off Mickey reached down and pushed at his leg.

'Move your feet.'

Jack knew what Mickey was reaching for and he reluctantly shifted so Mickey could lift his new portable tape recorder off the mat. Without asking, Mickey hoisted it onto Jack's thigh, glancing back at the road before checking it held the right tape. Once he was sure, he pressed play and turned up the volume until Hitler's voice filled the car. Mickey had several recordings of his speeches, and even though he didn't speak German, he liked to play them as they drove around. Jack slumped down, looking out through the open window, counting in his head as a way of blocking out the noise.

Mickey circled around the streets a couple of times before he found a parking space close to Shepherd's Bush tube. Jack expected him to turn off the engine and get things moving but instead Mickey sat with the back of his head resting against the seat, eyes closed. It astonished Jack how peaceful Mickey could look listening to Hitler speak. He must have heard this speech a hundred times already but he still listened to it until the end. He didn't care that it was sweltering inside the car and Jack was shuffling around in his seat, desperate to get out.

The moment it ended, Mickey got back to business. He ordered Jack to grab armfuls of newspapers from the boot and walked ahead of him to the station, where he greeted two other members by the entrance. Twenty-two-year-old Carl, a painter and decorator from Bow, and a boy with a silly quiff and heavily grazed chin who Jack knew was a bank clerk but whose name escaped him. He nodded at them both.

The four of them were quickly absorbed into the crowd. For nearly twenty minutes Jack tried to make eye contact with passers-by and talk up the party, but many looked away or actively changed the direction they were heading in. The station buzzed with people, and there was a great deal of jostling, so there was no warning when a coloured boy suddenly ripped the newspaper out of the hands of a woman in a nurse's uniform that Carl had cornered.

'Don't take it,' the boy told her. 'It's a hate rag. They're a bunch of Nazis.'

The woman's eyes widened. She clutched her basket to her chest and shook her head, then darted around them and across the street.

Jack looked at the boy. He couldn't have been more than seventeen, with pitted cheeks and a few dark whiskers above his upper lip. He was angry and talking fast about the White Defence League and the Notting Hill race riots.

'You lot beat up my brother.' He jabbed a finger in Carl's face.

'No, that's not true.' Carl smiled patiently. He knew how to react. In public they had to insist that anything bad that was said about the party was a lie.

'You broke his arm.'

The boy was drawing attention. People looked their way, some had even stopped to listen. Jack admired his courage. Then the boy lashed out and knocked the newspapers hanging over Carl's arm to the ground. They fell apart and scattered all over the pavement.

'How d'ya like that?' he yelled as he headed back through the crowd.

Carl and Jack quickly bent down to gather up as many

papers as they could, but Mickey was already by their side. 'He went that way. Come on.'

'Forget him,' said Jack. 'Let's just get on with the job.'

'Are you mad? Let a nigger get away with that?'

The cords in Mickey's neck tightened. There was no way Jack could get out of this. This was what Mickey was made for, what drove him.

As Mickey and Carl and the other boy took off, Jack ran after them. He had to keep up. If he didn't, Mickey would grow suspicious.

He followed them around a corner and down the street as the boy turned and noticed them, then broke into a run. Jack quietly swore. In the distance the boy was running furiously, arms batting the air. As he glanced over his shoulder, there was no mistaking his wide terrified eyes, and Jack prayed that he would be fast enough to get away.

'Jack, stay where you are,' Mickey yelled over his shoulder as they turned the next corner. 'Keep an eye out for coppers.'

Jack stood still while the others charged ahead. The boy pushed over two bicycles, and Mickey roared, leaped over them and knocked the boy to the ground.

Jack ran the few steps round the corner back to the main road, where he stood staring at the pavement, stricken by the boy's cries and unable to think what to do next. He knew how quickly Mickey could give the boy the sort of going-over that could seriously harm him. Or even kill him. A sour taste shot up Jack's throat and into his mouth. A few seconds dragged like hours. Knowing he couldn't wait a moment longer, he raced back down the alley in time to see the boy jerking around on the ground as Mickey repeatedly kicked him.

'I've just seen a police car,' Jack shouted through cupped hands as he raced towards them. His heart was in his mouth.

Mickey didn't seem to hear him and carried on kicking the boy.

'Come on.' Jack grabbed his arm. 'I said police. Let's get out of here.'

Mickey looked at him as if he'd finally registered what he'd said, gave the boy one last kick, then they all ran back the way they'd come and didn't stop running until they reached Mickey's car, breathless and swearing.

Three hours later, in a side street off the Walworth Road, Jack climbed into Barry's car and slammed the door so hard Barry winced. 'Easy.'

'I haven't got long,' said Jack.

Jack had thought he'd find comfort in Barry's presence. He'd wanted to tell him about the coloured boy, but now he was here he couldn't bear to mention the incident. Holding the images in his head was hard enough without describing them. All he wanted to do was push them away, smoke a cigarette and pretend it had never happened.

'How's things?' asked Barry.

'All right.' Jack nodded. 'Ralph took me aside. They want me to step up.'

Barry half-smiled. 'Well done.'

Jack lit a cigarette and wound down his window. He dangled his arm over the side and drummed his fingers against the car door.

'They're holding their first Spearhead training camp next week.'

'Where?'

'Somewhere in Kent.' Jack flicked his cigarette butt through the window and watched it land near a lamp post.

'Find out. I'll get a snapper from the paper down there.'

Jack stared at the open notebook on Barry's lap as Barry wrote himself a note in his solid, precise handwriting. He kept rigidly within the lines, as if he were still in school, unlike Jack, whose looping scrawl veered all over the page. Watching him write, Jack realised he'd been gone from *The Times* for almost five months and he missed it.

He missed the editors and the keen young secretaries from the typing pool. How warm and fresh a page of words felt in his hands when he tugged the sheet of paper from his typewriter. Sitting at his desk after everyone had left for the evening and reading his stories aloud in the silence, feeling that tingle of excitement if he'd written a half-decent piece, something that might move or inspire others. He had no idea he would yearn for it so much. Being at his desk opposite Barry, sharing cigarettes and banter and taking the mickey out of each other. Such simple, beautiful pleasures.

He glanced at his watch and opened the car door a crack. 'I'm off.'

'When's Jordan's next talk?'

'Not sure.'

'We did a good job turning over the one in Earl's Court.'

'You did,' said Jack. 'He went mad.'

As Jack put one foot on the pavement, Barry pulled on his arm. 'Did you see Vivien?'

'Yep.'

'And?'

'And nothing.'

'You know you can't see her again until this is over.'

'Of course.'

'You didn't tell her too much, did you?'

'No,' said Jack and got out, slamming the door hard again and gulping down the clean summer air.

13

Vivien knew she would have trouble keeping her happiness to herself. It was her turn to have Saturday off, and she'd woken thinking of Jack curled into her side, his feet pressed against her calves – and she hadn't stopped thinking of him all weekend.

Sitting at the kitchen table happily eating slice after slice of buttered bread, finger-painted with Nettie's home-made apricot jam, she remembered the feel of his warm skin and the taste of his sweet kisses. On the bus to work she pictured him kneeling in front of her, his head pressed into her skirt, arms wrapped around her thighs, and she almost missed her stop. Halfway down Wardour Street she recalled how beautiful and strapping he'd looked as he disappeared into the house, returning with a poetry anthology he'd plucked off the bookshelf, some of which he'd read to her in a low, lazy voice.

As she walked through Soho, the love oozed out of her, and she showered it all around. She smiled and said good morning to everyone who looked her way. She over-complimented and overtipped the waitress in the coffee bar where she bought her frothy coffee. A stallholder in Brewer Street gave her a hard-luck story about ordering too many carrots, so she bought a couple of pounds even though she had plenty in the pantry at home.

At work her new earrings and red top were immediately commented on. Lydia told her she looked wonderful and left it at that, while Maeve, not naturally as generous as Lydia, leaned in close, narrowed her eyes and said, 'No, it's more than that. You look different. And you sound different.'

In the afternoon, as Vivien watched the delivery boy carry sausages into the Polish deli opposite, the door swung back and a fair-haired girl, who she imagined was regularly described as beautiful, came in and asked for an appointment with Vivien. It was the first time a new client had asked for her by name and she blushed as Marcia called her over.

'I'm Nella Tyler,' said the girl holding out her hand. 'Ivy Wimpole said I had to see you. Could you be a darling and fit me in?'

Nella, who wore a wide red scarf over her fine blonde hair, was quick to announce that she was one half of the star entertainment at the Raymond Revuebar. But once she sat down, Vivien quickly saw that her hair colour did nothing for her. If anything, it made her skin look slightly jaundiced.

'What's your natural colour?' she asked.

'Mousy.'

'I think you should go dark.'

'Dark?' Nella repeated in a put-out voice. 'No one's ever said that before.' She pouted. 'I've been blonde for ever.'

Vivien smiled and nodded, remembering how Chrissie had said never to let the client think they looked anything less than marvellous. 'And you look terrific. But dark would suit your colouring a lot more. And I want to cut a fringe and take at least a couple of inches off.' She examined the ends. Dry as a bone. It was a wonder her hair wasn't breaking off. 'You've got such a lovely bone structure. Pity not to make more of it.'

'The punters like blonde,' said Nella thoughtfully.

'They'll like dark even better,' said Vivien. 'Trust me.'

Two and a quarter hours later Nella was turning her face and admiring her short stiff coffee-coloured bob and her new blunt fringe.

'You're a genius, Vivien,' she said. 'I bloody love it.'

Vivien blushed as she took off Nella's gown and listened to Chrissie clap gently somewhere behind her. But the moment Nella left, Maeve turned on her. 'Who is he?' she asked.

'What?' asked Vivien.

'You've met a bloke. It's obvious.'

'Yes, c'mon. Tell us,' said Marcia. 'What's going on?'

'Nothing. Honestly.'

'Something is definitely going on,' said Deirdre.

'Maybe she's been reading that naughty book.' Marcia tapped her foot against the floor. 'What the hell is it called?'

Barb leaned over the reception desk. '*Lady Chatterley's Lover.*'

Maeve snapped her fingers. 'That's it.'

'I have not,' said Vivien. 'I'm just happy, that's all.'

Just before Elvis Presley hit the last note of 'Surrender', Stevie returned the needle to the beginning of the record and lay back on his bed to listen to it again.

Three days on, the image of Vivien leaving the guest house still troubled him enough to wake him a couple of times during the night. He would picture her smiling and hear her loose joyful laughter, and he couldn't stand it. He hated knowing another man had brought her pleasure.

When there was a knock at the door, he shouted, 'What?' but no one replied, and as he swore and got out of bed he heard someone padding away. He opened the door and stared down at the tray on the carpet. His mum had left him cheese on toast, a cup of tea and two garibaldi biscuits. Now he felt guilty again. All he'd done these past few days was yell at her to leave him alone through his closed bedroom door, yet she still looked after him.

A few times, as he'd heard her pottering around downstairs in the kitchen, he'd considered confiding in her about Vivien. She was a good listener, but she was also so keen for him to meet a girl, he knew this would influence her advice. When his brother Gavin had brought back his fiancée, Diana, for the first time, they'd only intended to stop by on the way to the pictures for a quick casual introduction, but Mum hadn't let them go. She'd spooned them out a tin of grapefruit segments and put two steaks under the grill, insisting they ate at the kitchen table while she loitered quietly behind them, pretending to find things to do.

He bent down and picked up the tray. 'Thanks, Ma,' he called out, loud enough for her to hear, then kicked the door shut with the back of his foot and sat down on his bed with the tray. As he picked strings of cheese off the toast he realised he was sick to death of eating alone on his bed listening to music. Actually, he was sick to death of 'Surrender'.

He lifted the needle off the record, lit a cigarette and stood by the window, smoking and staring into the flats that backed onto his building.

Nothing much usually happened and today was no different. There was the stout bloke, whose tummy strained against his shirt as he reached down to stroke his cat. A coloured kid forking something off a plate and reading a book. The woman with the short cap of black hair ironing in her slip. A couple folding up towels and bedding in a silent, orderly manner.

As Stevie watched, he realised that all this stewing over

Vivien was getting him nowhere. He had to forget about her, forget about girls in general, and just get on with playing the drums. If he was playing his music, he'd start to feel like himself again. He might even start to feel good.

He stubbed out his cigarette and ate a garibaldi biscuit. He took pride in these new insights, enough pride to make him want to change out of his pyjamas and leave his room. It was as if he'd reached the top of a mountain he'd spent days climbing.

He pulled on a T-shirt and a pair of jeans and went in search of his dad, who was on the back step in a sleeveless vest, creaming up his brown leather shoes and listening to an afternoon play on the wireless. In the sun's shadow his dad's eyes were deep with creases and the doughy flesh hanging off his rail-thin arms made him look weak. Yet the opposite was true. He was old and decent and he deserved far more respect than Stevie had given him these past few days.

Stevie climbed over the step and stood in front of him. 'Sorry. I've been a brat.'

'It's your mum who deserves the apology.' His dad didn't look up. 'Everything she does is for you.'

'I'll make it up to her.'

'See that you do.'

Stevie clasped his hands behind his head. 'It's been hard for me. Everything went wrong. The girl I'm crazy about doesn't care about me. No one wants me in their band. I know it was my fault I didn't keep my job at HMV, but I can't find any work.'

He looked away in shame when he admitted the last bit. Dad wasn't work-shy. He'd always been employed, even if it meant selling eggs door to door, or gathering up bits of leather from the floor of his cousin's belt factory, like he'd been doing these last few months.

His dad picked up a shoe brush and swept it back and forth over the toe. 'Things will pick up. Always do.'

'I'm going to start my own band.'

'Good idea.'

'Do things my way.'

'You can do whatever you put your mind to.' His dad looked up. 'Ask your mother. I've always said so.'

An hour later his mum, looking happier than she had in days, fed them fish paste sandwiches and sang along to her Nina Simone records while he and his dad wrote out the announcement that Stevie had cobbled together to advertise the auditions for his new band. He planned to hold them in the room behind a record shop on Frith Street where the manager often let bands rehearse.

When Stevie remembered that the girl two doors down worked in the local library which had just bought a new Xerox photocopier, he charmed her into copying his notices for nothing, then the next day took them around all the coffee bars and pubs in Soho and Carnaby Street. He flirted with the barmaids and waitresses he knew and those he didn't, and convinced them to pin up the notices by the tills or near the toilets. Then he tacked notices to tree trunks in the side streets and even asked shopkeepers if they could display one on their counters.

Everyone was helpful and encouraging. They wished him luck and told him stories of their own dreams, and it all made him believe good things were possible and he could turn his life around. This helped him sleep well over the next few nights, and on Saturday morning he got up early, shaved and ate a bowl of porridge and two slices of toast. He took a bus into Soho and opened up the room behind the shop where he'd set up his drum kit the day before. Because the shop would be busy, he pinned a sign on the front door directing people around the back. Then he waited. This was all new to him and he kept glancing at his notebook to familiarise himself with the questions he'd written down.

By one o'clock, three hours after the auditions had officially opened, only four people had turned up. Two of them were guitarists and he could tell they were lousy from the first note they played. They were nice boys with hopes like his, and he liked them, but he'd go nowhere fast with them around. The third boy only really wanted to play jazz, and the fourth boy with the rage of orange hair and a long untidy beard liked himself a lot, and talked like he knew a thing or two, but the moment he began singing Stevie could tell he was another let-down.

Stevie waited for more people to arrive, sure that they would. Musicians were disorganised and couldn't be hurried. Time meant something different to them. He ate the sausage roll and boiled egg his mum had packed for him, and doodled on his notepad until he could tell that too many hours had passed and no one else was coming.

Then he screamed, kicked his kit over and punched the wall. Nothing was easy.

The doorbell cut through Jack's sleep. He jolted upright as if the disturbance was in his room, not outside, six flights down, separated by bricks and mortar. His pulse was thudding hard as he squinted at his watch. Twenty past eleven. No one had ever rung the bell this late before. Maybe it was kids messing around.

He punched the pillow and ducked his head down. He thought the doorbell wouldn't ring again but it did. This time it didn't stop. Whoever was down there had no intention of taking his finger off the bell. Once the room was flooded with light, Jack yanked on his trousers, grabbed his key and ran down the stairs, barefoot. Opening the door, he found Mickey swaying gently on the top step. Staring into his heavy hooded eyes, Jack couldn't decide if he was drunk or tired.

'Finally,' said Mickey.

'I was in bed.'

Mickey twitched his upper lip as if he was mimicking Jack's words in his head. 'Sorry to cut into your beauty sleep, darling.'

'What are you doing here?' Jack wrapped his arms instinctively around his chest. The moon's stark brightness shone over them. He shivered.

'Ralph wants you to ride along with me tonight.'

'At this time?'

'Yeah.'

'What for?'

Mickey pointed at Jack's vest and his open flies. 'Get dressed and you'll find out. Wear something dark.' He clapped his hands when Jack started to say something. 'Come on. Chop-chop. I'm parked over the road.'

Back in his room, Jack tried not to think the worst. He dragged on a white shirt, then quickly unbuttoned it and tossed it angrily into the corner of his room. 'Dark,' he said aloud, putting on a black pullover, black trousers, socks, shoes. 'Dark. Dark. Dark.'

He ran back downstairs then stood for a moment in the building's central hallway, preparing himself. He settled his hair with his hands, pulled the brim of his trilby low. Rearranged his jumper around his shoulders and neck. Formed a smooth, blank mask to hide the tension in his face. Finally, his mind felt strong. He was ready.

In the car he steeled himself for another of Hitler's speeches, but as he drove, Mickey started talking about his family, who lived a few miles away. His older sister, an unmarried office clerk. His younger brother, a carpenter, whose spastic son the family doted on. His uncle, a road sweeper, who had taught him how to fish. Mickey didn't have a bad word to say about any of them, and even at the traffic lights, when two West Indian men in flashy shirts laughed their way across the street, Jack was surprised that Mickey didn't curse or jeer at them through his open window.

He also noticed Mickey stayed off the main roads. He turned down side streets where barely anyone was about, streets where parents had put the children to bed, scrubbed all the dirty pots and pans and shut themselves away for the night. Jack had no idea where they were heading, but he didn't ask and made a point of displaying no curiosity.

'I played cards tonight.' Mickey took his hand off the wheel and patted his jacket pocket.

'Get lucky?'

'Too right.' He pulled over to the kerb. 'Here we go.' He pointed across the street. Between the silhouettes of clouds against the pale night Jack made out the low roof of a building.

'What is it?' he asked.

'A synagogue. Come on. Let's get this done.'

Jack fumbled with his door. Of course. Tonight he would daub swastikas on a shul, just like other party members had been doing for weeks. He should have guessed this was coming. Phil had warned him enough times. 'Expect to get your hands dirty,' he'd said. 'You'll have to prove yourself. They don't just take you on your word.'

Jack got out of the car. His conviction had barely flicker-ed when Phil had said he'd have to do this, so certain that he could put the necessary distance between himself and a paintbrush as he painted a swastika on the wall. But Phil was right to have reprimanded him for being cocksure. It was easy to be brave sitting in a comfortable wing chair in

Manchester nursing a brandy; an entirely different experience now Mickey was shoving a paint tin and brush into his hands.

In front of the railings Mickey told Jack to give him a leg-over. Once he landed, he disappeared through the trees. Jack followed. He twisted his knee a little jumping down, and as he straightened his leg and moved it around, moonlight broke through the clouds and helped him see the closed shul more clearly. The front door was padlocked, the lights inside were off, and the wall to the right of the entrance looked different, had been rebuilt in another, lighter brick. Jack reckoned it must have been bombed in the war.

The sign said it was a liberal shul in the care of Rabbi Allen. Jack wondered how Rabbi Allen would react when he learned that intruders had made their way onto the shul grounds. Since half a dozen other shuls in London had been defaced, he might have expected his own to become a target. Even so, he might still put down the telephone and weep to his wife, failing to understand what sort of people could do this.

Mickey appeared from around the corner and snapped his fingers at Jack. 'Get a fucking move on.'

Jack followed him to the far end of the shul, where Mickey stopped and grabbed the tin from him.

'I'll do it.' Jack took the tin back. 'I've not had the pleasure yet.'

'Be my guest. I'm busting for a piss. I'll be back in a minute.'

On his own, Jack stood staring at the wall. Now he was glad that Phil had made him practise drawing a swastika. It helped now that the nerves were getting to him, making his fingers shake. He dipped the brush into the red paint, moved forward and swept it across.

He finished the first and stood back, imagining Phil peering over his shoulder, like he had done in his office when he'd studied each of the ten swastikas Jack had drawn on a piece of paper.

Mickey reappeared as Jack was about to edge along and start another.

'Nice.' Mickey zipped up his fly and nodded admiringly. 'Top-notch.'

Somewhere between finishing his third swastika and tightening the lid back on the paint can, a darkness began to press down on Jack that hadn't been there before. Or if it had been, it was pushed to the edges of his life and he had been able to walk around it. Things had still felt ordinary. Now, as they left the shul, everything changed.

Outside his building Jack exited Mickey's car with an upbeat goodbye but he felt miserable. His walk up the stairs was sluggish. When he saw the shared bathroom on his floor was empty, he looked at his grimy, paint-flecked hands and decided to take a bath. For once he didn't care who he woke up; most nights he had to listen to a menagerie of sounds. Angry sex. Terrible music. Children sobbing, saying they were sorry. He'd heard it all. Let someone complain about the soft flow of water or him easing his body into the tub. He needed to be clean.

He collected a towel from his room, then went and turned on the bath tap, accepting he would get tepid water at best. As the bath filled, he sat on the floor smoking. Phil had told him to expect this. He'd talked about the double-edged sword of rising up through the party. You became relied on and trusted, but then you had to do things that took their toll. Jack was starting to understand this. The price was high. With every act he carried out, he could see he would be left with a little bit less of himself.

'Ow.' The cigarette had slowly smouldered away and

burned the side of his finger yellow. He stood up, flicked the butt into the sink plughole and ran his hand under the cold water. Get a grip, he told himself. You're not falling anywhere. You're just adjusting, that's all. Preparing for bigger battles ahead.

Vivien held out her arm for Nettie to grip while she wrestled her puffy feet into her shoes.

'Thank you, dear.' Nettie stared down at them and sighed. 'Elephant feet every summer.' Then she leaned forward to examine her face in the mirror next to the wall clock and appeared pleased with her reflection.

'Hadn't you better get a move on?' Vivien held out her landlady's cream handbag and short pale blue gloves as Nettie glanced at the clock.

'Goodness, yes. I don't want to miss my bus.'

As she scuttled down the path to catch her bus to Stamford Hill, Vivien stood in the doorway and waved, then rested her back against the shut door and closed her eyes, relieved. Every Sunday Nettie left at the same time to go to the pictures with her sister, which was why Vivien had been confident about asking Jack to telephone today.

With twenty minutes still to spare, Vivien went into the kitchen. She drank a glass of water and turned on the wireless. The song was unfamiliar but catchy, and she danced around barefoot, exhilarated that she was about to speak to Jack.

When they arranged the call in the guest house she had no idea that eight days of silence between them would feel so long. But it could, as she discovered, feel so intolerably drawn-out, she had begun to realise she might need to find some new hobbies if she was going to make a go of being Jack's girl.

When the telephone rang, she was already seated next to

it in the hallway and she quickly snatched up the receiver. 'Jack?'

'Hello, Vivien.'

'Oh Jack, I've been desperate to speak to you again.'

'Me too, baby.'

When he asked how her week had gone, she twirled the telephone cord between her fingers and told him about her visit to Kettner's with Maeve, where the waiter had stood next to their table and told them how the chef to Napoleon III had opened Kettner's as a restaurant a century before. Then she told him that Chrissie was trying to talk her into bleaching her hair ash blonde. She could hear herself jabbering on about things he couldn't possibly be interested in but was unable to stop, like a runaway train.

Eventually she found the brakes and caught her breath. 'How was your week?'

'Not bad.'

'What have you been doing?'

'Nothing much.'

'Really?'

'Vivien, don't ask about what I'm doing. I won't talk about it.'

'All right. I'm sorry, Jack.'

In the silence she looked down at her painted toenails and wished she could go back and start the conversation again.

'Are you wearing stockings?' he asked after a pause. 'I liked them.'

'No.' She raised a bare leg into the air and her gauzy green skirt fell back on her thigh. 'But I'll wear them again if we meet,' she said bravely.

It didn't cross her mind that he would agree to the suggestion, so when his breath shortened in the silence, she realised he might actually be toying with the idea and jumped out of her chair.

'Please, Jack, I'd do anything to see you. No one has to know,' she said. 'We can meet outside London. At the seaside! I love the seaside.'

'I don't know.' His voice was hesitant. 'It's a risk.'

'Please. I can't stop thinking about you.' She chewed a fingernail and waited.

'Well, maybe just once won't hurt,' he said, as if he were talking to himself. 'A man could lose his mind with just these lunatics for company.'

14

The curtains had been tied back, the windows opened and the early-evening sun cast the room in an inviting glow. Jack was amazed at the change in the appearance of the HQ front room. Someone with a sense of occasion had taken charge and spruced it up. The cat hairs had been beaten out of the rug, the sofa appeared to have received a similar treatment and the glass coffee tables, now free of dust and dirty rings, shone like new.

In front of the bay window a long table had been turned into a makeshift bar holding cans of beer, bottles of wine and mismatched glasses. Jack bent down to push the crate of beer he'd been carrying beneath the table. The day before, Ralph had taken him aside and invited him to hear Jordan read the party manifesto before it was publicly issued the following week.

It was the type of invitation Jack had been angling for since he signed up to the party, yet it was still a shock to receive it and realise he'd been asked precisely because of how convincing he'd become. He was obviously more suited to subterfuge than he realised.

'Jack.' Mickey stood in the doorway. 'Ralph wants to see you, me and Carl,' he said. 'Now.'

Jack's stomach dipped. 'Why?'

Mickey shrugged but didn't voice an opinion. Nor did he pace around restlessly while they waited for Carl to come up from the basement. He was both patient and reserved, which made Jack think he was also worried.

Once Carl appeared, Mickey led the trio up the stairs. He knocked on Ralph's door and after Ralph told them to come in, they lined up in front of his desk and waited for him to acknowledge them.

Jack stared straight ahead at the rows of military history books on the shelf. His collar felt damp and the pulse in his neck was thumping so loudly he was sure the others could hear it.

Ralph added a flourish under his signature, then laid his fountain pen on his letter and looked up.

'I had a call from Shepherd's Bush Police Station. About a coloured boy you put in hospital,' he said with barely concealed fury.

The instant he heard those words, Jack knew he was safe and his body loosened.

'Who was responsible?'

'The boy started it,' said Mickey. 'He had a go at Carl.'

'Who was responsible?' snapped Ralph.

'Me.'

Ralph stared at Mickey. 'We need our friends in the Met. And they're not happy. You went too far.'

Mickey nodded. 'Sorry.'

'Don't let it happen again,' said Ralph. 'Now get out.'

He picked up his pen, dipped it in the pot of black ink and began writing in his notebook without another glance in their direction.

Downstairs the guests had begun to arrive. Their cars were quiet and sleek, and one or two even had chauffeurs. Henry had been told to wait in the hallway and take people's jackets and hats, but it was a warm evening so he didn't have much to do.

Jack stood in the front room, shaking people's hands and

139

offering to fetch them something from the bar. Within half an hour he had counted twenty-seven of Jordan's allies filling the room with their chit-chat and braying laughter.

'Drink?' Mickey appeared unconcerned about Ralph's ticking-off. Jack nodded and Mickey handed him a bottle of ale.

As Jack lit a cigarette, he looked up through the smoke and noticed Ralph slip into the room and hover near the bar. With his thumbs tucked into his waistcoat pockets, he cleared his throat and asked for silence.

'Colin sends his apologies. Unfortunately he won't be able to make it.' A rumble of discontent started, but Ralph held up a finger, then paused theatrically before adding, 'He's waiting for a phone call from George Lincoln Rockwell.'

The room quickly buzzed with excitement at the mention of the leader of the American Nazi Party. Even Ralph's voice had quavered.

'I'd like to share with you, in confidence, of course,' continued Ralph, 'that Mr Rockwell will be joining us at the Spearhead camp and at the launch of the manifesto next week.'

The room broke into applause.

'Hitler showed the way ... The twilight of decadence lies over Britain. The grip of Jewish domination tightens ... The kings of chain stores, hire purchase and takeover are our real rulers ... The "free" press is no more than an enslaved organ of alien propaganda, and radio and TV debauch the public mind with the culture of the ghetto, the gutter and the jungle ...'

Jack only realised Ralph had finished reading the party manifesto because everyone started clapping again.

'Excellent speaker,' said someone behind him, adding in a whisper, 'far better than Jordan.'

The calm in the room had evaporated. Guests were talking among themselves and a few spoke directly to Jack, expressing disappointment that Jordan hadn't turned up, or agreeing with him that the manifesto was a work of brilliance.

As Jack glided smoothly around the room holding a bottle of wine in each hand, he smiled pleasantly and poured generous measures for those who asked while making small talk he felt no connection with. When an untidy-looking woman with stained teeth and a grey wiry plait asked him who he was and what he did for a living, he said his name was Jack Fox and he told her what he liked about the printers. He had nothing in common with these people; he didn't understand them at all and he was lying to them, but he didn't struggle to converse. He had his answers off pat and, as always, kept strictly to one drink.

Another half-hour passed before people began to leave and the conversation thinned out. Those remaining were either boorish and drunk or hanging on for the vague possibility that Jordan might appear.

Jack put his empty glass next to the others. He was restless and tired, desperate to be on his own. Besides, he had to write up his notes on who he'd met before he could go to bed. He wandered over to the fireplace, where Mickey was wiping a spill of ale from the front of his shirt, and clapped him on the back. But as he said good night, Ralph gestured to them from the doorway.

They waited for him while he kissed the hand of an elderly woman with a baggy powdered face and an expensive-looking fur stole draped over her shoulders.

'Boys,' said Ralph after the front door shut.

'Yes, boss.' Mickey thrust himself in front of Jack.

Ralph looked straight at Mickey, then switched his stare to Jack. 'I need you to go on a shopping trip. Colin wants you to deliver some goods to the camp.'

'No problem,' said Jack. 'What do you need?'

'Come by the day after tomorrow. I'll give you all the details then.'

Jack nodded.

'You can trust us,' said Mickey.

Ralph gave Mickey a swift, stern look. 'I do hope so.'

Early the next morning Jack sat casually on the train among people reading their morning newspapers as though his life was as ordinary and uneventful as theirs. At Bethnal Green he got off and headed south from the station.

He walked briskly. This was his fourth trip to the tailor's in as many months, and he knew he would pass the undertaker's and the kids' clothes shop, and now the bagel shop where the smell of hot salt beef always trickled out and weakened him. He glanced sideways as he passed by, registering again the WELCOME sign in both English and Hebrew, which hung crookedly on the door, and the handwritten notice taped to the fogged-up window reminding customers of the dates of Jewish holidays over the coming months when the shop would be closed.

Last time the door was ajar, and he'd glimpsed a row of customers huddled against the wooden ledge that ran the length of the shop, their heads lowered over their sandwiches, and he had pictured himself and his dad joining them one day. They both loved food. Eating out together was something they could usually get through without bickering.

As he walked on, he was surveying all the different fruits filling the front basket of a woman's bicycle when a bold voice rang out from somewhere behind him.

'Jack! Jack Morris! Over here!'

He kept himself stiff and upright, even though his stomach felt like it had caved in. The second time the man called out, his voice was so loud a woman next to Jack turned round to check where it was coming from. Jack kept his walk fast and steady, but once he'd rounded the corner, he dashed to the end of the street and hid in a doorway.

So alert to someone from the party catching him out, he rarely thought about bumping into someone he knew. It could have been a colleague from *The Times* or the *Hackney Gazette*. A school friend. A drinking pal. Someone from his Sunday cricket team. Just because he'd dropped out of sight didn't mean he'd been forgotten. He had friends, a life, people who knew him as Jack Morris and must miss him or, at the very least, be curious about his hasty goodbye and sudden absence.

He stubbed out his first cigarette and lit another. This was the last thing he needed. Something else to worry about. He let another ten minutes pass, then slunk out, back onto the main road, walking south again until he turned into a short narrow street where halfway down the sign A. CLEAVE, TAILOR & DRESSMAKER hung over a red door.

In the double-fronted window display a young coloured boy was crouched down low, sliding a dress over a mannequin. He stroked his fingers across the narrow bodice and down the flimsy layers of the pink skirt, his hands so tender it was as if he was caressing a lover.

Jack forgot what had just happened to him and pictured Vivien inside the dress, with its white floppy flowers stitched along the hem, and the intensity of his longing felt painful. He thought of her dark eyes with their hint of sadness, and how much he admired her for leaving behind everything she had ever known in order to make a life for herself here in the city. That took determination, he thought. And pluck. He shook his head gratefully. She was something else.

He was desperate to see her, to make normal conversation with someone he adored. And he could: he'd lied to Doug, saying he was sick, so that he could board a train in a couple of hours to meet her in Brighton. But now, given what had just happened, was that such a good idea? Was it safe?

He glanced over both shoulders again, then pushed the door open, careful not to step on the basket from where a chihuahua was yapping at him.

He leaned down and stroked the dog's quivering back while at the far end of the shop Alfie Cleave leaned forward in his chair, one hand clutching a pair of trousers. A cluster of pins was pressed between his lips and a tape measure dangled over his rounded shoulders.

'It's me,' Jack called out. 'Jack.'

'Good morning, sir.' The boy jumped from the window onto the shop floor. 'Can I help you?'

Alfie made a muffled sound and waved at the boy to get back to work as he took the pins from between his lips. When Jack extended his hand, Alfie sandwiched it firmly between his palms.

'You keeping well?'

Jack nodded, still a little shaky.

'They're already here.' Alfie released Jack's hand.

'They?'

'Sid's with him.'

'Ta.' Jack patted Alfie's shoulder and edged past him to the door in the corner. He could already hear high-pitched voices above the whine of machinery, and once through the door he was faced with four women hunched over sewing machines. Their nimble fingers pushed and glided fabric under needles, and their toes stepped lightly and repeatedly on the pedals as if they were following music, while behind them a coloured girl leaned across a table, scissoring red fabric from a roll.

144

'Morning,' he said.

They murmured a greeting in a scared, half-hearted way as he walked down the centre of the room, took a left just past the kettle and teacups on the low table and went through another door at the end of the corridor. He didn't bother knocking. He knew he would find Sid and Barry sitting among brown boxes and mannequins. They all shook hands, and when both the Kleins sat back down, they struck similar poses without realising it. Bulky arms folded over barrel chests, their bottom lips rolled out a little.

Jack took off his trilby and smoothed back his hair.

'What do you have?' Sid sat forward and pulled his shirt collar away from his neck. The stockroom was airless. Jack already felt sticky under his clothes.

'Something's going on,' he said. 'They're sending me shopping tomorrow. Want me to deliver some goods to the Spearhead camp.'

Barry's eyes darted around nervously and he swore. Jack watched Sid stare at the rolls of fabrics, his expression stony, and it might have appeared he wasn't paying attention, but Jack knew otherwise. Sid rarely gave anything away.

'Call Barry when you know more.'

'I will.'

'What else?' asked Barry.

'I had to paint swastikas on the side of a shul in Kensington. That was nice,' he said, and took a little satisfaction in noticing even Sid blanch a little.

'I'm sorry you had to do that,' said Barry.

Jack nodded, remembering the hour he'd sat in the bath, knees pulled up to his chest. 'Rockwell's visiting the camp. He'll also join Jordan when he reads the manifesto in Camden next week.'

'They let Rockwell into the country?' said Sid.

'Apparently.'

'How?'

'He came through Ireland.'

Jack remembered what else he was carrying. He unrolled his copy of the *Daily Mirror* and handed Barry the latest NSM membership list that he'd tucked inside. The day before Iris had left it lying on a stack of party newspapers in the living room.

Barry took the list and read the names on the first page while Jack checked his watch. 'I've got to go.'

Sid stood up. 'Things are heating up. You managing?'

Jack shrugged. 'I think so.'

'You look tired. It's a hell of a lot tougher than you thought. Am I right?'

Jack nodded.

'First time we talked I said you've no idea how lonely it is being brave. And you waved me away like I didn't know shit.' Sid put his hand on Jack's arm. 'Know you're doing an important thing. Hang on to that.'

'Good God.' Barry waved the membership list at Jack and pointed at a name. 'Not the actor?'

'Yep.'

Barry shook his head in disbelief and folded the membership list lengthways. 'Sandra won't believe it. She adores him.'

Now Sid's eyes were averted from Jack, his hands grabbing at the membership list. Most likely he had already forgotten what he'd just said to Jack. But Jack would remember. He would revisit Sid's words several times on the way to the station and as he boarded the train to Brighton. They would soothe him. They would keep him strong.

15

The road from Brighton railway station ran all the way down to the seafront. Vivien set off on foot, marvelling at the brightness of the day and how the water met the sky in such a silvery-blue haze she couldn't tell where one ended and the other began.

On the promenade, unsure of where Nancy's was, she asked directions from a man in a suit wearing a camera around his neck. They both laughed when he pointed at the sweetshop a foot behind her, its name in bright orange, a huge stripy stick of rock jutting up from the roof.

She retraced her steps and stood, as arranged, by the mermaid statue next to the shop, breathing in the sticky sweetness of candy floss and peanut brittle. Pressed against the railings, she stared at the children building sandcastles near the water's edge or splashing about in the sea, and at all the little boats, dark and sharp in the glare of the sun. People were enjoying each other and making the most of their lives, and it filled her with happiness.

Her only slight concern was that there was no shade. Worried about the sun beating down on her face, she took her sun hat from her bag and put it on. She might not have cared if she'd been in Soho Square with the girls, but today she couldn't bear for her make-up to run, for sweat to sour her skin.

She turned back to the promenade. Was she early or late? She wasn't wearing a watch and had no sense of the time. Turning to ask someone, she realised Jack was standing several feet away, in the middle of the road, waiting for a Morris Minor to pass by. His face was hidden by the tilt of his hat but it was him. She recognised his hard, spare frame and the way he clenched his fists in his trouser pockets. She took off her sun hat and waved, feeling the butterflies start up in her stomach again as he crossed the road and stood in front of her.

'Hello,' she said shyly. She could barely contain herself. All she wanted was for him to touch her, a feeling she couldn't imagine ever tiring of.

'Well, look at you.' He whistled gently. 'Pretty as a picture. I'm a lucky man.'

She put her hands on her waist and gave a coquettish sway of her hips. She did love her new red and white cotton summer dress with its scoop neck and big red buttons down the front, the *swish–swish* of the skirt against her legs as she walked.

He watched her without moving. His hands were still in his pockets, his body held away from her. Any second now, she thought, he's going to kiss me, or scoop me up, but instead he glanced around uneasily, took her elbow and guided her towards the edge of the road to hail a taxi coming in their direction.

'Let's go up the beach.' He opened the door for her. 'It'll be quieter in Hove.'

Once the taxi was moving, he sat close to his door, looking out through the window, one arm stretched across the back of the seat. When he made no effort to talk or touch her, Vivien stared at the back of the driver's head, unsure what to do. In her daydreams she had pictured them both laughing and joking, locked in a constant embrace, fighting to speak over each other. She hadn't imagined that within minutes he would be staring silently into space and tapping a box of cigarettes against his thigh. That he would be so closed-faced, so remote. She felt a long way from him and it hurt.

'Did you come by train?' she asked hesitantly.

'Yes.'

'Today?'

'Uh-huh.'

'On the 12.12?'

'No. Earlier. Some time around ten.'

'I took the 12.12.' She twisted her fingers nervously. 'My carriage was heaving. People were standing all the way down the corridor. I think everyone must be leaving London for the day.'

'Yes, it did seem that way.'

'How was your journey?'

'Fine,' he said.

He turned back to his window and didn't notice her smile fall away. She gave up. Fine? Fine didn't tell her very much. Fine didn't fill the space between them. It was odd. She couldn't read him. He wasn't being rude, he just wasn't engaging with her. Or with anything, she thought, glimpsing sideways at his smooth, set face. It was as if he wasn't there.

As the taxi sped past the crowded beach, Vivien gazed out at the stretch near the merry-go-round, where families were queuing up to try their hand at the lucky dip or ride the donkeys.

'It's not right,' she said angrily. 'Making those poor donkeys parade around all day. They must be baking.'

When Jack nodded but didn't respond, she blushed. It had been a daft thing to say, but without his help her head had emptied of everything she'd stored up to talk to him about. She chewed her lip and thought, that's it from me.

She didn't know why he was keeping himself from her, but she refused to say anything more.

Several minutes of silence passed, and then, as if he had finally been roused from a deep sleep, he squeezed her hand and smiled at her. Such a big wide slash of a smile, it took over his face, and although she didn't have a clue what had suddenly altered in him, she was relieved that it had.

'It is good being here.' He slid along the seat towards her and kissed her. 'It's everything I need. Over there, please.'

The taxi pulled over to the kerb, and Jack leaned across her and opened her door. 'Jump out.'

Vivien tried not to show her surprise. The wide clean promenade had tapered off into a loveless narrow strip with none of the colourful fanfare of activity of the main beach. There were no families collecting sand in buckets or parents towelling down wet children. Just a couple of lone sunbathers. And the promenade itself was deserted except for an elderly woman being pushed along in a wheelchair and a man with a little boy on his shoulders trying to grab at seagulls. No one came to this end of the beach for a day out. There wasn't a donkey or a carousel or an ice cream in sight.

Jack rubbed his jaw as he looked around. 'It's a bit boring, isn't it?'

'I don't mind.'

'It won't be like this for ever.' He stared down at her. 'I promise.'

On the beach she began walking towards the water, crunching the shingle underfoot.

'What fabulous weather,' she called out to Jack. 'Couldn't have asked for better.'

When he was slow to reply, she turned and saw he wasn't following her. He was striding off in the other direction towards a groyne. As he approached it, he opened the white beach bag he'd taken from her, then shook out her blanket and laid it down flat.

What was he doing over there? She understood that he'd want to be marooned away from the only other people – an elderly woman with a thick middle tucking her hair into a blue swimming cap and a man whose chest was white and shiny with sun cream – but the spot he'd picked was dreadful. Out of the sun's gaze and far from the water's edge. There didn't seem much point in coming to the beach. Yet, without knowing what else to do, she trudged over towards him, feeling another pull of disappointment. Oh God, had it been a terrible mistake to meet?

Now he was busy checking the contents of his wallet. She plumped down miserably on the blanket, her back against the rough wall.

'Are you hungry?' he asked.

'Yes,' she said flatly. 'A little.'

'I'll go get us fish and chips. I saw a place over the road. Cod or haddock?'

'Haddock, please.'

While he was gone she tied a scarf around her hair and put on her sunglasses. At least there was the sea to stare at and be soothed by. And, she conceded, the lack of people on the beach meant there was an empty quiet which was quite restful.

When he returned, cradling their food in a bundle of hot newspaper, Jack was holding a plastic flower on a stick that twirled in the breeze and a pink straw to push into her Pepsi bottle. His mood also seemed lighter – he made a joke about the colourful woman in the queue wearing her nightie and hairnet – which she took to be a good sign.

But he didn't say much else. He picked at his cod, then quickly put it to one side. He didn't touch his chips. He asked her about work and if she'd gone dancing, but she wasn't even sure he was listening to her. Certainly, he didn't seem to embrace the to and fro of normal conversation and gave one-word replies to her questions. So she wasn't surprised when he pulled his legs close to his chest and fell silent once more. He dropped his chin to his knees and stared at the sea for some time.

'I'm sorry,' he said eventually. 'I know I've been distant. Coming here was harder than I thought.'

'Why?'

'I haven't been around anyone ... anyone real ... for a while.' He pushed at the pebbles with his feet. 'I thought I'd be able to snap right back into all this.' He gestured with his hands. 'But it's like I've forgotten how.'

'Can I do anything?'

He shook his head.

'Is everything OK? I mean they haven't found out ...'

'No, nothing like that. Things are going ... as they should.' He sighed. 'It just forces you into yourself a bit.' He smiled and touched the end of her nose with his finger. 'I mean it, though. It's good being here with you.'

A man in a T-shirt and jeans walked into their vision, gently beating a newspaper against his palm and singing. His glance in their direction was vague and friendly, but Vivien noted how quickly Jack twisted around and pressed his trilby down on his head once more.

As the waves sloped gently over the sand, she huddled next to him and leaned her head on his shoulder. He did not move. They did not talk. In the confusing silence she wondered how her mum had dealt with her dad's work as an infiltrator. Maybe he just came and went, but told her nothing about the in-between. Or maybe she'd insisted he tell her everything because she was scared either way; at least knowing would bring them together and help fade the loneliness.

A black Labrador ran towards the water, barking loudly.

'Oh look, Jack!' She sat up and used her hand as a visor against the sun. 'Such a sweet dog!' His short happy barks made her smile. She didn't want to feel this sadness, she wanted to be in the water. She pulled out her pink bathing suit, contemplating how she could undress discreetly. 'Come on. Where are your trunks?'

'Trunks?'

'To go swimming.' She smiled.

'Oh. I didn't bring them. How stupid of me. Sorry.'

'Well, we'll go paddling instead. You can roll up your trousers. Can't come to the seaside and not dip our feet in the sea.'

He scrambled to his feet. 'That sounds like fun.' He took off his shoes and socks and turned his trousers up to his calves.

'Race you,' she said.

'Sorry?'

'Race you down there.'

She went as fast as she could but the stones hurt her feet and slowed her down. It would have been easy to beat her but instead Jack chose to stay close to her and to gasp loudly, pretending the speed was killing him. Charging into the shallow, foamy water, she lifted her skirt and ran in and out, kicking at the waves, and when he joined her, grinning, she could see a lightness had finally broken through.

They were still laughing when she stood on tiptoe to kiss him, and hearing his whispered thanks in her hair, she knew she'd helped lift him out of his mood, that he was comfortable with himself again.

He picked up a handful of smooth stones, then bent low and skimmed one perfectly over the water's surface, bouncing it far into the distance.

'Nice,' she said.

'Robert taught me.'

'Robert?'

'My dad's younger brother, Robert Morris. He was a journalist and a brilliant writer. He got me into writing. Bought me my first notebook when I was seven and told me to write about why I loved my dog Ruby. It was such a bloody waste that he didn't write again after he came back from the war. He said he sat for hours at his typewriter but nothing ever came.'

'How sad,' said Vivien.

'I know. Dad said he'd lost himself over there. He got promoted quite quickly and ended up with the Black Bull – the 11th Armoured Division.' He looked over at her. 'He helped liberate Belsen.'

'Poor man,' she said. 'No wonder he changed. Where is he now?'

'He killed himself,' Jack mumbled so quietly she wasn't entirely sure she'd heard him correctly. He glanced sideways at her, pulling hard at his bottom lip.

'That's awful.' She reached out and stroked his arm. 'I'm so sorry.'

'I owe him a lot.' Jack stared at a boat on the horizon. 'It was really because of him that I got my job on *The Times*. He made me send the piece I wrote on Kelso Cochrane's funeral to the news editor there.'

'Dad went to that funeral,' she said.

He'd been well then, four years ago. Strong enough to get angry and do something about it. The moment she heard on the news about the carpenter from Antigua who was stabbed to death by a bunch of Teddy boys, she knew Dad would be there. Bursting with fury on the man's behalf.

'So many people came. Around twelve hundred people lined up around the church,' said Jack. 'Coloureds, Jews, whites – this huge mix of people quietly pouring through the streets. It was extraordinary. A true show of solidarity. Do you know how easy it was for me to write about it? It flowed from here.' He put his hand on his heart. 'I was shaking when I finished. I still think it's the best thing I've ever written.'

The spray from a wave breaking fell on her. 'Can't you just be happy writing about what Colin Jordan is up to?' she asked.

He looked at her for a second. 'No,' he said slowly.

Another minute passed before she realised that he had fallen silent and disappeared back into himself again. She stood quietly thinking, then said, 'Look, here's an idea. Let's get a hotel room. Just to be on our own,' she added in a hurry. 'Nothing more.'

They walked back towards Brighton and went in and out of the hotels, asking for a room. There were so many hotels, she thought they would be spoilt for choice, but many of them, with snazzy names such as the Grand and the Queen's Hotel, were either too expensive or booked up. In the end, after the sun began to burn her arms, they asked for advice from a man in a sandwich board advertising accommodation and shows, and chose the Park Hotel, off the seafront, for no other reason than it was one of the closest and the flower arrangement outside the entrance was welcoming.

They took a double room without inspecting it first, then swiftly worked out they'd been conned by the flowers. The thick varnish on the dark wood bedside table was scratched and bashed in several places. The curtains stank of smoke and cheap perfume and there were two dead flies in the sink.

'Jesus. This is lousy,' said Jack. 'We should complain.'

'No, let's not. I don't care.'

'I do.'

'Well, don't. The main thing is we're together.'

'That's a nice sentiment,' he said. 'But when a man can't take his girl somewhere decent, it does matter. Bad enough that we went to the dullest beach imaginable.' He looked around. 'And now this dump.'

He turned on the cold water to flush the flies down the plughole. 'You really don't mind?'

'I really don't.'

'Even though this water is coming out brown?'

'I won't wash.'

He grinned. 'You're easy to please, Miss Epstein.'

She returned his smile. 'I am.'

'Well, as long as you're happy, I guess I can live with it.'

He perched on the edge of the bed and watched her while he unlaced his shoes. She was nervous now. It was their first time in a bedroom together – he had refused to set foot in hers back home, out of respect for her father – and the presence of the wide, bulky bed created a surprising tension. Even as she walked around it, Vivien was affected by the sight of the thin mattress, how Jack was now lying back with his hands pressed behind his head, scrutinising her. She pretended he wasn't. Staring through the crack in the net curtains, she made him laugh with her observations of the sweet old couples taking dance lessons in the hotel ballroom opposite. She opened, then shut the wardrobe door, then held up her hands and showed him the dust on her fingertips.

'Yuck,' she said and pulled a face.

He smiled at her. 'Come here.'

She ventured over shyly and with her back to him, slipped off her shoes, then lay down alongside him. As soon as she did, they lolled together because the mattress dipped so badly. Then they both giggled, her nervousness thawed and she felt sure of herself again.

'You have a tiny scar on your chin,' he said after he'd kissed her. 'I never noticed that before.'

'Fell off my bike.'

He pushed a strand of hair behind her ear and scoured her face. 'And is that a scar under your eyebrow?'

'Uh-huh. Hit my head in a swimming pool.'

'Well. Someone's accident prone.'

'I'm ridiculously clumsy.'

'That's hard to believe. You appear so graceful.'

'I do not!'

'You do. You're very elegant. I remember the way you took off your headscarf the first time I saw you. You didn't just unknot it and whip it off. You worked at the knot gently, then lifted it away from your hair like this.' He swept his hand through the air. 'I don't know why I remember that, but I do. It was lovely.'

'Is that tooth chipped?' she said, pointing at his mouth.

He nodded. 'I fought someone in the street for a girl's honour.'

'No!' she exclaimed. 'Tell me the truth.'

'I was carrying a television into my parents' living room and tripped. Smashed my mouth against it.'

She tutted. 'I almost believed you.'

As they kissed again, she felt his hand on her thigh. She didn't bother to articulate that his hand wasn't expected to roam anywhere else; she guessed he knew this wasn't the right time for anything more to happen.

'I'm sorry,' he whispered.

'What for?'

'For putting you in this strange situation. You should be out having fun with someone. Swimming in the sea. Cycling along the promenade. Drinking cocktails in some fancy bar, taking in the sunset. Not stuck in a grotty room with only ugly curtains to look at.'

'Now Jack, stop that. It was my choice to come to a hotel. No one is making me do anything I don't want to.' Pressing her body against his, she ran her hand up and down his arm as music started up in the room above them. Cliff Richard's 'We Say Yeah', one of Stella's favourites. Vivien smiled to herself. The vinyl must be worn through by now, the number of times Stella had played it.

When Jack slid abruptly off the bed, she felt cold as if the sun had rolled away from her. He stood by the curtains gesturing to her.

She sat up. 'What?'

'On your feet, lady.'

He reached over and pulled her to standing. Then he ringed his arm around her waist and laced her hand in his. He was humming the tune, occasionally joining in with the lyrics.

'I thought you didn't dance,' she said.

'I don't. This isn't dancing.' She felt the weight of his chin on her head, his breath like a breeze through her hair. 'I'm holding you while the music plays. See? I haven't moved my feet.'

'You're right.'

She rested her head against his chest. They stood like this for some time, long after the song had finished and several others on the album had played. Then he said, in a sad voice, 'I should probably be getting you to the station soon.'

'Already? What about you?'

'I'll get a later train. We can't travel together.'

'All right.' Her voice dropped to a whisper. 'If that's what you want.'

'Of course it's not.' He brought her close to him and kissed her head. 'I don't want to leave you for a minute. It's just how things are right now.'

16

The next day outside the hardware shop Mickey made it clear that Jack was only there to fetch and carry and should remain quiet while he did the talking. Now they were both silent as the lanky shop assistant stood on the stepladder and reached up to a shelf for two types of sodium chlorate weedkiller, then climbed down, clutching both tins to his chest.

Mickey grabbed one of them, nodding to himself and slowly moving his lips as he examined the label. He was not a confident reader and still put his whole self into it.

The shop assistant kept clearing his throat. Even reading silently to himself, Mickey filled the room with tension. Standing by the window, the sunlight revealed the mesh of nicks and scars on his face. He was proud of telling Jack that he'd never had to try to be a hooligan. He just was one.

Mickey now held a tin in each hand. 'Which one's best?'

'They both do the job.'

'There must be a best one.'

The shop assistant pointed at one. 'That's the most popular.'

'We'll take five.'

'Five?'

'You heard.'

Jack moved away from the conversation towards the door. He could still hear the scrape of the tins as they were removed from the shelf and Mickey humming loudly, so he took a stick of gum from his pocket and folded it into his mouth, chewing furiously to block out the background noise.

'Jack.' He turned to see Mickey pointing at the row of cans. 'Put these in the car.'

The assistant was writing out the bill. 'That's a lot of weedkiller,' he said in a shaky, high-pitched voice.

Mickey grinned. 'We've got a lot of weeds.'

When Jack opened the boot he had to move a cardboard box aside to make space for the cans. He lifted the flaps and looked inside, and when he saw one of several two-pound bags of sugar, all his strength drained out of him. He'd picked up enough knowledge on the news desk to know that explosives could be made by combining weedkiller with sugar. They might not always work but they often did.

He stared into the boot for some time, as though he were seeing it through thick glass, but when a car rattled by, reminding him that he was still on the road, he shoved the cans in the boot and slammed it shut.

Crouched down on the ground, he pretended to do up his shoelaces while he fought to catch his breath. He'd thought that he could handle whatever the party asked of him, but now he wasn't so sure.

'What are you doing?' Mickey barked at him from across the street. 'Could you be any slower?'

Jack swiped his sleeve across his brow, then stood up fast.

'Sorry.' He gestured to the boot. 'Couldn't get it open. It was jammed.'

'Yeah, well. There's another couple to bring over.'

'On my way.' Jack strode across the road, barely seeing the cars coming at him. He reminded himself that he didn't really belong to any of this. He was an outsider. An observer. Sent to bring these men to task. All he had to do was find out what they were up to. And he could do that. It was what he had been waiting for. So why did he feel so scared?

The following evening Barry held the elbow of Sid's secretary and guided her towards the front door. He helped her put her jacket on and patted her shoulder.

At the door she took two steps forward, then came back. A curl had escaped from her fringe; hairpins had to be rearranged. When she picked up her handbag and her package of meat, Barry opened the door wide and smiled as he mentally shooed her into the street. Please, he thought, do not tell me again about the lovely fresh brisket from the butcher and your secret way of braising it so it melts on the tongue.

Boy, could she talk. A well that never ran dry.

'Right-o Barry. I'll see your dad bright and early.'

'Night.'

Barry locked the door behind her and flipped the WELCOME sign to CLOSED, PLEASE CALL ANOTHER TIME. He unhooked the plastic clock – a tacky promotional gift from an insurance company – and moved the hands around so it read eleven o'clock, then hung it back on the door.

He glanced up and down the street. Now the men watching from their cars would know he and Sid were ready for them.

The six men from the 62 Group greeted each other warmly but didn't say much else. The mood was sombre, and once Sid had shut the door and poured each of them a whisky, they took their seats, impatient for Barry to start the meeting.

Barry switched on the fan, shrugged off his blazer and

sat down. 'Jordan plans to make firebombs at the camp.'

'Good God,' said Sid and swallowed his drink.

After a stunned pause everyone else began talking at once in heightened angry voices. Cigarettes were taken out and offered around. A couple of men were swearing.

Barry's head hurt. He took off his glasses and polished them with his handkerchief.

'How do you know?' Jeremy Hadden's calm voice forced everyone into silence.

Barry put his glasses back on. 'I can't say. But the source is reliable.' Sid shot Barry a look. 'Hundred-per-cent reliable,' added Barry.

They were the only ones in the room who knew Jack was the contact. Barry was certain he could trust the others, but he was dealing with a man's safety and he didn't want to take any risks.

'What do they want to torch?' asked Danny.

'We don't know yet,' said Barry.

'We need details.' Sid pulled a cigar from his inside jacket pocket. 'Soon.'

'I understand that.' Barry loosened his tie. 'No one's talking.'

'And the rally?'

The following week Mosley planned to take over the Ridley Road pitch, and a few hours later Jordan would hold an NSM rally in Victoria Park Square. It was the first time both men had made a public appearance on the same day and the anti-fascist turnout was going to be huge. Thousands of people were expected to make their way from all over the country.

Sid turned to Jeremy, who was now responsible for training the men and leading the street activities. 'So, what's our strategy?'

*

163

Jack woke up yelling and kicked the sheet down the bed. He lay on his back, snatching breaths and rubbing his eyes. Three nights in a row he'd dreamed about the kid whose birth certificate Phil had obtained for him – the child whose first name he shared, whose surname he had stolen. Jack Fox. Born 1951, died 1955. Phil didn't know why he had died but a child dying aged four was never good. A family had suffered.

From the start Jack had hated having to use a false name. It made him feel grubby. He understood the necessity – he needed a legend – but it felt like they were getting something out of a child's death. And all those feelings hadn't gone away. They still ruined his sleep. He stared at the cracks in the ceiling and tried to think of something else, but the last shreds of the dream hadn't left him. It was always the same. He would find himself waiting at a bus stop as the black-eyed boy with the smudge of chocolate around his mouth appeared at his side, asking him to return his name. 'It's mine,' he said. 'I need it back.'

When Jack ignored him, the boy would start crying so Jack ran off and the child, and another dozen identical-looking boys, quickly followed him. At this point the adrenalin would always cut through his sleep and wake him up.

He reached for his wristwatch. Ten past two. The street gave off almost no light and he was glad of the blackness because it would help him fall back to sleep. But half an hour later, still wriggling from side to side, he decided to go for a run. No one else would be around. The streets would be empty, his to own. He stood naked by the bed and finished off his glass of water, then pulled on a pair of shorts, a vest and his worn grey shoes with the soft soles.

Outside he didn't bother to limber up. He began to run as soon as he was down the steps. He started out slow but he wasn't slow; like his dad and grandad he always ran long and hard and made admirable time, as if the wind was at his back, propelling him forward. And by now he knew what he was capable of. He'd been running since he was thirteen when his mum insisted that he join his dad.

His dad wasn't keen, preferring to run long distances alone, but Jack's mum had made a big deal out of it being something they could do together. Almost every Sunday morning for years they had all piled into the car and headed down to a park a fair distance from the house.

Usually the conversation in the car was the best bit. At home his dad was often preoccupied or busy, eager to take his newspaper and coffee to his desk in the spare room. In the car they were all slightly sleepy and relaxed, and Jack could lie down on the back seat and say whatever came into his head, and his dad never seemed disappointed. He didn't chastise him. He listened and nodded. Sometimes he even appeared to be entertained.

Jack ran across an empty road. He wondered how his parents were and if his dad was less angry with him for what he was doing. His mum didn't like it either. She had sat in the armchair with her eyes shut, the blood draining from her cheeks as she twisted the rings on her fingers. But she hadn't flown at him like his dad had. 'It's bloody madness,' he'd shouted at Jack the morning he put his suitcase in his car. 'This is real life. You're not James Bond.'

A pleasant breeze came over Jack and he remembered running on mornings when the cold air made his breath steam and flakes of snow settled quietly on his hair. On those mornings his mum would wait in the car while he and his dad went round and round the park as many times as their bodies could endure. He recalled the whiff of sweat coming off them afterwards, the feeling of his lungs hurting and being tired in his chest, and how they put their arms around each other's shoulders to limp, tired but happy, towards the car.

Now Jack was running up a hill, past a derelict bus depot. He couldn't remember why he and his dad had stopped running. They just had. Probably Jack's teenage life took over and he couldn't be bothered. Probably something as small and stupid as that. By a postbox he bent over, clammy fingers pressed onto his knees, and hacked up phlegm onto the pavement. After he'd wiped his mouth, he straightened up and felt the thumping in his chest. It had been four months since he'd seen his parents and he'd do anything to see them again soon. He let the idea of it flood his mind, then quickly pushed it down. Seeing them was not something he let himself imagine that often, because no good came of these thoughts.

He crouched low and felt the rough surface of the pavement under his palms. Then he stood up. He should head back and get some sleep, otherwise he'd be in no fit state to drive to the camp in the morning. He began to walk slowly, shaking his aching legs, but he didn't really want to walk. Feelings were easier to handle when he was running. His chest might be hurting, his legs might get sore, but running fast downhill made him feel powerful, like he didn't really miss anyone and would never have another bad dream.

17

After a couple of hours of driving Jack turned off the stretch of grey road and the car rattled along a narrow track next to a private wood. Lofty trees sheltered the car from the sun and clumps of weeds bristled against the tyres.

At one point he panicked – the track seemed to go on for ever – and he considered turning back. He wondered whether he might have read the map wrong, but in the absence of a backup plan, he carried on. One cigarette and several minutes later the track came to an abrupt end. When a man left his position by a set of gates and approached him, Jack stuck his head out of the window and shouted hello. He recognised the man, an NSM member whose sister had dated Jordan for a couple of years. They saluted each other, then the man told Jack to drive through and park close to the woods.

There were no other cars, so either Mickey had come and gone or else Jack had arrived first. He got out of the car and stretched his arms above his head, relieved to have made it to the camp without any snags. He raised and dropped his shoulders a few times, then held on to his right shoulder and swung the arm around. That shoulder had always felt a little stiff, even more so today; he'd spent the journey hunched over the steering wheel, checking the rear-view mirror for police every few seconds, as if he was driving a getaway car.

In front of him was the barn where the training was due

to take place, and through the trees he glimpsed a derelict-looking house and stables. It must have been a decent-sized farm before it was abandoned and the woods took over. The large barn was in a bad state. The wood was rotting, the only window he could see was smashed, and bits of roof had fallen away, so that the sunlight shone in. It was ugly and in bad shape but Jack preferred it this way given what was going on inside. It was fitting somehow.

Yet there was also a stillness to the place, a bright nothingness. The sun was streaking, hot and glistening, through the trees, and a slight breeze shook the overgrown grass. Beyond the barn he could see a few cows and goats, a farmhouse set against the bottom of a hill and poppies dotted across the fields.

He opened the boot. He shouldn't be here for this purpose; he should have stumbled on this place on a day out with Vivien. Carrying a hamper and holding her hand as they sneaked through gaps in fences and climbed over stiles to find the perfect spot to enjoy a picnic.

He'd just taken out three cans of weedkiller when he heard the opening line of the 'Horst-Wessel-Lied', the Nazi Party's anthem, followed by the sound of marching. As he clutched the cans to his chest, the rhythmic drumming of feet grew louder and a line of about thirty men in uniform marched out of the far side of the barn.

Jack put the cans on the ground and straightened up, arms by his side. The men would take it as a sign of respect, but it also gave him a moment to compose himself as the familiar feeling of shock rushed through him. Some of the men had long daggers hanging from their belts, which banged awkwardly against their thighs. The weapons must be part of the Spearhead regalia, he told himself. They couldn't possibly use them.

As the men marched across the courtyard, they saluted

him and chanted, 'Sieg Heil!' Jack continued to watch them as they marched out of the gates and into the woods on the other side of the chicken wire. Once they'd disappeared, and he was sure he'd regained his composure, he picked up the cans. He wondered whether Rockwell and Jordan were here, and if he'd run into them, and the idea of it made him feel sick again.

He stared at the ground ahead of him and walked slowly until he reached the barn, where a bald red-faced man stood outside, leafing through paperwork held in a clipboard. Jack waited for a moment, his arms straining under the load.

'Jack Fox,' he said in a winded voice, but the man still didn't acknowledge him. 'Ralph Forster asked me to deliver these.'

The man looked up, then pointed towards a smaller barn around the corner. 'In there.'

Jack thanked him politely and walked away. He shoved the side of his body against the barn door until it swung open, then stood for a moment, letting his eyes grow accustomed to the dark, before edging into the room.

He dumped the cans on a table and noticed the bags of sugar stacked up on the floor. Mickey must have already come and gone. As he arranged the cans on the table, Jack saw that one had been tampered with: someone had replaced WEEDKILLER on the label with 'Jew Killer'. Jack turned the can in his hand and saw the official instructions for use had been scrawled over with 'Place a few crystals in a room of Jews'.

After he'd put the can back down, he looked around. A heavy blanket hung over the window, and at one end of the table were brass weighing scales and a book with slips of paper stuck between certain pages, its spine and cover concealed by several pairs of rubber gloves. He was trying to sneak a look at the book's title when he heard footsteps close by. He quickly pulled back. Don't take chances, he told himself. Remember who you are.

When he heard voices he walked outside to find a group of five men in their early twenties standing around smoking near the main barn. All of them were robust-looking, with tough stares, and he could only suppose they were the sort of men Jordan hoped to attract to Spearhead. Men who were not afraid of carrying out violence to prove their dedication to the party.

They returned Jack's salute, then a boy with a dull complexion and white-blonde hair stepped forward and shouted, 'Heil Hitler.'

From the grit of his voice through to the ironed creases in his brown shirt and the determination in his eyes, Jack could tell the boy was new to it all. He smiled at him, but the boy avoided his gaze and looked down.

Jack offered his packet of cigarettes around. When no one took one, he shook out just one for himself and waited for someone to strike up a conversation, but no one did. He wondered who they were and where Jordan had recruited them from. He was always on the lookout for boys of low intelligence or those who'd been let down or neglected. Boys who would do anything to be part of a so-called family.

He ground his cigarette butt under his heel and excused himself, then carried on walking to the car. It took him another few minutes to unload the boot, and after he'd finished he headed back towards the main barn.

The door was still closed but no one else was around. A box of brown shirts stood on the floor by the wall and lying on top was the clipboard the man had been studying. Jack knew he shouldn't touch it, and at first he just leaned casually against the door, smoking. He couldn't see the men returning but occasionally the wind carried their voices across the woods.

As he wondered what all this hard exercise was for, if it was preparation for the Victoria Park Square rally, he found himself edging closer to the clipboard. Then a noise startled him and he stepped away.

'What are you doing?' snapped the bald man, staring at Jack over his glasses.

'I'm looking for Ralph.'

'He's gone.'

'OK. I'll report back to him in the morning.'

'As you wish.'

The man stood aside and Jack slipped past him, praying the blotches on his cheeks and neck hadn't betrayed him. He walked briskly to his car, got in and left.

At the end of the track he drove aimlessly down several narrow winding roads. His head was full; his jaw hurt from clenching it so hard. He didn't recognise anything he passed and had no idea if he was driving in the right direction for London.

When he saw a pub, he parked on the grassy verge outside. He needed a stiff drink. The pub was quiet and cool. The top of his head almost scraped the beams on the ceiling. A couple of old men with a dog sat at the side of the bar, supping ale, not talking. It was the perfect location.

'Good day,' he said and tipped his hat at them.

The barmaid brought him his whisky, then went back to leaning her elbows on the bar and flicking through a copy of *Woman's Realm*.

He took his drink to a table in the far corner and as soon as he sat down, he raised his glass to his mouth and felt the trickle of liquid warm his throat.

His eyes lit on the narrow window opposite, the pleasant smudge of blue and green outside pressing against the mottled glass like an abstract painting. When this was over, he'd take Vivien on holiday. He'd show her Rome and Rimini and Madame Di Bernardo's guest house, where the air held the scent of lemons and they were minutes away from a beach with transparent turquoise waters. And it would be good for him because Vivien was considerate and understood that he liked his own company. She wouldn't buzz around him, demanding his full attention. She'd let him sit and read or gaze at nothing and enjoy the pleasures of shared solitude.

He took another sip of his drink. It was pleasant in the pub, listening to the old men mutter and the sound of the dog's tail brushing lazily against a bar stool. For a short time he almost forgot where he'd just been, but as the dog's bark rang out, it came back to him. The bags of sugar. The plastic gloves. The hardback book.

He put his glass down and pushed it away. Until today he had always been able to rationalise what he was doing. He could make it sound clear-cut and excusable in his head. He could accept painting swastikas. Going to rallies. The fighting. But this? Firebombs? The word hit him in his gut. And what if they asked him to throw the first one? He pictured them calling him in to tell him: Jack, you've made such a good impression. You've excelled. We'll bestow this honour on you.

He felt giddy. He was in too deep. Things were never meant to go this far. He pushed his elbows onto the table and put his head in his hands.

He tried to think about Madame Di Bernardo's lasagne and her zingy freshly squeezed orange juice, and not the dead Jack Fox and the men in the camp and the glitter of their daggers against their thighs. But when his mind came back to the brass scales, terror rushed up through him, into his mouth, and he had to run outside and throw up all over the grass verge where he'd parked.

Afterwards he went back into the pub and drank a glass of water, then walked outside to the public phone box, dialled *The Times* and asked the operator to put him through to Barry.

'Newsroom.'

'I want out.'

'What's happened?' Barry's voice fell to a muted whisper and Jack could tell he was clamping his hand over the receiver.

'I've just come from the camp,' he said. 'I can't do it.'

'Can't do what?'

'Fucking bombs. Arson. It's too much.'

'But you're doing a fantastic job.'

'Bullshit.'

'Have you been drinking?'

'I'm not drunk.' Jack stared through the glass at the heat haze curling off his car. 'I'm scared.'

After a pause Barry said, 'I know. And you'll be out of there soon. But we need you to find out what they're up to, Jack. What you're doing could save lives.'

A silence enveloped them as Jack watched several horses cantering across a nearby field where the grass had turned sandy from the scorch of summer. The horses tossed their heads and nuzzled each other, and he was awed by their magnificence and calm.

'Put someone else in.'

'There's not enough time.'

'I can't hurt anyone,' he said.

'Of course not.'

'I won't let it get that far. I'll walk before then.'

'Jack—'

'I mean it.'

'Jack.' Barry's voice dropped even lower. 'We wouldn't ask that of you. I'm your friend. Remember?'

'I know.'

'Good.' Barry paused. 'So I'm going to see your parents later. Your mum asked me to stop by. I'll send your love?'

Jack's eyes filled. He pictured Barry drinking tea with his mum, going on about how brilliantly he was doing so he could avoid her questions. His mum would flit between pride and worry as she hung on Barry's every word, and his dad would probably stay in the spare room working on his model boats, refusing to join them downstairs or even shake Barry's hand.

He strained against the glass, desperate to keep sight of the mesmerising horses as they faded from view.

'Yeah, do that,' he said.

18

With no other prospects on the horizon, Stevie found himself working in Alan's fruit and veg shop in Stamford Hill. It was only temporary – Alan needed an extra pair of hands for a week or two – but he said Stevie was welcome to put in some hours. He'd made a big song and dance about it, made it sound like he was doing Stevie a favour, and Stevie hated having to be grateful. It only made him angry with his mum for having asked Alan in the first place. It wasn't her business to find him a job. Maybe Stevie did need the money but he didn't want to be holed up on his own, sweeping dirt off a grubby floor in a poky storeroom.

He pushed the broom lethargically around boxes and sacks. Everything was such an effort. Ten days ago he'd thought he was about to put a great band together, but now that, like dating Vivien, seemed like just another silly pipe dream. He knew the best sort of men never gave up, but maybe those men understood something he didn't because he couldn't move himself on. He only had to picture Vivien's smile, see himself holding his notebook in the empty audition room or think about those people in the flats backing on to his, and the hope propping him up would vanish.

Who the hell am I? He stopped sweeping. A musician, he immediately thought, but it was over a year since he'd been in a band. He couldn't think of anything else except who he was to others – a son, a brother, a friend, a cousin.

Staring down at the squashed banana by his foot, it became obvious who he was. Little Stevie Pearlman, just another person on the planet, but that bit more of a schmuck because he'd fooled himself into thinking that he was someone special. Convinced himself he was destined for great things, yet here he was, cleaning out a storeroom, as ordinary as the people in those flats behind his, moving through their days cooking and eating and folding their bed linen.

With a heavy heart he got back to work. He threw down the broom to drag several large brown sacks out of a corner, and as he pulled them along, flecks of grime flew up and stung his right eye.

'For God's sake,' he screamed.

The door swung open and Alan rushed in clutching a bunch of grapes. 'What's happened?'

'I've got something in my eye.'

'Come here.' Alan pulled Stevie over to the window and gently lifted up his eyelid. 'I can't see anything.'

Stevie blinked and his eye felt fine again. 'It's gone.'

'Good.'

'Sorry I shouted.' He picked up the broom. 'I'm in a bad mood today.'

'We all have our off days.' Alan patted Stevie's back. 'What are you up to tonight?'

'Nothing.' Stevie started sweeping. 'Why?'

'Me and the boys are going to Camden.'

Stevie looked up, feeling brighter already. 'For a night out?'

'Not quite.'

'What then?'

'Colin Jordan's reading his party manifesto at the town hall.'

Stevie stopped listening the instant Jordan's name was

mentioned. He wasn't interested in rallies and meetings and politics. The government, the state of the country, the war – none of it meant anything to him. News like that always felt as if it was happening somewhere far away.

'We're meeting in the Rose and Crown pub in Camden at half seven. Come along.'

Stevie picked a mouldy pear off the floor. 'Not likely,' he said and chucked it in the bin.

At five o'clock Alan gave Stevie a day's wages and told him he'd done well. Stevie could always stand to hear praise, but he wished he was being complimented on his drumming and not his deftness with a broom. He took an apple and headed into the sunshine and down Stamford Hill. Although the sky was clouding over, it was still warm, and everyone looked browned and happy and filled with summery lightness, yet he didn't feel it and it only made him think of what he didn't have.

He stopped outside L.A.P. Motors, unsure of where to head next. He didn't want to go home. Mum wouldn't care that it was a nothing job. She'd be full of pride and he'd resent her for it, so when he saw a bus into town he ran to catch it.

Once he was in Soho, he wandered around aimlessly, not knowing where he wanted to go. The truth was he felt like some lovesick teenager mooning over Vivien, and nothing held much appeal except seeing her again. Because he had finally met someone he *really* liked. Someone he could imagine himself being with. He recognised that these feelings weren't mutual, but he felt so sure that if she just gave him a chance, he could change her mind.

He could also see he was far too absorbed in these thoughts; his reluctance to let go made no sense to him. He wasn't lonely. He had friends, places he could be.

He wasn't drowning in offers but there were always one or two girls he could ask out. Girls who wore the sort of pretty, skimpy sundresses he loved. Sweet-natured girls who enjoyed his chat and winning smile and wouldn't run away if he cuddled and kissed them in the back of his local pub.

But it was Vivien's kiss that he dwelled on and replayed until he felt frantic for another. He pictured her head dipped against his shoulder, his lips pressed on hers, and his chest would swell. Yet, just as quickly he would picture someone else removing her clothes and tracing her narrow curves, and the thought made him feel ill.

He was walking in a trance, out of Soho and down Oxford Street. His walk became so tense, he almost broke into a run and only slowed at the top of Tottenham Court Road when he heard a pounding coming from above the sandwich shop behind him. He looked up and saw the sign REES BOXING CLUB, then edged back towards the road to glimpse through the open windows.

From the gutter he could see a man skipping, another pounding a punch bag and two coloured men sparring in a boxing ring. They ducked and swiped and danced around each other, their bodies polished with sweat, and it was so beautiful to watch he couldn't take his eyes off them. And as he stared, something dawned on him. Even if it came to nothing, he needed Vivien to respect him and see him in a different light. She had to see he had courage.

There were twenty-seven men in total leaving the pub and they were all members of the 62 Group. Stevie had never heard of the Group before tonight and at first it made him uneasy to be part of an organised anti-fascist body. It was something you signed up for if you cared about the cause, not because you wanted to win over a girl, but he told himself he was doing some good and that mattered more than the motivation.

The men stood in discreet huddles down the street, forbidden to go into St Pancras Town Hall until it was their turn. For nearly twenty minutes Stevie waited with Alan and three others whose names he never learned because none of them was concerned with knowing Stevie or making small talk.

Eventually, a man called Jeremy came back over, told them how to behave at the meeting and what signals to listen out for. The others all nodded fervently and seemed to respect Jeremy, so Stevie tried to concentrate too but his mind kept drifting. Then he realised Jeremy had stopped talking and it was time to go.

They hurried down the street and into the building. As Stevie walked across the foyer, he had the urge to break into song and draw attention to himself, purely because he'd been told not to, but he thought of Vivien and kept his mouth shut and his eyes straight ahead.

In the hall he stopped thinking about messing around. There was a tense air about the place and far more people than he expected. He felt like telling Alan he'd had a change of heart, but their instructions were to populate the crowd and Alan was already on the move.

Stevie felt panicky as he looked around, so he stayed close to Alan, pressing against his back as they pushed forward together. The audience was a mixed bag: elderly men and women, sedate as churchgoers, and knots of young hip-looking people who, except for their placards, wouldn't look out of place in Soho.

KEEP BRITAIN WHITE. FREE BRITAIN FROM JEWISH CONTROL. HITLER LIVES ON. HITLER WAS RIGHT.

Once Alan came to a stop near the front, Stevie got a clear look at the stage. At either side red velvet drapes were held back by gold cords, and the polished wooden floor gleamed under spotlights. A long table, which could easily seat a dozen, was set in the middle of the stage, with an NSM party banner pinned across the front. Behind the table a portrait of Hitler was fixed to the curtain alongside a large black and white photo of a man who Stevie presumed to be the leader of the National Socialist Movement.

'Butterscotch?' The lady with the pinched nose and red lipstick to his right brandished a tin of sweets. He thanked her but politely refused, then saw she was clutching a copy of the *National Socialist*.

This is all wrong, he thought, recoiling. This was not for him. He should not be here. His legs were waiting for the rest of him to decide to make a break for it when the lights over the audience dimmed. A slight man in a waistcoat and matching blue trousers walked onto the stage. Clapping drowned away the chatter as the man pointed at some of the placards and gestured his approval, before tapping the side of the microphone and speaking.

'Good evening, ladies and gentlemen. My name is Ralph Forster. I'm with the National Socialist Movement.'

The applause that greeted him was so loud that men in brown shirts moved quickly around the room shutting all the windows.

'I'm delighted to announce a surprise guest this evening.' Ralph waited for the crowd to settle. 'George Lincoln Rockwell, the leader of the American Nazi Party, will be among those joining Colin Jordan on stage.'

The applause escalated. People stamped their feet and cheered. Stevie didn't know anything about Rockwell and he didn't understand the excitement, but he felt Alan stiffen so he knew it was bad.

A couple of men were making their way through the crowd handing out circulars. When one of them reached

Stevie, he didn't want to take a leaflet, but as he did he briefly glanced at the man shoving it at him and the sight of his face made Stevie look again.

Stevie recognised him. He just couldn't work out from where.

Squinting, he tried to get a better view as the man moved around, and then, as he thrust a circular into someone else's hands, it hit Stevie hard. It was him, the tall rakish man who'd stroked Vivien's jaw and held his arm around her waist as they left the guest house, scooping her up in the shadows by the bus stop and holding her in the air as if she were as light as a feather.

Stevie couldn't stop staring. It was definitely him. As the man edged out of sight, Stevie ducked around, peering over people's shoulders to try and keep track of him. It was incredible. He wanted to tell someone but there was no one to tell.

'It's Rockwell!'

The bellow from somewhere behind reminded Stevie that this was the signal, and suddenly the room was ablaze. Men he'd lit up a ciggie with in the alley some streets away were shouting and swearing and yelling. They were tearing through the crowd and sprinting to the front, and Stevie knew he should be among them. Instead he froze as he watched half a dozen men jump the stage and turn the table over, forcing the row of guests to shriek and run from their seats.

A brawl broke out. The men from the 62 Group were sure of their ground once their fists were up. They hurled themselves, punching and kicking, at the men in brown shirts circling the stage, then tried to duck the hard blows that came back at them. As most of the audience turned towards the door, Stevie edged along with them, glancing back over his shoulder.

He saw Alan twist someone's arm behind his back and at first Stevie thought he was shouting out because he was pleased with himself or because he'd scored a small victory, but then Stevie realised he was calling for help. Alan wasn't a natural fighter. He needed support and Stevie should have turned round and offered it, but he didn't. He didn't care if it made a man out of him, he didn't want to get involved. He wasn't brave enough.

Fighting for breath, Stevie shoved his way out of the hall, then sprinted across the foyer and into the fresh air, gasping hard and near to tears.

Jack hooked his hands under the man's armpits and threw him off the stage. As the man's legs kicked out, he let rip a stream of expletives and yelled that Jack was an animal, but the words passed over Jack because he'd heard it all before. He was just grateful the man hadn't lunged at him because that would have meant hitting him back.

From the stage Jack surveyed the room. People were getting hurt. A man had stripped to the waist and bunched up his shirt against his bloody forehead. Another was covering his face with splayed fingers, blood seeping between the gaps. A woman was holding up her friend, who was bent double and waving her arms around.

But the Group had done well. The meeting was a shambles. Now all Jack wanted was for the last stragglers to flee and for the final bits of fighting to end. About to turn around, panic rose in him when he noticed Henry wandering out of the door next to the stage. Henry had been allowed to sit next to Ralph but was forbidden to enter the hall at any other time.

Henry edged further into the room. His eyes were as wide as saucers, and Jack was ashamed that a young boy should see grown men behaving so badly.

Spotting Carl, Henry looked glad to see someone he knew, but as he charged over and pulled on Carl's trousers, Jack broke into a run across the stage. Carl was about to whack someone with a broken chair leg and Henry would get caught in the middle of it.

Jack jumped down and landed awkwardly on his ankle. He quickly scooped up Henry and lifted him away from the fighting just as a man with an open shirt and a Star of David around his neck came forward twirling a sock full of sand, which he smashed against Jack's thigh.

'Davy, enough! He's got a kid with him,' called out another man and held Jack's attacker back by both arms as Jack arched his back in pain but hugged Henry even closer.

Once they were through the stage door and the commotion was behind them, Jack set Henry down.

'Everything's OK,' he said gently, clutching his thigh.

'Henry,' shouted Ralph as he strode towards them. 'What the hell were you thinking of? I gave you strict instructions not to move.' He turned to Jack. 'I was only gone two minutes. I had to put Colin and Rockwell in a taxi.'

Ralph looked exhausted and undone. His stringy hair was stuck to his forehead and several buttons on his waistcoat were open.

Henry started crying. 'I'm sorry.'

'No harm done. You were just being nosy, weren't you?' Jack reached down to ruffle Henry's curls. 'You're as good as gold really.' He winked at Henry, then rubbed at the intense burning in his thigh as he straightened up.

'Thank you, Jack.' Ralph held out his hand for Jack to shake, and when Jack took it Ralph gripped it hard and stared directly at him. 'I mean it.'

And then he walked away, whispering something in Henry's ear which made Henry nod a couple of times and take his hand.

The men had planned to meet in the Rose and Crown afterwards. Stevie made his way there slowly, still feeling jittery. His mouth was dry and he kept thinking he needed a piss.

He ordered a pint of Guinness and sat down. Vivien's man was with the National Socialist Movement. It didn't matter that he didn't know any more than that. What mattered was that the man was a fascist, and that was enough for Stevie to drain his pint so fast he thought he might throw it back up.

There was no way Vivien could know, not in a million years, and Stevie decided it was his responsibility to tell her. I don't have a choice, he told himself. She'd want to know. He just had to find the best way to tell her.

When Stevie saw the men from the Group, he stopped thinking about his own life and got to his feet. He felt ashamed to be sitting down, nursing his second pint and looking fresh when they all appeared so battered and exhausted and shaken up. The 62 Group leaders had arranged for most of the men to have training in how to fight and defend themselves, but many of them had blood and gashes on their faces and hands. They looked like they'd earned the beers that Jeremy was lining up on the table, and now Stevie hated himself for leaving the hall and for not being brave like them.

He considered lying and telling whoever asked that he'd stayed and fought, but even by his standards that seemed low. Instead he shuffled out from behind the table and stood a few feet away from them.

Not that he needed to move. None of them paid him any attention. They were too busy talking about what had happened and reliving their own personal battles. When a teenage boy ran in twice to announce that police cars were heading in the direction of the hall, Stevie thought they'd be relieved to get away without being arrested, but they didn't seem to care one way or another.

'There you are.' Alan appeared in front of him. He had a cut near his mouth and his right hand was pink and swollen. 'Where did you get to?'

His expression was so compassionate, Stevie looked down and blushed.

'It's OK to be scared,' said Alan. 'I still am.'

'I don't want everyone to think I'm a baby,' whispered Stevie.

'No one's thinking that about you, Stevie. It's enough that you turned up.'

Turning his head slightly, Stevie noticed a pile of crumpled circulars someone had dumped on the table. He saw the words Victoria Park Square and the snapshot of Hitler, and he realised it was the same leaflet that Vivien's man had handed him at the meeting.

He gestured towards it. 'What's that about?'

'An NSM rally in Victoria Park Square next Sunday. A big one. And Mosley is holding a meeting at Ridley Road on the same day.'

Stevie looked at two men beside them. One was wincing with pain as the other fashioned him a sling out of a tea towel. They both looked done in, and not for the first time Stevie hated his own lack of guts.

'Count me in,' he said and looked Alan straight in the eye.

19

It was past five. The sign on Oscar's door had been flipped to CLOSED but Barb had discreetly asked Vivien and Chrissie to stay on. She wanted them to play around with ideas for dressing her hair on her wedding day.

'Nothing fancy,' she said bluntly. 'I don't do the look-at-me thing.' She waved her hands around like a party entertainer and pulled a face.

'But the bride's always the star of the show,' said Chrissie. 'Everyone will be looking at you.'

'You know what I mean. Understated. Classy.'

Vivien swivelled Barb's head round to face the mirror and held her hair up in one hand. 'Personally, I think your hair should be up,' she said, aware that a month earlier her voice might have wavered before giving an opinion. 'Pinned at the back. Backcombed here. And maybe a small hairpiece?' She pointed at Barb's crown.

Chrissie nodded. 'I agree.'

Vivien let go of Barb's hair. 'I've got an idea for the hairpiece.' She held out the top page of her appointment book for them to examine her sketch.

'Oh, lovely,' said Chrissie. 'I like the big curls. And the way you shape the hair into twirls at the front.'

'Very nice, Vivien,' said Barb admiringly. 'A few months more under your belt and you'll be ready for a competition. Won't she, Chrissie?'

'I reckon.'

'Really? Wow.' Vivien blushed. 'I wouldn't mind that!' It was her dream to win a competition.

'It's tough,' warned Barb.

'Tell me about it.' Chrissie sighed. At a competition in Kensington the week before she'd toiled for hours under hot lights styling her favourite model Julie in front of a huge audience but hadn't come away with a single accolade.

'I know,' said Vivien. 'But I'd love to have a go.'

'All in good time,' said Barb and gave her wet hair a shake. 'Well, that was easy. Can you do me a trim today?' She handed Vivien the scissors. 'We'll put in a date to do a practice run with the hairpiece.'

'I'm starving.' Chrissie clutched her belly. 'I'm going to pop out. Do you want anything?'

After Vivien and Barb said no, Chrissie grabbed her bag and left, while Vivien gently tipped Barb's head forward and began trimming the ends at the back.

'How do you like London, Vivien?'

'I love it. Dad always said I would.'

'Is he still in Manchester?'

Vivien held her scissors in the air for a moment. 'No, he died.' She moved slightly to tilt Barb's head to an angle. 'Not long before I came to London.'

'Oh, Vivien,' Barb gasped. 'I had no idea. I'm so sorry. Were you close?'

'Yes, very.' Vivien was aware how small her voice had shrunk. 'He brought me up. My mum died when I was very young.' She tried to speak normally, but the words still snagged at the sides of her throat.

Barb shifted in her seat. 'Vivien, that's just awful.' She reached out and grabbed one of Vivien's hands, clutching it forcefully in her own before letting it fall. 'You poor girl.'

Vivien nodded and carried on snipping, avoiding Barb's open gaze in the mirror. She carried out the rest of the haircut in slow, steady silence and after she had finished and checked the lengths were neatly even, Barb got up, put her arms around her and surprised her with a hug.

When Barb drew back, Vivien thought her eyes had glazed over and she looked a little melancholy. Barb took a cigarette out of her packet but didn't put it to her lips. Instead she stood flicking her lighter, watching the flame spark and die several times.

'Barb, I don't want to pry,' said Vivien quietly, 'but Marcia told me your dad hasn't been around.'

Barb said nothing, then nodded. 'He walked out. Left Mum for another woman. Well, I say woman. She's half his age. Twenty-six. A year older than me. She's a secretary in the office where he works.'

'I'm sorry. That's very painful,' said Vivien. 'Has he been in touch?'

'Yep. It only lasted a month. Now he's desperate to come home. I can see Mum considering it, and that drives me crazy. How dare he think he can leave and then flounce back in whenever he wants?' Barb threw up her hands. 'He's followed me here twice trying to get me to speak to him.'

With her hands on her hips, she stared around the salon with a sneer as if she despised the place.

'And did you?'

Barb looked at her incredulously. 'Of course not.'

'He loves you,' said Vivien quietly.

'Not enough.'

'He knows he was wrong. He's trying to make it up to you.'

'It's too late,' snapped Barb.

'No,' said Vivien. 'It's too late when he's in his grave.'

The instant she said it, Vivien wanted to walk out. She felt ashamed for speaking her mind, for letting her feelings

188

run away with her. 'I'm sorry. I shouldn't have said that. It's out of turn.'

Barb picked a boiled sweet out of the bowl on reception. As she popped it in her mouth and screwed up the wrapper into a tiny ball, she appeared to be lost in her own thoughts again. 'No, you're right,' she said, sighing. 'It's what Alan says. He keeps telling me that I've got to sort things out before the wedding.'

'You should.'

'I don't know if I can.'

'Make sure he's there,' said Vivien firmly. 'Let him walk you up the aisle. He's probably dreamed of that his whole life.'

The door handle rattled and Chrissie came through offering a bite of her half-eaten bacon roll and holding up a paper bag spotted with oil.

'Got us some chips.' As she went into the back to get a plate, Vivien tugged on Barb's sleeve.

'Barb, I would do anything to have my dad give me away one day.' Vivien's voice dropped and became rough with longing. '*Anything.*'

When Vivien arrived home just before eight, the door swung back before she had got her key out.

'You have a visitor.' Nettie spoke in hushed tones, and Vivien, who'd never had any visitors, realised the stir it had created. Nettie had removed her hair net, taken a comb to her curls and dabbed on a little pink lipstick.

'Oh really?' she asked. 'Who?'

As Nettie opened the door to the front room, Vivien looked inside and saw Stevie perched on the edge of the sofa. Gingerly raising his hand, he quickly got to his feet.

She shot him a quick puzzled smile and noticed how wide-eyed and scared he looked, like a boy half his age about to own up to something bad. That worried her. She couldn't imagine what might make him look so vulnerable.

'Sit down here, dear.' Nettie went over and patted a cushion on the armchair opposite Stevie. 'Stevie's just been telling me about being a musician. Sounds very exciting.'

'Yes,' said Vivien. 'I'm sure it is.'

'Well, I'll leave you both to it,' said Nettie.

'Thank you for letting us sit in here. It's lovely,' said Vivien, hoping Nettie wouldn't hear the lie in her voice. The room was large but very disorderly with far too many pieces of furniture. Sideboards, chairs and overstuffed cabinets were set against every bit of wall. Surfaces were cluttered with photographs, china rabbits and cut-crystal bowls, and piled up high on the settee around Stevie were balls of coloured wool and embroidered cushions. Even the star-shaped wall mirror next to the lamp had numerous postcards slipped behind its wooden frame.

As the door slowly shut, Vivien turned her attention to Stevie.

'I looked up your address in the salon book when Barb wasn't looking.' He kept glancing at her, then turning away and clicking each of his knuckles in turn.

The sound made her wince. 'Ouch,' she said and shuddered.

'Sorry.' He held up both his hands.

'Why are you here, Stevie?'

'Well, not to cause another scene.'

'Pleased to hear it.'

'I behaved like a real idiot that day in the street,' he said. 'Sorry.'

His voice was meek, she could tell he meant it, and she relaxed.

'Forget it,' she said, smiling. 'I have.'

'Good.' He exhaled noisily. 'I'm pleased to hear that.'

'Is that what you came to say?' she asked.

He didn't seem to hear her. 'Will you be at the rally? I'm going with Alan.'

On Sunday Jordan and Mosley were speaking at different rallies in east London. All week she'd been stopped by protesters in Hackney who handed her leaflets and pleaded with her to come along and show her support. She'd smiled agreeably but wouldn't dream of going. Not if there was a chance she could run into Jack.

'I don't know,' she lied. 'I'm not sure.'

In the silence she picked at a loose thread on the arm of the chair.

'I went to a meeting on Tuesday with Alan and the 62 Group,' he said.

'Oh. Did you?'

He nodded. 'My first one. A National Socialist Movement meeting at St Pancras Town Hall. They were launching their manifesto.' She had already stiffened when he added in a shaky voice, 'Vivien, there's something else.'

'What?'

He leaned forward, hands knitted, elbows poking out. 'Promise me you won't get angry with me.'

Her fingers curled against the lap of her skirt. 'OK.'

'I did something that I know was wrong. I was jealous.' He nodded frantically, as if reasoning with himself in his head.

She shifted in her seat. 'Stevie, what did you do?'

'That day on Old Compton Street –' he paused '– I followed you.'

She frowned. 'I don't understand.'

His eyes kept darting away from her face as if looking at her was proving too much for him. 'I followed you from Soho to that guest house in Camberwell,' he said.

'You what?' she said slowly, through a fog.

'I know it was wrong.'

'You followed me from Soho to Camberwell?' she repeated. 'You—'

'Please,' he cut in. 'Hear me out. This is important.'

She sat on her hands and gnawed at her bottom lip.

'Yes, I followed you. I waited in the square opposite and I saw you coming out of the guest house with that bloke. I figured he was your boyfriend ... Then I saw him again at the NSM meeting and ...' His pause was dramatic but nervous. 'And the thing is, Vivien, he ... he wasn't protesting. He wasn't with Alan's lot. He was handing out leaflets for Jordan.'

She gasped but couldn't think of anything to say as he stared at her, eyes flashing. He still looked scared, but also strangely excited as if he expected her to share in his horror.

'I know. You probably can't believe it. I mean, I had to tell you, didn't I? You had to know. He's a fascist, for God's sake.'

Stevie dipped his head briefly, then looked up. 'It was wrong to follow you. I've never done anything crazy like that before and I won't do it again ... But you can't trust him. He must have told you some terrible lies ... And yes, I know it must be strange hearing it from me, and it's true that I'm mad about you, I can't get you out of my head ... That's no excuse, I know, but ...'

As he rattled on, air slowly began to fill her lungs again, and she could think clearly about the implications of what he had told her. Her only concern was whether Jack was safe. Stevie thought he knew the truth but he didn't. He only knew what Jack wanted everyone to believe.

She drew herself up in her chair, baulking at Stevie's actions, and how involved he seemed to think he could get in her life. As he reclined comfortably on the settee, she realised that spotting Jack had benefited Stevie the most. It was perfect. Now he could believe he was saving her from a terrible calamity. It made him a hero. Yet he couldn't be sure, she reminded herself. He had no real proof.

Finally, he fell silent and waited for her to speak.

'I don't have a boyfriend, Stevie,' she said. 'I don't know what you think you saw but—'

'You don't?'

'No.'

'But I *saw* you.'

'Yes. With an old friend from Manchester who's in town.'

'He didn't look much like an old friend. He had his hands all over you.'

'Not that I should have to explain myself,' she said in a mannered voice, 'but he was a boyfriend many years ago. We're still quite affectionate with each other, that's all.'

'But he's a fascist.'

'Rubbish,' she said, covering her mouth as she pretended to laugh. 'He most certainly isn't. What an imagination you've got! He doesn't even live in London. He was just passing through. Anyway, when was the meeting?'

'Tuesday,' said Stevie.

'Well, that solves the mystery. He was with me again. Met me up west. We went to the Curzon to see the new Peter Sellers film.' She was worried her voice might start shaking if she carried on with the lie, but now there was no going back. All she could do was dig herself in a little deeper. 'We ended up at La Crème.'

Stevie rubbed his jaw and stared at the carpet in bewilderment. 'I was sure it was him.'

He was still staring at her, eyes narrowed. She wanted to look away but forced herself to focus her attention on him. Make him believe you, she told herself, smiling. Make him think the mistake is entirely his.

Eventually he slumped down as if every bit of air had leaked out of him. 'Jesus, I'm sorry. I've got it all wrong, haven't I?'

'Yep.' She raised a knee beneath her skirt and ringed her arms around it.

'Can you forgive me?' He put his head in his hands. 'I'm so embarrassed.'

'Yes, but you shouldn't have followed me. What were you thinking? Don't do anything like that again, please.'

'I won't.' He shook his head. 'I promise.'

'OK.' She stood up. 'Come on. Let's put it behind us.'

'I mean, I just saw this bus and I was hurt and I ...'

'Stevie,' said Vivien, simply. 'It's fine.'

They walked out of the room and into the hallway.

'Look, Vivien, maybe you'll laugh in my face,' he turned his childlike gaze on her, 'but do you ... do you think we might start again, as friends?'

She felt so numb inside that she agreed to it before she knew what she was doing. Then she glanced over, caught sight of his wide smile and his dimple, and felt a little sorry for him. He was like everyone else really. He just wanted to be accepted.

'Thank you. Promise I'll do everything right from now on,' he said. 'I won't mess up again. Maybe see you on Sunday? At the rally?'

He reached out tentatively, as if he was about to put a hand on her sleeve, then reconsidered and pulled it away as she said goodbye and shut the door.

As Jack raised his hand to ring the bell at party head-quarters, he heard Ralph's raised voice. Carl answered the door, and when Jack asked him what the shouting was about, he gestured towards the kitchen. 'We're in there.'

In the kitchen Jack stood by the door next to Bill, Carl's

twin brother, and glanced around, swiftly noting that with every visit these days there were new men he'd never seen before.

'Look at this.' Jack caught the folded newspaper Ralph threw at him. 'Page six.'

Jack recognised *The Times* masthead at a distance. He opened the paper and stared at a photograph of Spearhead men marching across the courtyard. Good job, he thought. The photographer had even managed to capture one or two of the daggers.

'God,' he said. 'How did they get this?'

'Someone's talking,' said Mickey.

'Really?' said Ralph in mock amazement. 'Listen to Einstein over there.' He leaned in close to Mickey and screeched, 'Of course someone's bloody talking.'

Mickey recoiled and pushed back his seat so hard the chair scraped noisily against the floor. His half-rolled cigarette escaped from his fingers and specks of tobacco fluttered down over his trousers. Ralph stepped away and paced the room.

'Too many meetings have been sabotaged,' he said. 'And now this.'

Jack waited for the fear to leave him but he knew it wouldn't. It had nowhere to go. He'd been dreaming about this moment for months, and what surprised him most was that he could still hold things together in his mind and notice everything going on around him. The cat leaping off the wall in the garden. The shiny notes of a violin being played next door. The low hum of the old fridge.

He fixed his eyes on Ralph and kept his hands in his pockets. He felt Carl fidget next to him. The man who'd guarded the camp gates was tapping a foot. They were all waiting for Ralph to do or say something, they were all worried, but Jack knew full well he was the only one truly holding his breath. The only one with something real to fear.

Ralph took the newspaper from Jack and laid it open on the kitchen table. As he smoothed his palms over the pages and stared at the photo, Jack heard footsteps in the garden and Henry came into view clutching a bucket and spade. He was sun-kissed, his T-shirt and shorts were grimy and dishevelled, but he looked and sounded like a contented child, chatting to the governess who occasionally brought him there after school. Noticing everyone in the kitchen, he jumped around and waved, and even Ralph smiled briefly as Henry ran to the back door and let himself in.

'I found three worms,' he announced cheerfully.

'Well done. Good digging.' Ralph looked around the room. 'I suggest everyone here starts doing the same. That will be all.'

Everyone murmured yes, sir, thank you, sir, and as Jack filed slowly out behind the others, he told himself he no longer cared what sort of a life he would have, as long as it was far, far away from here.

At five o'clock the next evening sirens rang out from the factories in the neighbourhood as puffs of black smoke dirtied the sky.

Jack stood on the factory steps rolling a cigarette. At least it was the weekend. He wanted nothing more than to go and hide for the evening in his bedsit, but if he stayed away it might look like he had something to hide.

On his walk to party headquarters he kept glancing over his shoulder. His mental state had nosedived since Ralph had guessed the party had a mole. His sleep the previous night had been non-existent. He was jumpy all the time. He felt the burn of eyes on him everywhere he went and he was constantly talking himself down. You're being ridiculous. No one knows, no one cares. Get a grip.

But it didn't matter what he told himself; nothing shifted the paranoia. He'd just have to put up with it. It wasn't about to go away any time soon.

As he approached the house, the front door opened and a group of men trooped past, on their way to hand out leaflets advertising Sunday's rally. Jack greeted them warmly, then breathed a sigh of relief when he got inside and realised no one else was downstairs.

In the living room he stepped around two empty beer bottles and a dirty soup bowl and spoon. Through the grubby nets he saw the day was still bright but he had to fight the urge to draw the curtains. He was fidgety and out of sorts, and he didn't know what to do with himself so he turned on the television and adjusted the aerial, pleased to find an episode of *Z Cars*.

Sitting on the sofa with his feet up on the worn pouffe, he heard scuffling and bent down to see Henry on all fours, pushing two cars along the carpet.

'Jack!' He shook a car in the air. 'Will you race me?'

'Sure.' Jack stifled a yawn. 'Why don't you watch this programme with me first?'

Henry shook his head. 'I'm not allowed to watch television. Daddy says it's controlled by Jews.'

Jack felt himself stiffen. 'I'd heard that too.' He walked over to the television. 'Let's switch it off.'

Henry pushed a car across the rug, then turned it over to spin each of the wheels. 'Daddy says Jews are maggots feeding on society.'

'Jews are not maggots,' snapped Jack, filled with an anger that he couldn't hide. 'Well, a lot of Jews are,' he added quickly. 'Your father's right about that.'

He glanced down at Henry and faked a smile but Henry

wasn't looking. Pushing his cars around, making raucous *vrroooming* noises and announcing near-fatal crashes, he didn't seem to be paying attention to anything Jack said or did.

The following afternoon Jack was back at party head-quarters helping with preparations for the next day's rally. Hundreds of old copies of the *National Socialist* were languishing in the attic and his job was to fill a lorry with them so they could be handed out to supporters in Victoria Park Square. Mickey hadn't shown up to help him so Jack had been making the same trip up and down three flights of stairs for over an hour. But he wasn't the only party member who was busy. Several men had made dozens of new placards, and one man, a senior copywriter in the advertising industry, had spent hours writing and editing Jordan's speech.

There had been such a big build-up to this rally, it was making everyone jittery. If they got it right, Jordan hoped for a tenfold increase in national and local membership. Two foolishly heated arguments had already broken out over the wording on the placards, and whether the banner should be rolled up tight or folded, and it probably didn't help morale that Jordan had appeared twice at the top of the stairs to bark out orders and questions as they occurred to him. The tannoys need testing. How many men would be available to give out newspapers? Where the bloody hell was his speech?

By eight o'clock, Jack had locked up the lorry and was planning to go home and get some sleep. He'd just started the engine when Carl walked in front of his car and motioned at him through the windscreen.

What now, thought Jack wearily, rolling down his window.

'Ralph wants you.' Carl's face was relaxed but his voice was a little brisk. Jack nodded and turned off the engine.

By the time he'd climbed out of the car, Carl had disappeared back into the house so Jack went in alone. He took off his trilby and hung it on the banister, ran his hands over his hair and steadily made his way upstairs. In Ralph's study Carl was standing by the window, looking quite pleased with himself – chin jutting, arms folded over his chest.

Ralph looked at Jack. 'Close the door. I don't want anyone else to hear this.'

Jack shut the door and turned back.

'Colin's been under a lot of pressure from the Met about the coloured boy Mickey assaulted,' said Ralph. 'He's still in hospital. It's a volatile, if unwanted, section of our community. Events like those are very awkward politically.'

He walked over to his desk and sat down. 'I've decided to let Mickey go. Colin agrees. He's got no self-control. He's become a liability. I need you both to take over from him.' Ralph leaned back in his chair and tapped his fountain pen on the wooden armrest.

Take over what, thought Jack, nodding. 'Of course.'

'Yes, sir.' Carl dropped his arms to his sides and straightened up.

'So far we've been rather tentative, wouldn't you say?' said Ralph. 'Lots of rhetoric but little else. That's about to change.' A smile played on his lips. 'After tomorrow we'll be in a position to send a clearer message.' He rose from behind the desk. 'We'll meet after the rally. I'll have more details for you then.'

'Yes, sir,' said Jack.

'Now go home and get some rest. You've a big day ahead.'

At the bottom of the stairs Carl turned and whispered to Jack, 'Shit. Didn't expect that.'

'No,' said Jack.

'Mickey's a bloody nutcase.' Carl shook his head. 'He had it coming. D'ya fancy a quick pint?'

Jack had intended to find the nearest telephone box and call Barry, but instead he pushed his trilby firmly onto his head and nodded.

Carl wasn't a man who could be trusted, but he was a man Jack could drink with, and Jack needed a drink.

20

The midday sun beat down on Stevie and made him feel weak. It was far too hot to be standing around in Ridley Road, waiting for the meeting to start. He scanned the crowd. Scores of men from the 62 Group had arrived the night before to claim the pitch so Mosley wouldn't get a look-in. None of them appeared to be struggling in the heat. They looked keen and strong and ready to fight.

But everyone was still waiting for a speaker to show, and Stevie was already restless. An hour had passed and nothing had happened. He told Alan he was going to stretch his legs for a bit, then wandered down Ridley.

Without the din and chaos of the market, the street had a lonely, abandoned feel, as if a lover had just left. Shops were closed up, rotten fruit lay in the gutter or was trodden into the faint hopscotch marks chalked on the pavement. Standing in the shade, Stevie watched two teenage girls bat a tennis ball against a crumbling wall with their hands.

All he really wanted was to go home, but what if Vivien turned up? He'd already envisaged her appearing, lithe and tanned in a pretty sundress, sunlight flashing on her hair. He couldn't miss the chance of seeing her and finally putting his stupid behaviour behind him, so instead he walked up and down the side streets off Ridley Road for a while. When he got back to the pitch, the crowd had doubled, and a member of the 62 Group had taken the platform and was rousing everyone with fierce, heartfelt words about working together to get the filth off the streets. He'd almost finished when Alan appeared at Stevie's side.

'Jordan's men are on their way over to try and take the pitch, so Jeremy has split us into groups,' he said breathlessly. 'Some of the other lads are going to stay here and keep them out. You and me are with the lot heading up Dalston Lane to Victoria Park Square in time to end Jordan's speech.'

Alan's hands were plunged into his pockets. He was bouncing on the balls of his feet and his voice had shifted up a notch. Stevie could feel his fear and it was infectious. He felt it race through him.

'OK. Jeremy's signalling,' said Alan, blinking fast. 'Let's go.'

Stevie lost sight of Alan almost as soon as they set off up Dalston Lane. There were hundreds of men and they walked fast and in silence.

If he glanced up, the sun got in his eyes, so he stared at the heads of the men in front and imagined himself behind his drum kit on stage, thrilled to be performing to a packed room of young people, for whom music was an identity, a way of shaping themselves.

Then the atmosphere abruptly changed.

There was a rallying call, a few wild cries and the group splintered. Men were running everywhere, there was a piercing scream, then he spotted the fascists approaching in a pack from the opposite direction. There weren't that many of them, but as fighting quickly unfolded all the way down the street, he felt scared and small.

He ran to the edge of the road and watched. Punches were being thrown everywhere he looked. Men were hurling themselves against each other, ignoring the warnings of the police on foot or those on horseback. Someone had a tightly rolled newspaper bent in half and was smacking it against a man's head. Others were chucking sticks and bottles. At the sound of a bottle smashing behind him, Stevie jumped, wanting to cry at the savagery of it all. When a cricket bat cut through the air close by and someone screamed, he knew it was time to run, but after a couple of steps, a hand shot out of nowhere and punched him in the face.

'No, not me—' he shouted.

He tried to stay on his feet but his attacker hit him again. He cried out, expecting another punch, but it never came. Instead a big man with heavy cheeks took hold of his attacker's arm, threw him to the ground and kicked him until he couldn't get up. Then he disappeared back into the crowd.

Stevie ran. His heart was pounding, his lip had split and he was terrified, but he made it to a row of parked cars fifty yards away, squeezed himself in between a Rover and a taxi and leaned back against the car's bumper, waiting for it all to end.

From the pauses between the noise Stevie could tell the trouble was fading. There were a few sirens and panicked voices, and some people came running by, their legs whipping past him in a blur, but the fighting had stopped.

He stayed squatting against the bumper, desperate to go home. His thoughts were everywhere. This was no place for him. He didn't have the bottle for fighting, and he never would. It didn't even matter any more what Vivien, or anyone else, thought of him; he just needed to accept who he was.

He crept out and looked around. He was right, it was all over. Apart from a few stragglers the street had emptied, and the last of the coppers were climbing onto their bus.

Stevie stood up, dusted himself down and wiped his face on his handkerchief.

'Got a fag?'

He turned and recognised two scrawny boys from Ridley. 'Sure.' He shook one out of his packet.

'We're going to the square,' said the short one. 'There's hundreds of us down there. You coming?'

Stevie shook his head and watched them race off before he began walking in the opposite direction. His face felt puffy and tender, and there was dirt all over his hands and clothes. He planned to go home and take a long bath. After that he'd play some records, get nicely drunk and feel good about the life he had.

Hearing footsteps behind him, he turned, thinking the boys were back for another cigarette, but instead three men in brown shirts were rushing at him. He screamed.

'Get the yid,' one shouted.

Stevie screamed again and tried to run but he didn't stand a chance. They were on him in seconds. One of them kicked him hard in the back so he fell face down onto the road, gravel pressing into his cheeks. Then he was lying on his side, looking at the wheels of a car. There was the thud of heavy boots against his body and the side of his head. The skin on his face was tearing. All he could see were strange shards of brilliant colour behind his closed eyelids. He didn't know who these men were or where they'd come from. He just wanted them to leave him alone.

'Should have gassed the bloody lot of you.'

'Nah, waste of gas.'

'Another useless yiddo.'

They kicked him as if he weren't a live thing, just an empty sack of nothing, and as he pleaded with them to stop, he felt himself sliding into a white-hot pain so terrible he wondered if he was going to die, because this time he knew no one was around to help him.

Jack pulled the curtains across the window in his bedsit. Along with everything else in the room his landlord had scrimped on these, and the fabric was an inch too short at the bottom. He stuffed a pillow and two pullovers against the glass until the room was so dim he could hardly make out what was in each corner.

A man was shouting out of his window onto the street while a woman above was rowing with her husband about him flirting with her sister, but Jack paid little attention to their loud, brittle voices.

He took off his filthy shirt and threw it to the floor, then poured himself a whisky and moved the wrapped steak pie off the bed and put it on the cooker top. He hadn't eaten since the day before but he still wasn't hungry. It was ridiculous to have stopped in at the pie shop on his way home. He couldn't imagine his appetite returning any time soon.

He sank heavily onto the bed. It wasn't my fault, he told himself, draining his tumbler and swiftly pouring himself another drink. He couldn't have guessed how things would turn out.

He thought back to the huge crowd waiting for Jordan in Victoria Park Square, how the trouble began when the lorry carrying Jordan backed up against the platform. As Ralph whipped everyone up, Jack had thumped the lorry door twice, signalling that it was safe for Jordan to get out. He could still hear the outrage as Jordan emerged and the police struggled to contain the crush.

He had leaped off the stage to join the others, and moments after he landed among the protesters near the front a man had charged at him and punched him so hard in the stomach it took his breath away. Before he had time to reconsider, he'd lunged back and hit the man in the face.

He just wished he hadn't hit him so hard. The man was bony and slight. With one punch he had gone sprawling and lay still on the ground, his kappel hanging down over his cheek. Jack had silently pleaded with the man to move, to get up. *Just do something*. A minute later he still hadn't stirred, and a number of people had come together to carry his limp body to a place of safety.

Jack held his hands to his face. What had he done? The man might be a stranger but he was also a Jew, and Jack cared about him for that reason alone.

He sank to his knees by the bed.

With his hands clasped against his chest, tears dripping down his cheeks, he bent his head and prayed for the young boy and for the love of God.

And then he prayed for himself, for forgiveness.

Two hours later he was slunk low in his car a hundred yards from his home in Golders Green. He knew he shouldn't be there. It was breaking the rules to be anywhere near these streets, but after three whiskies his judgement had deserted him and he no longer cared enough to do the right thing. The image of the man on the ground was still in his head and it was making him crazy. He was confused and lost and lonely. He needed to come home.

He wasn't sure how long he'd been staring at the thick, lush surround of hedge outside the house when he saw his parents appear, but he knew they were about to embark on their early-evening walk.

Hanging over the steering wheel, he craned towards the windscreen. He supposed they must be tanned from the week they spent in Bournemouth every August, but his mum still didn't look well. He was shaken by how, even at a distance, her slender frame had turned scrawny. That was because of him. It had to be. The feeling of purpose that had whipped him on these past few months, filling him with a righteous belief that he was doing something good, meant nothing right now. Forget helping others – what about what he owed her? Her longed-for only son disappearing into a life fraught with danger. What had he put her through?

He thought back to the days before he left, his refusal to get sentimental or be swayed by her tears. It didn't matter how hard either of them had tried to persuade him, he wouldn't back down. He wouldn't change his mind. Yet, look what it had come to! Weeping alone in his car, yearning for them to hold him close.

They'd only walked a few steps away from the house when his dad stopped abruptly. He patted his blazer pockets, checking for something, a forgotten wallet or a handkerchief perhaps. Jack's mum lingered by the irises, rearranging her white cardigan over her shoulders as his dad threw up his hands, turned and ran back up the path to the house.

Jack clutched the steering wheel. His mum was alone. He could rush over to her and feel her arms around him. That's all I need, he told himself. That would nourish me. That would keep them both going.

He was fighting with himself now, his fingers curled around the door handle. He could be at her side in seconds, then run off so quickly no one else would ever know. Yes, he thought, I'm going to do this, it's a risk worth taking. He quickly opened the door and was about to get out when his dad came running back down the drive.

Jack pulled his leg back in and slammed the door shut. He watched them disappear from sight, then turned the car around and drove away in the opposite direction.

He shouldn't have come. It was a ridiculous idea. He had thought it would help him get the man out of his head, but instead it had made him feel worse – being so near yet not being able to draw comfort from them – as if he'd died and was watching them from somewhere above. A pain spread across his chest. It was all too much to bear.

Several streets away, outside a telephone kiosk, Jack got out and brushed cigarette ash off his shirt and trousers. By calling Barry at home, another rule was about to be broken but he didn't give a damn. He needed a friend. He dialled the number and was attempting to light another cigarette when a spray of matchsticks fell from the box onto the floor.

As soon as he heard Barry's voice, he said, 'It's me.'

'Jack? What's … It's OK, honey. It's for me.' Holding his hand over the mouthpiece, Barry's voice grew blurry. 'Hold on.' There was a noise as if Barry might have dropped the receiver, then Jack heard a door close.

'What's wrong?' asked Barry.

'I hurt someone at the rally.' Hearing it aloud overwhelmed him and he couldn't keep the fear from his voice. 'A Jewish man. I hit him because he hit me, but I hit him too hard. He was unconscious.'

'I'm sure it looked worse than it was,' said Barry quickly.

Frustrated, Jack took the receiver and banged it several times against the wall. 'Is that all you can say?' he shouted when he got back on the phone. 'I want out.'

'You'll be out soon.'

'No. I want out now. Today. Tell Sid. Get someone else to do this.'

'You can't mean that, Jack. Not when we're so close.'

'I do mean it.' Jack rested his forehead against the cool glass.

'Look,' said Barry calmly. 'If it's about this man, I'll make some enquiries. Find out if anyone at the rally was taken to hospital. But you need to put him out of your mind.'

'It's not just the man. It's the whole thing. I can't handle it any more.' He shut his eyes and tried to keep hold of himself.

'Yes, you can. It's been a bad day, that's all. Hang in there a little longer. We've almost got them. You're a strong man, Jack.'

'Yeah? So why do I feel so weak?'

Barry exhaled. 'Jesus, Jack. Stop drinking. Stop with the big questions. Go home and get some sleep. That's an order.'

'I can't. I've got a meeting with Ralph.'

'Shit. Why?'

'I don't know yet.'

'Well, pull yourself together. You can't go in this state.' Barry's voice grew harder. He was almost shouting down the phone. 'We're relying on you, Jack. You're the only one who can tell us what they plan to do with the explosives.'

Jack stared out of the window.

'Jack?'

'I'm still here.'

'It will be over soon,' said Barry.

'Yeah,' he said and hung up.

Downstairs, the house looked closed up. The porch light was off. All the members must be at the pub, celebrating. Jack took a step back and glanced up. The curtains in Ralph's study were drawn but a stream of soft light escaped at one side. He tried to imagine himself being in the room, attempting to stay neutral and detached as he absorbed Ralph's instructions. He was worried he was going to feel out of his depth, possibly not have the strength to pull it off, but he didn't have much of a choice. He couldn't walk away – Barry had made his expectations clear. And now he'd calmed down, he knew he had to go in. He would never forgive himself if he didn't follow things through.

The glint of car headlights rounding the corner startled him and made him blink. A car pulled over, two doors slammed. He heard high heels teetering up the neighbour's path, then casual chit-chat about unhappy gardenias and dry-looking soil beds. After he'd collected himself he raised his hand in the couple's direction and called out a greeting. It was no surprise when they ignored him.

Turning back to the door, he tucked his shirt neatly into his trousers. Almost as soon as he rang the bell, the door swung back and he found himself staring into Carl's dead-pan face. If he too was struggling with the world they were in, he didn't show it. He didn't show anything. But at least he didn't bother with small talk on their way up the stairs. As they reached the landing, Jack heard Jordan's favourite music, Wagner's 'Ride of the Valkyries', and a snippet of Jordan's nasal laughter, and he was relieved when he was inside Ralph's room, the door shut behind him.

Ralph was bent over the round table near his bookcase, so engrossed in examining a large sheet of paper, they stood waiting for a moment before he noticed them. As he straightened up, the floor lamp behind him illuminated his sharp features, and from his grin Jack could tell that he was still heady from the day's events.

'Today went well,' he said. 'Very well. We're delighted.'

'It couldn't have gone any better,' said Jack.

Ralph took out his case and offered each of them a cigarette. 'Come and look at this,' he said.

They gathered around the table, smoking. 'What is it?' Carl pointed at the hand-drawn map.

'The Karl Marx memorial at Highgate Cemetery. Our first target.'

As Ralph carried on speaking, Jack nodded enthusiastically but all he could hear was the word 'target'. Suddenly he became aware of the smallness of the room and how close he was standing to Ralph. He felt like a snared animal.

'... the memorial is in the East Cemetery. Very close to the entrance on Swain's Lane.' Jack forced himself to listen and focus, standing back so Ralph could use his pen to point at relevant markings on the drawing.

'Nice and easy,' said Carl.

'That's the intention.'

Jack flinched at the voice behind him. He hadn't heard the door open and was startled to see Jordan, since he rarely mixed with members except at large public functions. They might hear him at his typewriter in his office or showering in the bathroom, but if they met him on the stairs or in the kitchen he would only make token conversation before slipping away.

'Good evening, gentlemen.'

He shook Carl's hand first, then Jack's. A brief, tentative shake, a man acting out of duty. He didn't smile. He didn't want to make eye contact. Still in the uniform he'd worn at the rally – brown shirt, military boots and a Nazi style armband – he had a bloated look around his pockmarked cheeks, and smelled faintly unwashed.

'Good evening, sir,' said Ralph. 'We were just commenting on what a successful day it has been.'

Jordan nodded and picked up the red glass paperweight on the desk. At first he seemed to be admiring it, then he tossed it from hand to hand.

'A good turnout. Hundreds of new supporters.' He still hadn't smiled. 'I see Ralph's been briefing you about Highgate.'

'Yes,' said Carl.

'Good. Now the real work can begin.'

'Yes, sir,' said Jack.

'I think this calls for a drink, Ralph.'

'Indeed.' Ralph was already holding a bottle of brandy and pointing to four tumblers lined up on the bookshelf.

'We'll start with the Marx memorial.' Jordan took his glass and swilled the drink around. 'Then move on to the synagogues. Not that you've heard me say that. We can't be seen to have any direct involvement in such activities.' He held up his glass. 'Here's to the future.'

'I'm ready, sir,' said Carl.

'Yes.' Jack raised his glass. 'Me too.'

Once the meeting was over, Jack was desperate to go back to his bedsit, but Carl insisted they join the other party members at the Raven, a local drinking hole.

Sure that Carl would want to talk to him on the walk over, he was relieved when he didn't seem to have anything to say. It meant Jack could try to absorb the plans that had just been hatched, while Carl happily jumped up and grabbed branches on every tree they passed, shaking the leaves to the pavement, then breaking into a sprint as the pub came into view.

Carl tried to make a big entrance. He barged through the door, clapping his hands above his head and yelling out that he'd arrived. Behind him Jack paused before forcing out the smile that would be plastered over his face all night. About three dozen party members were crowded around tables, and he shook hands with men he recognised and some he didn't, and after he'd agreed in his loudest, heartiest voice that they'd given the yids the going-over they deserved, he turned to the bar.

Waiting to be served, he thought it was Carl who had sidled up alongside him, but it was his brother Bill. Both were plain-looking. They shared the same piggy eyes and disappearing chin, but the couple of times Jack had met him, Bill had struck Jack as a quieter and more intelligent version of his brother.

Bill clapped him on the back. 'Evening, Jack.'

Jack smiled. 'Bill. What can I get you?'

'That's good of you. I'll have an ale, ta.'

When their drinks arrived, they toasted the party, then made light conversation. Jack's one-drink rule had been laid aside hours ago, but after Bill had bought him two vodkas, Jack realised he couldn't remember the name of the song Elvis was crooning on the jukebox. He wasn't nearly as drunk as Carl, whose words were bleeding into each other, but he was endangering himself, so he said his farewells and didn't let anyone talk him out of leaving.

When the pub door slammed behind him, he walked briskly down the street until he was out of sight. Then, slumped against a wall, he tried taking deep breaths. His thoughts turned to Vivien, his lovely Vivien, before returning to the image of himself stealing through the darkness into Highgate Cemetery.

He knew he had to tell Barry that he would get out of the party after this job. No question about it. He didn't care if the decision was met with protest or if Barry tried to coax him into staying. He had to save himself. He genuinely felt his sanity would be wrenched from him, possibly irreversibly, if he carried on doing this any longer.

He stood up straight and took another long, deep breath. He set out walking slowly as the night was balmy, but then he gathered speed and started to run. His bedsit was half an hour away but he ran all the way back without stopping.

21

Vivien applied tint to Anita Hill's hair and forced herself to titter and nod appropriately to stories about her job in the cheese shop on Frith Street. But as soon as she could make her getaway, she called Lydia over to carry out a manicure. Then she darted into the back, wedged the door open with a brick and took a cigarette from her overall pocket. While Maeve sorted out the dirty washing, Vivien leaned into the doorway, smoking and worrying.

Jack had intended to call her the night before. She kept thinking the phone would ring and he would make some silly excuse. He'd been delayed running an errand. Something urgent had come up. He couldn't find an empty telephone box. Because he hadn't missed a phone call yet – had never been late by more than a few minutes. Instead she had sat at the top of the stairs for hours, picking off her nail polish and thinking about Jack and about how hard the waiting was.

Now her imagination was getting the better of her. So many protesters had been arrested or hurt at the rally; news of it had been splashed across the front page of the *Hackney Gazette*. In the bus queue that morning she had overheard someone talking about her husband's broken leg. Stevie had been taken to hospital, Alan was lucky to have escaped with a sprained wrist ...

She turned and stubbed her cigarette out in the new

floor ashtray that Barb had picked up in the market, just as Deirdre came through.

Maeve caught Vivien's eye. 'Any plans tonight?'

'Not yet.' Filing a police report, she thought. Calling around all the hospitals. Visiting a morgue.

'Mick will want to watch television or go to his mum's.' Maeve sighed. 'He's like an old man. Last night he just wanted to eat his tea and fill out the pools.'

'Well, let him,' said Barb, who had come to drop an armful of dirty towels by Maeve's feet. 'You'll be out.'

'Will I?'

'Yes.' Barb circled them all with her finger. 'This morning the three of you said you'd come and see Stevie with me.'

'I forgot about that,' mumbled Vivien.

'Me too.' Maeve screwed up her face. 'I suppose we should. Poor sod.'

'Lydia and Chrissie can't come, so I'm relying on you to make up the numbers,' said Barb on her way out of the room. 'We'll leave around seven.'

'Where's that bottle of peroxide I left out?' Deirdre tapped the door of the store cupboard and glanced around. 'For my blonde.'

Vivien gasped. 'Oh no! I thought it was mine. I was sure I got a bottle out.'

She leaped over the mound of dirty towels and ran as quickly as she could to Anita Hill, but she could already see that her usually dark hair had, in that short time, begun to lighten.

'Barb!' Vivien's voice struck the air so urgently, it immediately caught Barb's attention.

'I am so sorry, Miss Hill,' she said and faced Barb, who was now by her side. 'Barb, it appears I used a slightly higher-volume peroxide than I should have and ...'

Barb got it. She smiled and in a flash began a thorough

examination of Miss Hill's hair. 'No harm done,' she said. 'You still have beautiful hair, Miss Hill, just like your sister. We'll get this sorted straight away. Lydia, please wash Miss Hill's hair.'

While Lydia shuffled the confused client over to the sink, Barb put her hands on her hips and stared at Vivien.

'Well?'

Vivien felt the sobs chase up her throat. 'I'm so sorry.'

'What's the matter? It's not like you to make this sort of a mistake.'

'I've got things on my mind. But that's no excuse.'

'Do you want to talk about it?'

Vivien shook her head.

'Go home then. Or take a walk. Whatever does the trick.'

'But you're so busy.'

'Yes, too busy to watch you.'

Vivien nodded as Barb shooed her towards the door. 'Go on. Take off your overall. Marcia, get Vivien's bag, please. Come back when you've got your wits about you.'

Barry sat at a table at the back of Bloom's near the kitchen. He was the only lunchtime diner left, and a waiter taking his break at the table nearest his was recounting the story of Cliff Richard's recent visit. The queues of hysterical women pressed against the front. A photographer from the *Jewish Chronicle* crawling in through a toilet window. Barry laughed and made all the right noises, but he was relieved when the man eventually left him alone to eat his chopped liver and latkes.

Five minutes after he'd started he was finished, and immediately wanted to order something else. It was obvious to everyone, including himself, that he was far too greedy. Eating had become a compulsion, something he turned to when he was aggravated, which was much of the time these days. He would tear apart a roast chicken or tuck into a huge slice of Sandra's famous sticky honey cake, and while he was wolfing it down, the worries burning him up inside would disappear.

He pressed the tip of his finger into leftover crumbs and put it to his lips. Dad, Danny, Jeremy – they took everything in their stride, whereas he was more torn about what the 62 Group was doing. He didn't like to think that by training street fighters they were putting good men in danger. After last week's rally, scores of men had needed stitches, casts and patching up. Three had been hospitalised with concussion; one still hadn't been discharged. And many of them weren't strangers. He'd met their parents and their wives, and he knew that, like him, they had young families.

He could see why some members of the Jewish community might consider the Group thuggish but he still believed theirs was the best way to fight fascism. You couldn't be reasonable about it, he would say to his critics. Gentle persuasion won't make these people go away. The Board of Deputies Jewish Defence Committee, a body of representatives from the Jewish community, might organise outdoor meetings and print anti-defamation leaflets, but that wasn't going to keep everyone safe. At least the Group was out on the street, doing something.

'Sorry I'm late.' Sid squeezed Barry's shoulder from behind. 'Is it me, or are there more cars everywhere these days?' He pulled out a chair opposite Barry and looked at his empty plate. 'What did you have?'

'Chopped liver and latkes.'

Sid reached out and touched the arm of a passing waiter. 'I'll take the salt beef, please. You want anything?'

Barry shook his head.

'And a black coffee. Nice and strong.'

'Yes, Mr Klein.'

'How's Sandra and the kids?' asked Sid.

'Good.'

'Lawrence's cough better?'

'So-so.'

'Your mother says I'm to remind you of our telephone number.'

'Sorry. I'll call her tonight.'

'Wednesday night is taken care of.' Sid leaned forward and drummed his fingers on the white tablecloth. 'There'll be about a dozen of us at the East Cemetery from nine thirty. When Jack and the others get there at ten thirty, we'll be ready for them. We've shown photos of Jack to everyone involved. They know to make it look convincing. Give him a few cuts and bruises. Nothing serious.'

'Good, because he's planning to leave the next day.'

Sid nodded. Barry had already told him of Jack's decision to get out of the party. 'What if the police turn up?' asked Barry.

'They won't show unless someone calls them.'

'But if they do? If Jack is arrested?'

'I've already spoken with our guy at the Met. He'll make it go away for Jack.'

'Are you sure?'

'Why would I lie?' barked Sid. 'Of course I'm bloody sure.'

'Sorry.' Barry tried to smile. 'Everything's getting to me.' He stared at Sid rubbing his jaw and yawning. 'How can you be so calm?'

'How can I be so calm?' said Sid incredulously. 'I think about the war. What they did to us. Everything else is easy.'

'What if—'

'There are no what ifs.' Sid smiled up at the waiter, then down at his plate. 'Thank you.'

Barry watched him push the gherkin slices neatly to one side.

'In two days' time we're going to nail those bastards,' said Sid. 'You hear me? There are no what ifs.'

Barry nodded, his breath tight as a fist in his chest as he reached over, picked all the gherkins off Sid's plate and dropped them into his mouth.

Sid threw up his hands. 'What, now you're eating off everyone else's plate?'

Vivien mouthed another apology to Barb as she closed the salon door, then put on her sunglasses. A breeze was gently lifting her skirt, but the sun was still hot on her arms and face so she crossed over the street and walked in the shade.

By the French House she stepped around a gang of men jostling on the pavement. It had just gone midday – this was the lunchtime crowd. Laughter flowed around her, some slurred compliments about her shapely legs. She looked ahead as she carried on walking. Their advances weren't welcome. She'd bet good money they had wives and kids to go home to.

Some way down the street their wolf whistles were still ringing in her ears when a hand grabbed her wrist.

'What do you—'

'Ssh,' said Jack as he pulled her into a doorway. At first she was unable to speak and clung to the lapels of his jacket. When he asked her to go and flag down a taxi for them, she couldn't bear to let go of him.

'Go on,' he said, gently ushering her onto the pavement, then moving back into the shadows.

When a taxi pulled over, he shot out into the street. He hustled her into the back, gave the driver an address she didn't catch, then climbed in beside her. She watched him glance gravely through the windows.

'Jack, what's happened?'

'Nothing.'

'Something has. I can tell.'

'Nothing for you to worry about.'

'How can you say that when you've just turned up out of the blue?'

'I missed you, that's all.'

'I don't believe you. Look at you.' She held his wan face. 'You're done in. And so thin.'

'Nothing a good sleep and few home-cooked meals wouldn't cure.' He tried to smile.

'I waited for your call.'

He sighed. 'I forgot. Lost track of time.'

'Jack, tell me.'

'Vivien, not here.' He glanced at the head of the driver. 'OK?'

'OK.' She nodded. 'It's just that I've been so worried.'

He put his face into her neck. 'Sorry,' he whispered.

They kissed. She tasted whisky on his lips and smelled tobacco in his hair. She tried to remember that he was alive. He was here. For now, his presence had to be enough. She fitted every bit of herself against him, welcoming him, and with her head resting on his shoulder, gazed through the window at the shoppers on Tottenham Court Road.

'Where are we going?' she asked.

'A hotel I know.' There was a hardness in his voice that told her he didn't want any more questions. He didn't want to speak. He just wanted to stare at the road ahead. She fitted her hand into his and, for the rest of the taxi ride, stroked the grazes on the spurs of his knuckles and didn't say another word.

*

Just before he got to Warren Street station, the driver overtook a bus, then turned into a side street and slowed to a stop. Jack paid him as she got out.

'It's not the Ritz,' he warned as he pushed open a weathered door.

'I don't need the Ritz.' Smiling at him over her shoulder, she went through into the foyer and nearly went flying. A bucket of soapy water and a mop had been placed just inside the door. A cleaner came rushing over to apologise, but Vivien told her it was her fault and rearranged her dress as a dog tied to the leg of a chair barked at her, then returned to the job of trying to paw at a basket of new toilet rolls placed just out of reach.

Behind the reception desk, a sleepy-looking man was listening to a race on the wireless and eating a pie. Vivien wondered what sort of people stayed here.

'Mr and Mrs Fox,' said Jack. 'I telephoned earlier.'

As he said it, she blushed and looked down at her shoes. It probably happened all the time in a place like this but she was still embarrassed. She'd felt the same way in Brighton. A bit cheap, as if she was his mistress, a bit excited.

Not that the man noticed. He was only interested in the race commentary. He turned to take a key off a hook behind him, gave it to Jack, then pushed a register across the desk for him to sign.

Jack dangled the key against his palm then led Vivien towards the stairs. 'First floor.'

The room was small but well kept. There was a light, citrusy smell of air freshener. The pillows were nicely plumped. It was all quite pleasant, but when Jack tried to lock the door behind him it wouldn't close properly and he grew vexed. He shoved against it and swore under his breath and she was daunted by the sight of this angry, slightly haggard-looking man taking out all his unhappiness on an old door.

After he got the key to work, he drew the thin curtains together so hastily she worried they might slip off their track. Now they were finally hidden and alone, she expected him to relax and speak more freely. Yet he was still on edge and didn't say a word. It was difficult to know what to do. He appeared so deep in thought, so serious, she wondered if he still registered that she was with him.

He sat on the edge of the bed and after several minutes of staring at his back, she went over and joined him. She reached for both his hands and pushed them into the lap of her skirt.

'I'll need to go away soon.' He looked her straight in the eye. 'Will you come with me?'

Her grin came easily because she was overjoyed to have been asked. 'Oh, darling, of course.' But then she quickly buried her face in his chest because she was also confused and didn't want it to show. This was all so unexpected and far too soon. She wasn't ready to leave London, she'd only just unpacked. She'd barely made an impression. And when she thought of the girls hovering around another awkward new stylist, or Nettie cooking egg and chips for someone else, she was filled with sadness.

Jack must have sensed it. He gently pulled away from her and held her chin. 'You don't look very happy about it.'

'I am.' She wasn't really lying; she would go anywhere with him. 'Of course I am. It's just sudden. That's all.'

She leaned in and for a time they kissed fervently, swaying down onto the bed before quickly pulling themselves back up. Then she hung her arms around his neck and stared hard at him. Her pulse was hammering and she could tell neither of them knew what to do next.

'I want to,' she said in a small voice.

'We don't have to,' he said quickly.

'I know.'

'I mean it. We don't have to do a thing. I'll wait for ever,' he said, then quickly added, 'well, maybe not for ever.'

They both laughed and hugged. She was scared, but the anxiety over her decision had gone. They kissed again and she felt desire coursing through her, heating her skin as she drew away from him and pulled back the bed sheet.

She crawled under it, unbuttoned her dress and pushed it down her arms and body until it lay in a heap under the sheet. With the sheet pulled up over her white cotton brassiere and knickers, she watched him take off his trousers, vest and socks, then slide onto the mattress next to her.

'I think about you every night as I close my eyes,' he said, pushing the hair away from her face.

'You do?'

He nodded. 'I think of your eyes. You have such beautiful eyes. And this.' He stroked her neck. 'Such a long, graceful neck.' His hands cupped her breasts. 'And these.'

As he pulled her close and kissed her deeply again, she felt his hardness pressing into her thigh and quickly broke away.

'I'm scared,' she blurted out.

'We don't need to do anything,' he repeated and took his hands off her.

'I want to. I just needed to tell you I'm scared.'

'You can tell me anything.' He planted kisses on her shoulders and her arms, sucking her skin so gently, she thought she might explode.

They were not awkward with each other, she was no longer frightened, but it was all so unfamiliar. She couldn't help worrying about what she was doing, whether she was doing everything right, but when he raised himself gently over her, she moved her legs and smiled up at him and stopped thinking about anything much at all.

Afterwards he shut his eyes and held her against him. 'That was wonderful.'

'Perfect,' she whispered.

The moment it was over she had wanted to do it again. She pressed against him and shared his cigarette, then leaned on an elbow and stared at him.

'Why do you want to leave? Have they found out? Has your cover been blown?' The words sounded ridiculous to her, like something straight out of a film.

He shook his head. 'No. I just want out. And I've got the chance. I've told Barry.'

'Just like that?'

'Just like that.'

'When will we go? And where?'

'Thursday.'

'In three days' time?' she gasped. 'So soon?'

'I need to leave then,' he said. 'I thought we could head back to Manchester.'

She could barely contain her surprise. 'Manchester?' she repeated, fixing a smile on her face.

She could see it made sense but it also made her want to leave even less. She could picture the dank, empty house and Dad's cold slippers in front of the television. His shaving brush still on the bathroom shelf, the neat rows of balled-up socks in his chest of drawers. Without Dad, Manchester wasn't home. It was just a place she had left behind.

'It will be great to see Stella,' she said, and meant it.

'You really don't want to leave, do you?'

She shook her head. 'No. But I'm coming with you.'

'We'll be back,' said Jack. 'I promise.'

'Really?' She felt more optimistic again.

'Yes. After things have settled down.'

Jack lay very still while Vivien fell asleep on him. It was quiet all around except for the occasional tread of footsteps up and down the corridor. Only once did he hear voices, two cleaners complaining to each other about the mess in room 11's bathroom. Vivien slept soundly, barely moving as he caressed her, but he knew he wouldn't sleep. He'd begun to realise what he'd done. Grabbing Vivien off the street in the middle of the day and carting her off to a hotel was idiotic.

He'd gone from taking no risks for months to taking too many in a matter of weeks. He was losing the self-discipline that had seen him through for so long, and yet now he was in so deep, he needed it more than ever.

His arm was dead beneath her. He dragged it out, shook it to life, then got to his feet. He pulled on his clothes and watched Vivien turn over, her dark hair streaming across the pillow. He leaned down and smoothed it out with his hand, then trailed a finger down the knots on her spine. Her beauty was in not knowing quite how beautiful she was, he thought.

Looping his belt through his trouser waistband, he carried on watching her, then whispered her name a couple of times. 'Time to go, sweetheart.'

When he opened the curtains the room was awash with light. Vivien looked around groggily, then stretched her arms above her head and yawned. He leaned over and kissed her, smiling briefly as she tried to put her arms around his neck and pull him down.

When he resisted, she grabbed his wrist.

'Come on, Vivien.' He unclasped her hand. 'We need to go. It's nearly four.'

She let go of his hand, and when she yawned again and stretched, catlike, he gathered her clothes off the carpet and tossed them onto the bed. 'I mean it. Let's go.'

At the sharp change in his tone, she got up and pulled on her dress with the clipped speed of someone who was silently angry. He took her chin in his hand and said sorry and kissed her one last time before they left. Outside he put on his trilby and tugged the brim low over his eyes.

'Meet me at eleven o'clock on Thursday morning at Euston station. On the platform for the train to Manchester Exchange. I'll get the tickets. Just bring whatever you can carry.'

He caught sight of a taxi, put two fingers in his mouth and whistled for it. When it stopped for him, he took a note from his wallet and handed it through the window to the driver. 'Take her wherever she wants to go.'

'Dean Street, please,' she said to him, then turned back to Jack. 'I need to give my notice in straight away if I'm leaving so soon.'

'Thank you for being patient with me,' he said. 'You've put up with so—'

'Jack, I love you.'

'I love you too.' He felt a tightness in his throat. 'Things will be different soon.'

As the taxi inched away from the kerb, she swivelled in her seat and faced the back window. But when she waved he could not wave back. He found, instead, that his hands were trembling in his pockets and he couldn't move from the spot. As people crossed the road in front of him, the taxi wove into the traffic and disappeared from sight. A few more days and they would be together, he told himself, but even that thought did not bring him any great comfort. Nothing could.

*

A little further up the street Mickey leaned over his steering wheel. About time too. They'd been in there for hours. At least now he could get a good look at her.

Jack had never said he had a girl, but then, thinking about it, Jack never said very much at all. She could be a tart. It wouldn't surprise him, not when he saw how crummy the hotel was. And she did have a cracking little body.

When Jack waved down a taxi, Mickey snapped back into action. He sat up straight, turned on the engine and put the car in gear as he watched the fancy little brunette get into the back of the taxi alone.

Bingo, he thought, and set off behind her.

22

'Keep up, Vivien,' Maeve shouted. 'It'll be Christmas at this rate.'

Vivien stepped up her pace. Maeve had scolded her twice for lagging behind since they'd left Oscar's, but then she didn't realise how reluctant Vivien was to visit Stevie.

Barb stopped and waited for her. 'Maeve would make a very good headmistress, don't you think?' She tucked her arm through Vivien's. 'Scaring the kids into doing their homework on time.'

Vivien laughed. 'She is bossy, that's for sure.'

'Thanks for coming,' said Barb. 'I know you didn't really want to.'

'I don't mind,' she lied, wishing she'd gone straight home after dashing from the taxi into the salon to give Barb her notice. But Barb had been so kind, listening to her garbled made-up story about urgent family business pulling her back to Manchester. She hadn't pushed for details. She had rubbed at a smear of tint on her hand, buying herself a little thinking time, then simply nodded and said she would try her best to always have a job for her.

'I forced you into it,' said Barb, adding in a whisper, 'but Stevie did ask me several times if you were coming. I think he has a soft spot for you.'

Vivien looked down at her feet. 'I don't think that's true.' Her voice sounded a little squeaky.

'Don't feel you have to stay for ages.' Barb smiled. 'You've probably got a lot to pack.'

'It shouldn't take too long. I didn't bring that much stuff.'

'Oh, that's good. You don't want to have to worry about all that. Not if you have other things on your mind.'

Vivien looked up at Barb. She hated this. At least one positive thing about going was that she would be free of all these lies. 'I'd tell you if I could,' she said.

'I know. Don't worry.' She patted Vivien's arm. 'See, that's where I live.' She pointed at the house next to Stevie's. 'When you get back you'll have to come round for tea.'

'I'd like that,' said Vivien as Maeve charged up the steps and rang Stevie's doorbell. When the door opened, Stevie hobbled forward and smiled. 'Ladies,' he announced happily.

Vivien gasped. What a mess his face was! She hadn't expected that.

'Come on inside.' He turned his smile on all of them but his eyes kept flickering to where she stood at the back.

'Great to see you,' he said as she slid past him. But as he shut the door, then shuffled ahead of her into the living room, she had the terrible feeling of being trapped.

'Grab a couple of those chairs, Deirdre.' He pointed his crutch at the straight-backed wooden chairs surrounding the dining table.

Deirdre looked over her shoulder. 'Nah, we're all right, Stevie. We'll sit on the floor, won't we, girls?'

'I'll bring them over,' said Maeve. 'You're a right lazy cow when you want to be, Deirdre.'

'That's a bit bloody rude!'

'Well, stop yawning and help me with the chairs.'

'Now now, children. Play nicely,' said Barb. 'Do you need a hand, Stevie?'

'No, ta.' He made his way round to the front of the

sofa, grimacing as he lowered himself carefully onto the cushions.

Finally, they were all sitting in an awkward semicircle around him, taking in his bloated, bruised face and his bandaged ankle. A bone in his left hand had been fractured, so his hand was in a splint, and his arm was pinned against his chest in a white sling.

He must have felt all their eyes on him because he suddenly seemed self-conscious and pushed his dank, floppy fringe off his forehead. 'Sorry, I don't look my best today. I slept badly.'

'Me too,' said Deirdre. 'The heat's unbearable.'

'I meant bad dreams.'

'Of course.' She blushed. 'Sorry.'

No one had much to say. Barb drifted off to stand and smoke by the window, waving at people she recognised on the street. Vivien kept lifting her hair away from her neck. Maeve was fanning herself with her hands and puffing out her cheeks. Even with the windows open, the air in the room was sweaty and close.

'Keeping busy?' asked Deirdre drily. She held up a heap of girlie magazines that were balanced precariously on the far arm of the sofa.

'Give me those.' Stevie blushed as he took them from her and chucked them under the coffee table. 'A friend dropped them by. I would never buy them.'

Maeve got out a tin of fudge and two bottles of beer. 'Didn't know what else you'd need. Figured you were probably sick of grapes.'

'Thanks,' said Stevie. 'But seeing your lovely faces is enough of a tonic.'

'Bloody charmer.'

'Oh, I think that's sweet,' said Deirdre.

'I can't believe what they did to you, Stevie,' said Vivien. 'It's awful. I wish they'd stop all this fighting.'

She'd barely finished the sentence before he launched into a blow-by-blow account of his attack. He was angry and emotional and she felt for him. Understandably, it was still very much alive in his mind, but she was so used to Jack's economical way with words when out of sorts, that she was taken aback by Stevie's non-stop talking.

'I might have permanent nerve damage.' His voice trembled. 'No more drumming for me.'

'Don't say that.' Barb turned and pointed her half-finished cigarette at him. 'I keep telling you. That's loser talk.'

'Yeah, I give you two weeks,' said Maeve, getting up, 'and you'll be back, good as new, annoying the hell out of us.'

She wandered over to peer at the framed photos on the shelf above the television, then laughed loudly, took one down and stuck it under Vivien's nose. 'Look at him here. Sweet enough to eat, don't you think?'

Vivien stared at Stevie and his older brother as teenagers. They were lying on a bed on their stomachs, ankles crossed in the air, smiling at the camera. Stevie hadn't changed that much. The puppy fat had dropped away from his cheeks, but he still had an endearing smile and lovely soft green eyes.

'Hey, which photo is that?' Stevie looked upset as he strained towards Maeve. 'Let me look.'

Maeve held it up to his face. 'See? You were gorgeous.'

'Put it back, please. It was taken years ago. I was completely different then,' he said, glancing at Vivien. He stared down at his hand, then up at Maeve. 'Can you light me a smoke?'

As Maeve lit one and passed it to him, the front door

opened. When a slow, large-boned woman wearing a flowery housecoat and slippers came in, Stevie rolled his eyes and mumbled, 'Mum.'

'My goodness,' she announced in a breathy voice. 'More visitors, Stevie! You are popular,' adding, 'Hello love,' as Barb went over and kissed her cheek. Everyone else stood up and said their names.

'Well, I've forgotten them already.' She laughed. 'Call me Marion.'

Clutching a pint of milk to her chest, she talked for some time about the heat and then, blotting the corners of her eyes with a tissue, about how lucky Stevie had been.

'Mum.' Stevie gave her a warning look. 'I can take it from here.'

'Of course.' She made her way to the door. 'Tea, anyone?'

There was a chorus of 'No, thank you.'

'Well, I'll bring in some water.'

'Mum! We're fine.'

'Sorry,' he said once Marion had left the room. 'She tries too hard.'

'She seems very nice,' said Maeve.

'She is,' said Barb pointedly. 'She's smashing.'

'How about some music?' Stevie winced and held his side as he reached for a brown bag on the coffee table. 'My friend Ray bought me the new Billy Fury single, "Letter Full of Tears".'

'Good idea,' said Vivien, standing up. 'I'll put it on.'

She slipped the record out of its sleeve and put the needle in place. With her eyes shut, she swayed to the music and thought happily about seeing Jack again. Once the song had ended, Stevie started talking about all the records he'd dug out to play that afternoon. He seemed much brighter too, as if something about this life might suit him after all.

They played the record twice and Vivien was about to set the needle back into the opening groove when Deirdre said, 'Tell Stevie your news, Viv.'

'What news?' he said.

She steeled herself, then turned around. 'I'm leaving in a few days, Stevie. Heading back to Manchester.'

'Why?' he barked.

'Urgent family business,' she said.

'You've only just got here,' he interrupted. 'You can't leave yet.'

'I'll be back.'

'When?'

'I'm not sure exactly.'

He fiddled with the bandage around his hand. 'You're really going?' When she nodded, he shook his head and sighed.

'You've still got us, Stevie,' said Maeve. 'Aren't we good enough any more?'

'Of course you are,' he said, but he couldn't take his eyes off Vivien, and she blushed when she saw Barb glance between them and raise her eyebrows.

'Look, I've got to go,' Barb said abruptly. 'I have a scintillating evening ahead of me, arranging the reception table plan with Mum. Sorry, love.' She ruffled Stevie's hair. 'I'll pop in again tomorrow.'

'Me too.' Vivien grabbed her chance to leave. 'Got to get on with some packing.'

'We'll stay for a bit,' said Maeve. 'Won't we, Deirdre. Got any cards?'

'Don't forget to leave your glad rags out for Wednesday,' Deirdre said to Vivien. 'Got to give you a send-off you won't forget.'

'Will do.' Vivien leaned down to kiss Stevie's cheek. 'Bye-bye, Stevie. I really hope things get better for you soon,' she said hurriedly and headed out of the room before someone tried to stall her.

Once Maeve and Deirdre had left, Stevie stood by the window staring up and down the street. He couldn't remember the last look Vivien had given him. He could picture her clutching her bag and craning towards him, but then he shut his eyes and that was it. Now it mattered desperately, like the last frame of the most important film of his life was missing. As he hobbled back to the table to find a smoke, he heard the clatter of a train in the distance and thought of Vivien boarding hers back to Manchester.

He just had to accept that she'd never been his, that she'd never wanted to be.

'Damn it.' The cigarette packet was empty. He crumpled it in his hand and threw it onto the carpet as his mum came in holding a mug of tea. At first he ignored her and picked up his crutch, then he muttered he was off to the shop.

'But I've made you some tea,' she said.

'I'll be back in ten minutes.'

'Let me go for you, Stevie,' she said. 'You're not well enough.'

'I need some air.' He walked past her into the hallway then slammed the front door behind him.

It was his first time outside that day and he was surprised at how jolting it was. Night was falling but heat still shimmered off the pavement. He had to go more slowly than he expected. This was the furthest he'd walked since the attack and he felt woolly, as if all the stuffing had been knocked out of him.

After a few steps he stopped to gather himself. He wiped his red, heated palms on his trousers and rearranged the crutches under his arms. He was about to set off again when he felt a hand grip the back of his neck.

'Make a sound and I'll smash your other arm,' someone whispered in his ear.

As Stevie was shoved into the back seat of a Rover, panic shot through him and all he could think was, Oh God no, please no. They've come to finish the job.

The forty-eight hours since he'd put Vivien in a taxi had passed unbearably slowly for Jack. He'd gone to work. He'd dropped by the party headquarters twice. He'd stayed away from the booze, even though he often felt an urge to drink, knowing it would cloud his mind.

Today had been the worst. He woke up around dawn sweating, then couldn't get back to sleep, thinking about what was ahead. As he leaned against the pillows he imagined himself climbing over the cemetery wall that evening, carrying explosives, so he got up and went for a ridiculously long run.

He'd had egg and chips in his local café, then returned an hour later for a cup of tea. He'd tried, and failed, to read the entire newspaper. He attempted a crossword. He'd played marbles on the step with the kids from the basement, then pulled them up and down the street in their home-made go-kart. Afterwards, he did burpees and press-ups in the narrow strip next to his bed until the woman downstairs pounded the ceiling with the end of her broom.

And still the hours had dragged by.

The highlight had been packing his case, but that didn't take long. It wasn't as if he was taking much – a pair of navy trousers, three short-sleeved shirts, a few vests, two British history books, wire-rimmed glasses that he should wear for reading but almost always forgot, and half a bottle of top-quality whisky that was a treat to himself.

But placing the train tickets on top, fastening the catch and leaving the suitcase under the bed signalled a clear change. The end was in sight. Soon he could write freely in his notebook without fear of someone else reading it. He could go to the pictures and not hide away in the back row. Spend Sunday morning playing cricket and in the afternoon take long walks or sit in coffee bars reading his book. He could make love to Vivien in a comfortable bed that was theirs, and not panic about falling asleep and leaving her unguarded.

Fifteen minutes. That's all that remained until Carl pulled up outside the building and sounded his horn. And now he just wanted to get it over with. The night before, he had dreamed that his foot had got caught in a bear trap while he was carrying a lit firebomb. He couldn't move, Carl had run off and no one else came to his rescue. He was left lying on his own, yelling for help as the fire which had started small now caught on dry wood and leaves and quickly spread. When the flames began to engulf him, he had woken up screaming.

He looked through the open window at the row of dark roofs against the dimming sky, then down onto the heads of the few people going about their business. It was a peaceful evening. No rattle of factory doors. No kids kicking a ball around. Even the harmonica player, sprawled out on the corner most days, wasn't there. It was as if Jack was the only person in the world for whom everything was about to change.

Ten minutes. He edged back from the window, put his glass on the shelf, then sank to his knees. With his eyes shut, he pressed his fingertips together and prayed. But tonight he did not rush through the words in his head. For the first time since he had moved in, he said a prayer aloud in a normal clear voice.

Afterwards he opened his eyes and got up. He was ready now. He would wait on the step outside, smoke a cigarette and gather his courage. With his hand gripping the edge of the door, he thought ahead to the next time he would be in this room. A taxi would be waiting downstairs for him, the engine running as he raced up, picked up his suitcase and left for good.

The thought didn't make him want to linger or have one last glance over his shoulder. He couldn't stand the place and he didn't want to remember a damn thing about it.

At eleven thirty the atmosphere among the three men in Barry's car shifted. It had been a long night of waiting. In the two hours they'd spent parked up opposite the entrance to the East Cemetery on Swain's Lane there hadn't been a single sighting of torchlight or the flicker of a match in the darkness. They'd run out of excuses as to why Jack and Carl hadn't turned up, but it was clear nothing was happening.

'Shall I walk around?' said Barry. 'See what's what?'

'Absolutely not.' Still puffing on his cigar, Sid turned sideways. 'Sit tight for a bit longer.'

'For what? Dad, they're not coming.'

'I think Barry's right,' said Paulie in the back.

A knock on the window jolted Barry. He wound it down and came face to face with one of the fourteen men from the 62 Group who had been allocated between four cars.

'What's your thinking, boss?' The man leaned into the window. 'It's getting late.'

Barry and Sid exchanged glances.

'It's a set-up,' said Barry flatly. 'I don't think they're coming.'

The man nodded. 'We've been thinking the same.'

Sid didn't say anything.

'For God's sake, Dad. You know I'm right.'

When Sid reluctantly nodded, Barry was momentarily stunned. As much as he'd wanted him to agree, Barry was also desperate to be contradicted – for Sid to bark at him to be patient and reassure him that his thinking was all wrong again.

Panic made him clumsy. He dropped the car keys by his feet and fumbled around for them. He had to find Jack, know he was safe. He found himself gasping for air as he turned the key, and when the engine coughed noisily but wouldn't start, he turned the key again and again until it did.

Jack had only expected to find Carl in the car, but Carl's twin Bill stood by the boot, rubbing pigeon crap off the back window with a tissue.

'Bill needs a lift.' Carl's door was open. He glanced up from where he sat on the edge of the driver's seat, his legs thrust out of the car, staring idly at the gutter.

'All right, Jack?' said Bill.

'Yes, thanks.' Jack opened the passenger door. 'Get everywhere, don't they?'

'Filthy bastards.' Bill tossed the tissue into the road and climbed into the back seat.

Tonight, because Carl was in one of his slippery moods, Jack appreciated Bill's presence. Either Carl was swearing at Jack to blow his cigarette smoke out of the window and stop talking about football, or he was cracking terrible tasteless jokes, like the one about empty buses and Auschwitz, and expecting Jack to roar with laughter.

Not that Jack cared, really. In a few hours he would never have to set eyes on him again, and for a moment this glorious thought lit him up inside like a firework, before quickly burning out as he peered through the windscreen, then at Carl's deadpan face. They were not heading in the right direction.

'Carl, you're going the wrong way,' said Jack.

'No, I'm not.'

'Yeah, you are. Highgate Cemetery is—'

As Jack made to turn in his seat and point through the back window, Bill extended his arm, tightened it around Jack's neck and brandished a long knife in his free hand, the tip of which he twisted in front of Jack's face like a precious jewel.

'Shut the fuck up, yiddo.'

Jack didn't speak. He didn't move. He had no idea how or when they'd found out, but they knew, and they despised having him in the same car as them, warming the front seat with his Jewish backside.

But none of that mattered. They could do whatever they wanted to him as long as Vivien was safe, and he silently, fiercely prayed this was the case. Then Bill squeezed his neck so tightly, his eyesight went fuzzy and he wondered whether the black lorry moving alongside them was the last blur of traffic he would see, and if the images of Mum and Dad and Vivien that were flashing through his mind like a photo carousel were going to be his final thoughts.

At Camden lock Bill dragged him out of the car and both brothers pushed him down the steps onto the path by the canal. As they walked along, Bill clutched Jack's arm and pressed the tip of the knife in between his shoulder blades. Jack tried to stay calm. He walked with his head high, telling himself that he was proud of who he was and what he'd done. No one could take that away from him.

The stream of lights coming from the houses and pubs behind them kept Jack's breathing steady, but then they plunged further into the darkness and he wasn't calm any more. His teeth were chattering. A pulse thumped in his neck. His impulse was to break away, run as fast as he could, but he knew he wouldn't get very far and would only make things worse for himself.

239

When he stumbled over a rock or stone, Carl yanked him up and forced him on. When he slowed down because he couldn't see that far in front of him, Bill gave him a shove. He heard water rushing alongside him, then the sound of fish making their way to the surface.

'Hello, Jack.'

The voice came first, and the instant it rang out Jack felt his insides slump. He might as well leap in the canal. His time was up.

'I've missed you,' said Mickey.

Mickey would want him dead. Mickey, who stood in front of him in a nifty new denim jacket, looking as relaxed as if he were on holiday or taking a late-night promenade before turning in.

Jack pictured Vivien naked in the hotel bed, her hair falling around her face as she shouted out her happiness. He thanked God he had known what it felt like to love, and be loved, as Carl crooked his arm around his neck and Mickey punched him so hard in the mouth that he spat out blood and a tooth.

Mickey kept punching him until he was too weak to stand. When he collapsed to the ground, they dangled him over the edge of the canal and dunked his head in and out of the filthy black water before they set about kicking him.

They must have kicked him for a while, and their heavy boots hurt, but then nothing hurt any more. He wouldn't even have known there was a dog licking his face if Carl hadn't shouted over the barks, trying to call Mickey and the dog off.

Still hearing voices, Jack rolled over and vomited up water. He wanted to keep on vomiting because water was swilling through him, flooding his lungs, but then suddenly everything stopped and went dark.

23

'Do you really have to go?' asked Chrissie. 'I mean, really really?'

'Yes, I do.' Vivien nodded. 'But I'll be back.'

'You still haven't said what the urgent family business is.' Maeve pushed her boobs around in a tight black top. 'We're dying to know, aren't we, girls?'

'No,' said Deirdre. 'You are.' She looked around, grimacing. 'All I want to know is when we're going to Le Noir.'

A raucous hour had been spent in the back of the salon, drinking Babycham as they tarted themselves up. But now that they were on the soft drinks in Le Macabre, their mood had drooped. It had been Lydia's decision to swing by. She'd pleaded with them. She needed to do something about her crush on the bespectacled Spanish man who worked behind the counter.

'Yeah, I want to get out of here too.' Marcia picked at her sticky black lashes. 'This place gives me the willies.'

Vivien was on the fence about the strange, sombre interior of Le Macabre. It was a curious place, stylish but a little morbid – skulls hung from the ceiling and cupped lit candles stood on the tables. And by table, she really meant that her elbows, their drinks and the candles rested on the lid of a dark wood coffin. But it was popular enough, especially with students, like the grubby-looking boy and the pretty long-haired girl whose face was powdered as white as rice, laughing their heads off just next to them.

Vivien didn't mind the students, she could find something interesting about most people, but they got on Maeve's nerves.

'The music's good,' said Chrissie, bouncing in her seat to a Juliette Gréco tune on the jukebox.

'Lydia, you have exactly five minutes to talk to him,' said Maeve. 'Otherwise we're leaving without you.'

Lydia blanched and straightened her top. Her hair was twisted high on her head, and her eyelids shimmered blue.

'How do I look?' she whispered to Vivien.

'Smashing.'

'Really? I feel done up like a dog's dinner. It doesn't suit me.'

'It does.' Vivien nudged her. 'Go and speak to him.'

When she left, Chrissie moved into her seat and tugged Vivien's arm. 'Please don't go, Viv! I'm just getting to know you. We'll miss you so much.'

'And I'll really miss all of you too.'

'So you say,' said Maeve.

'I will! Of course I will.'

'Barb should be here,' said Marcia, touching up her red lipstick in her hand mirror. 'It's not the same without her.'

'It's not her fault,' said Vivien. 'It was all a bit last minute.'

Only Vivien knew that Barb was going home for tea because her dad had moved back in that morning. He'd asked Barb to meet him halfway, which meant her making an effort to be civil, and she'd agreed. She seemed as spirited as ever but more relaxed, and had even begun to talk about getting married as if it was an event she was looking forward to.

'She'll miss you something rotten,' Marcia added, snapping her compact shut.

Vivien felt this was true. At closing time Barb had hugged her and insisted she came back for the wedding.

'Well, we're still going to have a giggle tonight, aren't we, girls?' said Maeve. She winked and smiled. 'Give Viv something to remember us by.'

Chrissie and Marcia clapped and Vivien smiled broadly, but only because it was expected of her. After all, they were out on the razz in her honour. But the memory of how strained Jack had seemed during their goodbyes outside the hotel took the edge off her happiness. Roll on tomorrow, she thought. It was exhausting to worry about him all the time.

Deirdre came back from the loo and sat down scowling. 'I shouldn't have worn this.' She stared down at her flimsy blue dress, which caught every curve. 'I'm all lumpy.'

'Oh no, you look lovely,' said Chrissie. 'It's such a beautiful dress.'

'Yeah,' said Deirdre. 'On someone else.'

Marcia nudged Vivien. 'See. She's making progress.' The Spanish man acknowledged something Lydia was saying with a quick smile, then pointed at the detailed illustration of skeletons chalked on the blackboard on the far wall.

'Maybe he's explaining why the bosses like that monstrosity.' Marcia stared at the drawing and shuddered.

Maeve got to her feet. 'Right. I'll go tell her we're off. If she doesn't like it, she can catch us up.'

They waited for Maeve to whisper in Lydia's ear, for Lydia to nod and for the Spanish bloke to smile at Lydia and lightly touch her hand. And then they were all on their feet, slapping change on the table and tugging a grinning Lydia out of the door, twisting and laughing as they poured down the streets towards the club.

Barry drove as fast as he could to Jack's bedsit. It was his first time there but he had the address written on a tag attached to a spare key in his wallet. He double-parked and shouted at the others to stay in the car, then raced up the stairs. He banged on the door, knowing Jack wouldn't answer, then fumbled with the key and let himself in.

A terrible sense of dread came over him as he stood there, listening to the baby cry next door. He had been sure he'd find a clean and plain bedsit, not a for ever sort of place but somewhere that suited Jack's purposes in the short term. Yet this was truly miserable. It didn't feel like anyone had ever properly lived here, just a procession of lost, transient souls who couldn't be bothered to make their mark or lend it any love.

As soon as he stepped inside and shut the door, he was almost on top of the bed, which was small, like a child's bed, and took up most of the floor space. The wallpaper, where there was wallpaper, was a deep muddy grey which made Barry feel even more hemmed in. The cooker was inches away from the pillow, hidden behind a curtain. There was a sink, no fridge, and Jack had left half a pint of milk on the floor in the corner. On the ledge above the bed was a chipped mug holding a few knives and forks, and above that a framed tapestry of Big Ben.

Jack had to wake up to this, every evening he came back to this, and in between he lived a life he'd grown to hate. Barry felt ashamed for what they'd put him through, but then he forced those thoughts down and pulled himself together. This was no time to get sentimental.

He got on his knees. Seeing the suitcase under the bed, he pulled it out and opened it. On top of Jack's clothes was a pair of train tickets back to Manchester in the morning. He threw the tickets back in and slid the case away. Where the hell was Jack?

The following morning Nettie walked Vivien to the bus on her way to a fundraising meeting in Norwood. They sat on a bench and Vivien's hand went to her hair. Every strand was coiled perfectly into a gleaming knot. The style of it, like her snazzy emerald-green dress and her green and black bag, had been chosen for the exciting and significant train journey ahead.

Nettie rearranged her hat to sit back off her forehead and pressed her palms gently to her cheeks. 'I might have to leave the washing today. That kitchen's a furnace when the machine's going.'

'I think you can treat yourself to a day off,' said Vivien.

Nettie smiled. 'I think so too. Now, you must write and let me know how things are.'

'Yes, of course.' It was as uncomfortable lying to Nettie as it had been to the girls. 'I wish I could explain properly.'

'No, no,' said Nettie. 'I quite understand. Some things are private.'

Vivien thought Nettie would keep talking but she sucked hard on her mint and said nothing more. Vivien liked this. There was something lovely and comfortable about their silence and Nettie's reassuring hand on her knee.

Noticing the red of the bus flash in the distance, she dragged out the suitcase from between her legs and jumped up. Nettie stood and Vivien pulled her close and hugged her, breathing in the smell of talcum powder and peppermints.

'Thank you for everything, Nettie.' She clutched her soft hands. 'I've loved staying with you.'

'It's been my pleasure. You're my star lodger.'

'Goodness, really?' said Vivien.

'Yes. Your parents would be thrilled with the way you've turned out.'

Vivien shut her mouth and tried not to cry. 'I will miss you.'

'Me too. I hope you'll keep your word and come back and see me.'

'Of course I will.'

'Good. I shall look forward to that.'

On board Vivien held on to the rail and waved at Nettie until the bus started moving. Then she took her suitcase up to the top deck and stared through the back window until Hackney became a blur and then was lost from sight.

On the platform Vivien clutched her gloves and used them to fan her face. With her case by her feet, she smiled automatically at people who glanced her way, as if she was perfectly at ease waiting on her own. Why was he so late? She kept wondering if she'd got the time wrong. She didn't really believe she had but the last few days had been strange. It was possible she had become confused.

There was a long blow on a whistle. The thud of several doors slamming. The train was ready to depart. Girls dangled their arms through rolled-down windows and held on to their men for as long as they could, savouring those last few intimate moments.

As Vivien turned away from them, she saw him approach. At first she didn't recognise him. It had been over fifteen years and they had been children then, but when he came up close and calmly said her name, she realised how much he resembled Sid, and every part of her ran cold inside.

'Where's Jack?' she asked. 'Where is he?'

Barry Klein reached for her but she couldn't bear to be touched. She jolted away and knocked her suitcase onto its side. 'Where is he?'

The whistle kept blowing. People rushed around them. The platform controller was shouting all aboard and Barry was holding her shoulders, telling her why he was here and Jack wasn't, and she kept trying to wriggle out of his grip.

Her high-pitched scream scared passers-by. Her gloves

dropped to the ground as she crouched down and put her head in her hands. She didn't know what she was thinking. There was no language in her head that made sense. It was all just noise.

Barry grabbed her under her armpits and pulled her up. He told a policeman that she was fine; there had been a family upset but he could manage. In between he told Vivien he was there for her, he wouldn't leave her. He wouldn't let go.

She wanted to be strong, but she just went limp. Her mouth opened but no words came. She couldn't even be sure what time of day it was any more, because everywhere she looked was so white and so bright ...

24

When Vivien saw him, she said his name. She said it again as she held weakly on to the side of the bed. She did not cry. She sat down, took Jack's hand, warm from the light streaming in through the window, and held it tight. Then she stared at his mouth. He was thin and pale and bruised, but the delicate beat of his breathing reminded her that he was only unconscious. He was still alive.

She held his hand against her cheek and tried to remember what Barry had said. A blade had cut in between his ribs. A kneecap was smashed, his leg swathed in a tight bandage. His right eye was hidden beneath a cotton pad because the iris had been damaged by a chip of stone. There was internal bleeding too, some concern over his spleen, but she couldn't recall the details and now she was thinking about him wading into the sea with his trousers rolled up. Refereeing the kids playing football on her street. Encouraging her with a gentle nod when she was sharing something that was on her mind. She only wanted to think of him as he was worth remembering. Not like this. Not broken and stiff under a sheet.

She leaned over and kissed him on the mouth.

'You'd better wake up soon, Jack Morris,' she whispered and felt the tears on her cheeks. 'I'm all packed and ready to go.'

The sound of wheels on the hard floor startled her. She heard the low *thrum* of women's voices behind the curtain, then a short grey-haired nurse came through and smiled.

She walked round the bed, lifted Jack's wrist and found his pulse.

'Why does it keep beeping?' Vivien sat down and motioned towards one of the machines. 'Is something wrong?'

The nurse stared at the fob watch pinned to her breast pocket. 'It's monitoring his heart.' She laid Jack's wrist gently back on the sheet.

'His lips look very dry,' said Vivien. 'Is he getting enough fluid?'

The nurse came up behind her. 'We're doing everything we can for him,' she said gently.

'I know.' Vivien nodded and folded her arms across her chest. 'I'm so sorry. I didn't mean to suggest that ...'

She pressed her hand to her mouth and tried to contain herself, but as soon as the nurse put an arm around her shoulders, she leaned her head back against the woman's comforting bosom and sobbed uncontrollably.

When Barry came back, she was holding Jack's hand again. She had not cried or moved for a while. She could hear Barry speaking to the boy from the 62 Group who sat on the other side of the curtain pulled around Jack's bed. Somewhere behind that a patient was doing an impression of an actor and making a nurse chuckle. Dad immediately came to mind. He would always find time to joke around with the nurses on his visits for radiotherapy treatment.

Vivien shivered. Her cardigan was draped over her shoulders. She pulled the edges together and closed her eyes. She was so tired of everything.

Barry came through the curtain. 'Are you all right?' She opened her eyes and looked up at him. No, she wanted to say, getting to her feet. Life is too much for me right now. It's swallowing me up. Leaving me empty.

'He's a fighter, Vivien.'

'I know.' She took in his kind face and shock of un-brushed brown hair, and a childhood memory came to her of the time when he got stuck in a locked bathroom during a game of hide-and-seek. It was a memory which would amuse Jack, she thought, but then she saw him grey and unmoving before her and the pain came back to her. She felt more alone with herself than she had ever done before.

'I should have told Jack about Stevie,' she said again.

In the car to the hospital, shock flooding her words, she had told Barry about Stevie following them. He had done his best to make her feel better. He kept repeating that it was not her fault, that Stevie didn't know the truth so he couldn't be the reason Jack had been hurt. But who could say what might have prevented Jack ending up in hospital? No one knew anything, except that Jack was in a coma. It was entirely possible that this was all her fault. At the time she'd decided it wasn't relevant to tell Jack that Stevie had followed them, but maybe that was the worst decision she'd ever made. If she'd warned him, would he now be lying in this hospital bed?

'You'll definitely speak to Stevie?' she said again.

'Yes. Either today or tomorrow,' said Barry.

'Thank God that woman walking her dog found him. I mean, if she hadn't ...' Tears trickled down her cheeks again. 'We must thank her.'

'We will.' Barry nodded and patted her arm. 'Jack would hate to see you like this.' He took a handkerchief from his back pocket and handed it to her. 'Come on. Dry your eyes,' he said.

When the curtain moved aside, she lifted her head from Barry's shoulder and blinked the tears away before turning to see who it was. Her first feeling was one of shock; it was clear she was standing in front of Jack's parents. There was no mistaking the man's resemblance to Jack. He was as tall and robust-looking as Jack with the same intense, dark stare. His mum was much fairer with very light sad grey eyes. She smiled wanly at Vivien.

'Vivien, this is Esther and Bruce Morris,' said Barry.

'Hello.' Her mouth was dry as corduroy.

Bruce barely registered her presence. He nodded, then swept by her and peered at Jack.

'Hello, dear.' Esther's voice came out gravelly, so she cleared her throat as she walked around to the other side of the bed. 'Pleased to meet you. We've heard all about you.' She smiled over her shoulder at Vivien, then kissed Jack's forehead and combed her fingers through his hair.

'I'm so sorry about Jack,' said Vivien in a rush. 'It's awful.'

Esther nodded, but then she drew herself up and glanced across the bed at Bruce. 'But I think he has more colour this afternoon, don't you?'

'I ... I don't know, Esther. I don't think so.' Bruce wore a raincoat buttoned up to the neck. He looked smart but Vivien couldn't imagine how hot he must be. 'He looks the same to me.'

Esther nodded but her lips twitched as though she might cry.

'Jack's a fighter,' Vivien said, echoing Barry's words.

'You're right. He is.' Esther nodded furiously. 'I must keep telling myself this.'

'Look, I'm sorry. I have to leave.' Barry checked his watch. 'I'm due at an interview. I'll be back later with my dad. But you'll telephone me at work if there's any change?'

'Of course.' Esther pushed her crumpled tissue up the sleeve of her shirt and walked over to where Barry and Vivien stood.

Jack had said his mum had been a model when she was younger but even with her career long behind her, her looks had not betrayed her. Her shoulder-length fair hair was streaked with an even paler blonde, complimenting her yellow trouser suit and the blue silk scarf coiled around her neck. She knew something about style.

'Esther ... I'm sorry.' Vivien heard Barry's voice catch.

'Ssh.' She took his hands in hers. 'I don't want to talk about that now.' She looked over to Jack. 'I just want him to wake up.'

When visiting hours drew to a close, none of them could bear to leave. They begged the nurses to let them stay but the nurses refused, insisting they would call the house if there was any change.

Esther pointed at Vivien's suitcase at the end of the bed. 'Where are you off to?'

Vivien's mind went blank. She had no idea. She'd forgotten that she had nowhere to go. She supposed it made sense to telephone Nettie; she would want to look after her.

'Come back to us first,' insisted Esther after Vivien told them about her landlady. 'You can telephone Nettie, and Bruce will drop you back there later.'

'I don't want to be a bother,' Vivien said, glancing over at Bruce's sour expression.

'Not at all.' Esther picked up Vivien's suitcase, bringing the discussion to a close.

It was strange to be on her way to Jack's home in the suburbs without him. She did not enjoy climbing into Bruce's expensive car, especially after he'd brushed down the back seat with a handkerchief before she sat down, then told her in a sharply unpleasant voice to watch where she put her feet. Perched on the edge of the seat, no one beside her, she was gripped by sadness. Jack should be with her, getting ready to show off his childhood trophies and his favourite books. Squeezing her knee playfully under the table during tea, running his socked foot up and down her calf.

At least there wasn't any pressure to talk in the car. No one spoke. This suited her fine as she didn't feel like talking, and it probably suited Bruce too. Beneath his leaden expression was a fury that she felt was directed at her in some way.

It was a relief when he finally pulled over in a neat, pretty street. She briefly registered the charming house and how well kept it was, with a basket of mauve-yellow flowers hanging over the door and the square of grass framed by tidy beds of marigolds and pansies. It was almost picture-perfect.

And it was the same inside – nothing was out of place. Not that she was paying much attention. She couldn't have cared less about the paintings and the furniture and the number of rooms. What did any of it matter? She stood in the kitchen, completely drained, waiting for someone to instruct her, to tell her what to do.

'Have a seat, Vivien,' said Esther and pointed at a kitchen table big enough to sit six comfortably. A round light hung down low over the centre like a soft, tired full moon.

'I don't think I can eat,' said Esther flatly.

'Nor me,' said Vivien.

Esther took a bottle of white wine from the fridge. 'We need this,' she said and filled three glasses to the brim.

Vivien sat in the chair opposite Bruce and drank. Bruce had yet to utter more than the odd word, but Esther was talking enough for all of them. It was hard for Vivien to keep track of the conversation – something about the garden, the shed, Esther's sisters – because she was too busy picturing Jack. A young Jack running amok in the kitchen. Flying a paper aeroplane or helping Esther fold flour into a sponge. Traipsing in as a teenager, bleary-eyed and surly after a night out.

Vivien liked imagining him among them. It helped her believe everything was normal even though there were three glasses on the table and the only thing Esther hadn't talked about was how ill Jack was.

When Bruce took a report out of his briefcase and started scribbling notes in the margins, Esther paused mid-story. 'You're being rude.'

'Sorry?' Bruce looked up at her over his glasses, his pen poised in the air. His calmness suggested that he had no idea what he'd done. 'The London Society of Ophthalmology is meeting next week. Being secretary comes with certain duties.'

'But why do it now?' asked Esther.

'It's important,' he said. 'And I'm not sure what else I'm supposed to do.'

'Vivien is here, Bruce.' Esther turned her back to him and said to Vivien, 'He's not angry with you. He's angry with Jack.'

'Esther—'

'Don't Esther me. It's true.'

'Vivien doesn't need to hear this.'

'Yes, she does. She's his girlfriend. I want her to think we're nice people. If you won't explain, then I will.'

'Fine, let's tell the world our business, shall we?' Bruce slammed his pen down and took off his glasses, then stood up, but he was slow to speak again.

'Well, Vivien, I don't agree with what Jack's been doing,' he said eventually. 'He had a wonderful job on *The Times*. And what does he do? Goes and throws it all away.'

His voice was strong and emphatic, but he kept moving his head around and loosening his tie, as if it physically hurt him to admit it.

'He was brave,' said Vivien. 'Doing something he believed in.'

'He was an idiot,' shouted Bruce. 'I knew that one day the phone would ring with terrible news.'

'Bruce!' said Esther sharply. 'Remember what the doctor said.' She lowered her voice and whispered to Vivien out of the corner of her mouth, 'High blood pressure.' Then she turned back to him. 'Stop this right now. I mean it. I won't listen to another word. Jack is going to be fine,' said Esther. 'And you're frightening poor Vivien.'

'I'm sorry.' He sank back down into his seat. 'I'm just angry. It's such a bloody waste.'

Esther went over to him and kissed the top of his head. 'Jack's got a will of iron,' she said fiercely. 'He takes after you. And he'll be back here crossing swords with you in no time.'

When the telephone in the hallway rang they all looked at each other before Esther ran off to answer it.

'It's just Dad,' she called out, and Bruce looked as deflated as Vivien felt. She twirled the stem of the wine glass in her hand and thought about smoking a cigarette but was too scared to ask for an ashtray. She wished Bruce would just pick up his report again.

Then suddenly he leaned over the table. 'What are you wearing?' He looked pained.

When he pointed at her throat, her hand went to it and she realised Jack's necklace had got caught up around her dress collar.

'It belongs to Jack.' She released it and dangled it towards him.

'I know,' he said. 'I bought it for him for his eighteenth birthday.'

Her hands shook as she tried to undo the clasp. 'You must take it.'

'No, it's fine.' He shook his head. 'Jack gave it to you.'

'I'd much rather you had it.' She took Bruce's hand and pressed the necklace into it. 'Give it to him when he wakes up.'

'I …' he started to stay, but fell silent and nodded, his eyes luminous with tears.

25

The next day Alan marched ahead of Stevie towards Sid Klein's pawnbroker's. A few feet away from the door Stevie suddenly stopped and held on to a lamp post. His chest hurt. 'I can't do this,' he said, puffing slightly. 'I'm getting pains. You go in and tell them.'

'They're good people,' said Alan. 'You've nothing to be afraid of. Just tell them what you told me.'

'But Jack's in hospital because of me.'

'How many times do I need to say it? You made a mistake. This isn't your fault.'

'I'm sorry, Alan.'

'I know. Enough with the apologies. Now do I have to prise you off that lamp post or are you going to walk in on your own like a man?'

Inside, Alan announced their arrival to the redhead behind the counter, who turned her pretty smile on them both. 'Mr Klein's expecting us,' said Alan. She told them to take a seat.

Alan sat next to Stevie and flicked through the *Reader's Digest* while Stevie went over and over in his mind what he was going to say. He'd start with the two men asking him about Vivien and Jack and end with them shoving him, barely conscious, out of the car and into the gutter, laughing as they drove over his crutches, shattering them to bits.

All he wanted was for things to go back to normal. For the chance to practise his drums, to watch television with his mum while she noisily sucked on segments of an orange, or to buy everyone in the pub a round of drinks with money he didn't have.

'He's here.' Alan nudged him and put down his magazine, standing up the instant a man lifted up a hatch and waved them over.

'Good morning, Mr Klein,' said Alan.

'Sid, please.' He stole a look at Stevie as he shook Alan's hand.

'You must be Steven Pearlman.' When he shook Stevie's hand he didn't smile, but he leaned in so close Stevie could make out tobacco stains on his front teeth. 'Follow me.'

Sid was a big, burly man but he lumbered along like he was slowing down inside. His white shirt tails were crumpled, hanging out of his trousers, and it occurred to Stevie that he might have slept in his clothes.

As he entered the meeting room, Stevie recognised one of the two men standing there. Jeremy had instructed the 62 Group on the night of the NSM meeting in Camden. Stevie felt a little steadier seeing him. Jeremy could vouch for him turning up that night and trying to do some good, even if Stevie's motives had been dubious and the evening hadn't turned out as he'd hoped.

It wasn't even 10 a.m., and Jeremy was pouring fingers of whisky from a cut-glass decanter and handing them round to everyone. One sip was enough for Stevie. Alan didn't even touch his glass. He sat with his arms crossed, looking at Sid and making a strange clicking noise in his throat, which Stevie knew he automatically did when he was anxious.

A plump man with damp spots under his shirtsleeves and a birthmark as big as a shilling on his cheek, pulled up a chair next to Stevie. 'I'm Barry Klein. Thanks for coming in, Steven.'

'Tell Barry what you told me.' Alan squeezed Stevie's shoulder, rushing him like an anxious parent.

Stevie moved his lips but the words didn't come. He'd lain in bed for hours rehearsing everything he was going to say, but his throat had dried up with all their eyes on him.

'Stevie, don't be scared.' Barry had a notebook in front of him.

'We know you want to help us,' said Sid.

'I do,' said Stevie, earnestly. 'I really do.'

'Dad, I'm dealing with this.' Barry motioned for Sid to back off. 'Let me get you started. From what Vivien told me, I understand you followed Jack Morris and Vivien Epstein to the Arnot Guest House. A few weeks later you saw Jack again at the NSM meeting in Camden and assumed he was a fascist. So you paid Vivien a visit and told her what you had seen.'

Stevie kept nodding as the heat rose up his neck and jaw. 'I shouldn't have done it. None of it.'

'What happened earlier this week?' asked Barry.

Stevie had to sit on his hands to stop them trembling. 'Two men put me in a car.' He paused to clear his throat, remembering how they had pushed him into the back and slammed his forehead repeatedly against the passenger seat until the pain had stopped him thinking straight.

'They said they'd seen Vivien visit me and they wanted to know who she was. And if she was Jewish. They showed me a photo of Jack and asked me if I knew him or if I'd seen him and Vivien together.' Stevie looked down. 'I asked if Vivien was all right but they only seemed interested in Jack. They smashed my forehead against the seat and punched me until I said I thought I'd seen them coming out of a guest house together but I couldn't be sure.

'I've been terrified,' he added. 'One of the men said he'd

come back for me if I told anyone about him. I didn't know what Jack was involved in. I swear I didn't.'

Stevie's voice kept cracking. He turned to Alan, who reached over and gently wrapped his hand around Stevie's fingers.

'I didn't want Jack to get hurt. That's true, isn't it, Alan? I wouldn't want anyone to get hurt.'

They'd been driving around the streets near Jordan's house for almost an hour and a half. Stevie had said he would accompany Barry and the three other men from the 62 Group for as long as they wanted. But now it felt pointless, going up and down the same wide streets. The workday was ending, people were darting here and there, and he was sure he wouldn't be able to spot the men who'd grabbed him. And the longer it went on, the more the strain became visible. The men in the back were growing restless, Barry kept exhaling loudly and even though he'd just pulled over so Stevie could take a piss behind a bush, Stevie already needed to go again.

Another jab of a knee in the small of his back jerked Stevie forward. It was obviously intentional – the beady-eyed lad behind had given him a nasty look as soon as he got in. Stevie wished he had something else to say to him, to all of them, but he couldn't think what. He'd already said sorry a million times to whoever would listen. Sorry for what he'd done and the terrible trouble he'd caused. Sorry for messing things up for Jack. Sorry for being alive.

A sudden shot of pain burned up his leg and made him wince. Barry was going to notice something was up, the way Stevie was rubbing at his ankle and gently moaning. 'It's the injury,' he explained.

Barry cocked his head in a tired fashion and shrugged as if he didn't really care. 'Keep your eyes peeled.'

Stevie massaged his ankle and stared out of the window.

'Hang on a sec.' The man buying a newspaper from the seller on the corner looked familiar. Stevie stuck his head close to the open window but quickly pulled back. 'Sorry, false alarm.'

'Right,' said Barry a little archly. He sounded as if he thought Stevie might be winding him up – clearly he didn't understand Stevie's state of mind. Didn't he realise how badly Stevie wanted to find these men and put them behind bars? He'd barely left his room since he'd been jumped, petrified that someone was still out there gunning for him.

They drove down the road, but as they turned again into the quiet winding street where Jordan lived, Stevie allowed himself to drift. His mind pulled towards Vivien and Jack. Now everything was out in the open, he still cared deeply about what Vivien thought of him, but his concern over Jack verged on the obsessive. In between meeting Barry this morning and driving around with him this afternoon, he'd called Alan twice for an update. And he'd even dared to telephone the hospital, but a stern-sounding nurse had refused to tell him a thing because he wasn't family.

'How's Jack?' he quickly asked Barry before he lost his nerve.

'No change.'

Stevie nodded. He was about to probe further when he was distracted by someone getting out of a car on the other side of the road. 'Pull over.' He slouched down in his seat. 'Now.'

After a few seconds he forced himself to peep out of the window at the back of a bald man with a thick neck who was sauntering along the pavement.

'It's him.' His voice sounded small, tangled in his throat. 'Who?'

'The bloke who grabbed me.'

'Sure?'

Stevie nodded.

'He's gone. Get up.'

Stevie was shaking so badly, it was an effort to sit up properly. Barry pulled out and turned the car around. 'Which one's his car?'

Stevie looked at each of the cars alongside them. He pointed at the green Rover. 'There,' he said, then quickly averted his eyes.

'Sure?' said Barry.

Stevie nodded.

'Take down the number plate,' Barry called over his shoulder. The man in the middle scribbled it down, then pressed his body into the gap between the two front seats while Stevie cracked his knuckles.

Barry pulled over to the kerb, opened the glove compartment and shoved two sheets of paper at Stevie.

'Recognise any of these names?'

'What's that?' piped up the bloke from behind.

'A recent list of NSM members.'

Stevie ran through the list. He'd already told Barry he was fairly certain one of the men was called Mick or Mickey, but none of these names was familiar.

Barry took the papers from him and tossed them back in the glove compartment.

'Sorry,' said Stevie. 'I wish I knew.'

'Thanks.' Barry pulled away from the kerb. 'Let's get you out of here.'

26

'Morning, miss.'

Each day Barry sent a different boy from the Group to sit on the hard chair outside Jack's curtain. Yesterday's boy, whose face Vivien had already forgotten, whose name she never knew, had been replaced by a small tidy-looking boy with freckly cheeks. He stood up, clutching a pen and a newspaper which had been folded down and over so all he could see was the crossword.

'Morning,' she said, and gave him a half-hearted smile which fell away the instant she slipped through the curtain. It had been four days and nothing had changed.

She stood wrestling with the truth, trying not to deflate. She might have dreamed that Jack was awake and had telephoned her to say, 'Prepare a picnic; I'm coming to get you in my new car', but a dream was just a dream. It didn't mean anything.

Her swallow felt hard in her throat but she kept smiling and talking to him in an upbeat voice about whatever nonsense came to mind. She folded back her shirtsleeves, then sat down on the chair and stroked his leg for some time before a familiar ache started up in her chest again.

You could go along for a while believing you'd stopped feeling lonely, she thought, but it didn't take much to remind you that you still were and probably always would be.

The tea trolley stopped close by. There was the clatter of

cups, a man groaning loudly, then a nurse with a plummy voice called out to her colleagues for help.

The groaning carried on but Vivien tried her best to ignore it. She combed Jack's hair and wiped his face with a damp cloth. She went and refilled the jug of water and returned just as a nurse she didn't recognise was checking the bag of fluid at his side and making notes on the clipboard at the end of his bed.

'When will he wake up?' Vivien asked in a measured voice.

'I can't say, dear.'

'You'll wake up soon, won't you, darling?' she said. 'It won't be long now.' Once the nurse had slipped away, she bent over Jack and said in a quiet voice, 'You come back to me, do you hear? You come back and give me everything you said you would.'

When Jack's parents arrived, Vivien headed out for a walk and a bite to eat. Eastern Hospital was too far from Nettie's to pop back for lunch, so she picked up an apple and a white roll from the shops on Homerton Row. To avoid the grubby glare of Homerton High Street, she stuck to the quiet tree-lined streets nearby and walked at a slow, constant pace. The fresh air did not cure everything but it cheered her up a little. Then, as she stopped in at the tobacconist's for a Jubbly, the realisation that she was only one street away from Stevie's house came to her in a flash.

She immediately regretted having walked this way but reminded herself that Barry had told her not to worry. He'd been quick to reassure her that both she and Stevie were safe, they were of no importance now. The people who'd followed them were only concerned with confirming their suspicions about Jack. Though it wasn't surprising how nervous she still was. It was hardly any time at all since Jack had been hurt, and with the events still so clear in her mind, she was not going to stop worrying quite yet.

As she walked on a bit further, she remembered that Stevie had said there was a shul at the other end of his street and she found herself heading that way. For the first time since she had arrived in London, she had a keen urge to pray. She hurried alongside the black railings and through the unlocked gate, noting that a square of large window had been replaced by a board of pale wood. When two small birds flew past she spotted faded paint marks on the brick wall, and whatever anxiety she had been entertaining gave way to anger. The marks were in the shape of a swastika.

She knocked hard on the double doors, but when each of her knocks was met with silence, she crouched down and peered through the letter box.

The foyer was shadowy and vacant, but the door to the hall was open and she could glimpse the Ark in the distance. The sight of it made her even more determined to go inside, but still no one responded to her knocks. About to give up, she heard the clank of keys and a pair of slippered feet slowly appeared in her line of vision.

The door opened and a small elderly man in caretaker's overalls peered out through the gap. 'Not open.' His accent was foreign and unfamiliar.

'Please, sir,' she said. 'I just want to come in for five minutes.'

'Not open. We clean.'

Her lips trembled. 'Please, sir, I won't be any trouble. I need to come in.'

He leaned in even closer and examined her face. 'OK, you come,' he said kindly. 'You don't stay long.'

'I won't.' She shook her head. 'Thank you.'

He let her in and handed her a headscarf and prayer book from the pile in the foyer. She thanked him, draped the scarf over her head and walked down the aisle. Her gaze was fixed on the Eternal Light which hung above the Ark because it was this that she had always been drawn to as a child and needed to see. The light that always burned as a symbol of God's presence. Only now no adults and restless children packed out every seat like they did during the Saturday morning service back home. When the air hung with bitter breath and whispered gossip. Now it was just her and God.

Sitting down close to the front, Vivien looked into the light. She apologised to God for not having been to shul since Dad's funeral, and begged him to show Jack mercy. Then, lowering her head to turn the fragile pages of the prayer book, she saw a tatty teddy bear out of the corner of her eye. It was balancing at the far end of the row. She edged along and reached for it, sad for the child who was without it, knowing how bereft she would have been to lose her own childhood bear.

Vivien got up when the caretaker arrived, swishing round a mop and glancing in her direction. She put the bear back, gave the caretaker the prayer book and wished him a pleasant day as he locked the door behind her.

Back on the street, the air was close. Everyone kept saying the weather was about to turn, but she couldn't imagine what it would be like when it did finally rain again. She walked for a while, trying not to let difficult thoughts overwhelm her, but as she approached Hackney Downs, she decided to sit down on the bench near the bowling green and reread the letter she'd received from Stella that morning.

It was a reply to the letter Vivien had sent a few days ago, in which she had told Stella everything about Jack and his work and what had happened to him. She had not set out to fill four sheets of paper, but getting up and writing in the middle of the night had brought Stella into the room and made her feel that she was not entirely alone in the world.

Stella's reply was short, just one page, and consisted almost entirely of how shocking the news about Jack was, how Vivien must stay strong and her conviction that Jack would make a full recovery. The letter ended with a heart-shaped trail of kisses and a firm promise that they must see each other soon.

Vivien reread the letter several times, but when two chatty women sat down on the bench beside her, she got up and began walking again, not much caring where she was going. Picturing Stella running down the street after her boys, she couldn't believe how homesick she was. Today she felt she would do anything to turn her back on this city and return to her small, safe, manageable life on that street.

She could not face going back to the hospital just yet, so instead she decided to take a bus to see Barb and the girls. She missed them all, especially Barb, who knew everything from Alan and had already telephoned and invited her to come over and talk whenever she was ready.

But, arriving in Soho, she wasn't sure she had made the right decision. It held none of its usual charm. Everything infuriated her. It was a chore to push her way through the tourists and the shopkeepers and to watch out for the street cleaners and barrow boys. She didn't want to stop and point the Dutch man with the stutter in the direction of Nelson's Column or the Irish family towards Piccadilly Circus. She wanted to slip by, undisturbed.

As she approached Oscar's, she saw Chrissie bidding a client goodbye. She looked lovely and delicate in her little white skirt and top, and as she stood in the doorway the sun flowed around her, lighting her up like a pale angel. Vivien quickened her step, relieved. Suddenly she needed these women, their kindness and gift of friendship, and their sturdy arms which they would be quick to put around her once they heard the anguish in her voice.

By the time she arrived back at the hospital, Esther was already there in the chair by the window, forcing a smile. Neither of them pretended they wanted to talk. Esther had a headache and looked drained. Vivien just wanted to hold Jack's hand and picture him as he was, but it was getting harder every day, and she wondered if Esther felt the same.

She was reluctant to leave before the nurses ushered them out, but Sid was picking her up to take her home for Friday night dinner. She didn't really want to go. She was tired of company. Once inside Sid and Elaine's flat she asked to use the loo, where she sat for some time, listening to them talk to each other from different rooms. Eventually she unlocked the door and made her way into the living room.

'Don't just stand there; come in.' Sid sat in an armchair by the television thumbing through the *Hackney Gazette*. 'Make yourself at home.'

As she sat down, Elaine came through from the kitchen, stirring a wooden spoon around a bowl.

'Do you want a drink? A piece of challah?'

'I'm fine thanks, Elaine. Can I help with anything?'

'No, darling. Put your feet up.'

Elaine had laid eight places at the table. She'd polished the Shabbos candlesticks with a soft cloth and placed them on a silver tray in the centre of the table, next to the loaf of challah and jars of rollmops and pickled gherkins.

Sid got up and poured himself a whisky. 'You want one?'

'Sid, she's a young lady,' said Elaine. 'What does she want a whisky for?'

'You want a soft drink? A Pepsi?'

'Nothing, thanks.'

'You hungry?' said Sid. 'Elaine's cooked up a storm.'

Vivien nodded, although she hadn't had much of an appetite for days.

'Me too,' said Sid. 'I could eat a horse.'

'You're too thin, Vivien.' Elaine put the bowl on the settee armrest and removed the large roller from her fringe with a frown as if she'd just remembered it was there. 'Tell her she's too thin.'

Sid didn't look up. 'You're too thin.'

When the doorbell rang, Elaine leaned through the kitchen hatch, put the bowl back on the counter, then untied her apron and pushed that through too. As she was leaving the room, she pointed to the television. 'Turn that off,' she told Sid. 'We've got company.'

'What? We're standing on ceremony for our own kids now?'

'Danny's going to be a little late,' she said over her shoulder.

'Big news.' Sid shook his head. 'Danny's always late.'

Vivien sat down on the edge of an armchair. She was apprehensive about being present at a big raucous Friday night dinner. When she was feeling good she appreciated other people's families, but when she felt this low, they reminded her of what she had to go through life without.

Barry's two kids ran in first, and Sid picked each of them up in turn, tickling their stomachs until they shrieked with laughter and begged him to stop. Sandra and Barry followed and both greeted Vivien warmly.

'Who wants what?' Sid pointed at the bar.

'Gin and lemon, please,' said Sandra.

Elaine knelt down on the rug. 'Where's your kiss for Grandma?'

'No kisses.' Lawrence shook his head and began walking the toy soldier he was carrying over the arm of Barry's chair.

'Really?' Elaine pouted. 'Well, I suppose you won't want the trifle Grandma's made for you.'

'Trifle?' Lawrence flung his arms around Elaine's neck and showered her in kisses.

When everyone else laughed, Vivien felt Jack's absence and her smile dipped away.

Barry reached over. 'OK?' Without waiting for an answer, he patted her hand. 'I popped in on Jack before I went home.'

'Any change?' she asked hopefully.

He shook his head in a slightly embarrassed way, then sighed.

'How are you?' asked Sandra, looking consolingly at Vivien.

'Fine.' Vivien tried to smile.

'Well, I don't imagine that's true,' said Sandra. 'Can I do anything?'

As Vivien shook her head, Sandra's attention had already shifted back to her father-in-law.

'Sid, stop it. She'll be sick.' Sid was swinging his grand-daughter Susan upside down by her legs and pretending that he was about to drop her. 'Tell him, Barry.'

Barry was reading Sid's newspaper and yawning. 'Dad,' he said without looking over, 'she'll be sick.'

'Ready!' Elaine clapped her hands. 'Everyone to the table. Danny will have to catch up when he gets here.'

'It smells great,' said Sandra. 'I've been saving myself for this all day.'

'Oh, it's nothing I haven't made a hundred times before.' When the telephone rang, Elaine was instructing Vivien and Barry to pull the table out from the wall.

'You get it,' Sid said to Elaine. 'It will be your mum.'

'It might not be.'

'Course it is. The moment we sit down to eat, she rings. Never known timing like it.'

Elaine waved her hand dismissively at him as she walked out into the hallway. Everyone started to argue over where they wanted to sit, and Lawrence was about to swap with Barry when they heard Elaine yell, 'Vivien, quickly! Jack's awake!'

Vivien still hadn't seen his face. Barry had dropped her off in the car park, and she'd run all the way through the hospital to his bedside, yet she couldn't get close. Several doctors and nurses were gathered around him, discussing what they saw on the machine, his pulse and heart rate. Then the machines got shunted back into the corners and they raised the head of the bed.

One doctor pulled at the stethoscope around his neck and asked Jack to follow his finger. Another ordered blood tests. Their voices were low and serious but there was hope on their faces.

Vivien stood on tiptoe next to Esther and watched Jack's arm being lifted up, then dropped. At least there wasn't the usual clamour of the ward behind them. Most of the patients were sleeping and the room was pleasantly cool.

When Barry charged in, Esther repeated for the umpteenth time the story of how Jack had just opened his eyes while she'd been pouring herself a glass of water. He'd blinked until he could focus, attempted to clear his throat and then, in a rough, barely audible voice, he'd uttered Vivien's name.

'He knew his own name and date of birth,' said Bruce.

'And what had happened to him.' As Esther spoke, the doctors started to drift away.

'Go on.' Bruce prodded Vivien's arm.

She looked up at him in alarm. All this desperate waiting for Jack to wake up, yet now she felt completely unsure of herself. There was something a little overwhelming about baring herself to Jack in front of a room full of people, most of whom were strangers. As she edged towards his bed, fists clenched by her side, a panicky feeling flared deep in her gut.

Then she looked down at him and forgot about everyone else. 'Oh God, Jack.'

'Vivien.' Just hearing him say her name was enough. She hadn't been sure she'd ever hear that again.

He reached up and drew her face down, then held it just above his and kissed her.

His lips were dry, but it was the best kiss she'd ever had.

27

When he heard Vivien's voice asking him to wake up, Jack stopped shouting and opened his eyes. He was still in the armchair by the living-room window. He punched off the blanket someone had draped around him while he slept and leaned forward. His back was drenched in sweat.

Vivien knelt at his side. 'Same one?' Her hand lightly cupped his knee.

He nodded and groped around for something to say. It had been nearly ten days since he'd woken from the coma and five days since he'd arrived home, yet he still dreamed that he was by the canal, face down in the brown slimy water, trying desperately to breathe through the clumps of pondweed stuck in his throat.

Sitting back on her calves, Vivien nodded sympathetic-ally. She looked like she wanted him to talk to her about it, but she wouldn't ask. He was grateful to her for how well she handled him and how she knew exactly when to back off. Because he wasn't himself yet. After he'd regained consciousness he was so happy that he could still think and speak and feel – *that he was alive* – he thought nothing would trouble him again. But fear still pushed down hard on him all the time, infecting him, ruining every moment he was with Vivien.

As he wiped the drops of sweat from his forehead, the rain sloped down against the glass and made him think back to being on the ward, listening to it beat against the window above his bed while someone's wireless played in the background. Thank God he was out of that place. All those men groaning and crying or looking for company. He couldn't find a moment's peace. Turning back to Vivien, he noticed the shine of raindrops on her hair and leaned over to touch them.

'Do you want to go and have a lie-down?' said Esther. He glanced at the chair by the writing desk in the corner. He hadn't noticed his mum sitting there, squeezing her hands together between her legs. 'Maybe you've overdone it today.'

'I've only come downstairs and sat in here. Hardly the Olympics.'

'Well.' His mum nodded. 'You know best.'

Her face had that faintly wounded look it had begun to wear all the time. He didn't blame her. He was shamed by the brisk and offhand way he kept talking to her but he seemed locked into his behaviour and couldn't snap out of it. And yet he'd missed her all the time he was away and was delighted to be home. The mess of his emotions bewildered him.

'Esther said your eye's a bit better,' said Vivien.

He nodded. 'I think so.' When he'd changed the dressing that morning he could have sworn everything looked sharper, less creamy.

'I'll go and make us all a cup of tea.' His mum stood up. 'Did I say that some of your cousins are coming over at the weekend? Ruth's kids. Maybe Carol's too. Everyone's dying to see you. I think I may just put on a bit of a spread and make it an open house.'

He could feel Vivien's hand press firmly against his thigh. A coded message, he thought. Understand her. Don't shout her down. Don't go on the attack.

'Sounds fine.' He hoped that she was too busy lining

up magazines on the coffee table to notice how quickly he stopped smiling. What no one except Vivien understood was that his life for the past six months had felt like being in prison. All he'd done was watch his back and consider every word that came out of his mouth. He'd forgotten how to make small talk and be easy around others.

'Jack?' his mum said.

'What?'

'I asked if you wanted something to eat?'

'No, thanks.'

'But you barely touched your lunch.'

'I'm not hungry.'

'Let me at least—'

'Later,' he said. 'OK?'

She smiled brightly and pushed a strand of hair away from her mouth. 'Of course.'

As soon as she walked out, he wanted to call her back. She was sweet and loving and deserved better. She'd struggled to help him out of bed that morning and got him to the toilet just in time. In the bathroom she'd washed his face and combed his hair. She'd made him a boiled egg for breakfast and good-naturedly accepted his complaint about the hard yolk. He wanted to call her back and tell her he loved her. He just wasn't ready for her yet.

On their own, Vivien pulled herself to her feet and sat on the arm of his chair, her legs bent to the side. She kissed his head. 'You won't believe what it's like out there.'

She told him about the shopkeepers who'd gathered by their windows to witness the dramatic downpour. How no one wanted their hair done when it would be ruined in minutes, so the salon had been empty for most of the afternoon.

'I saw.' He'd watched from his bedroom window. Cars

slashing down the black road. Rain springing off car bonnets. A neighbour running down the street holding a soaked newspaper above her head. For the longest time he had just sat and watched the raindrops drip down the glass until he realised he should probably go and do something.

'I'm being difficult, aren't I?' he said.

'Course not.'

'I'm sure Mum thinks so.'

Vivien sighed. 'She just wants everything to be all right.'

'So do I.'

'She's your mum, Jack,' said Vivien gently. 'This is really hard for her.'

He nodded, then sighed. 'I'm on such a short fuse.'

'Of course you are. Everyone understands that.' She paused. 'Look, you would say if this was really all about … well, if you were still angry with me?'

'When was I angry with you?'

'In the hospital when I told you about Stevie following me and seeing you at that meeting.'

'I was never angry with you about that.'

'Well, you should have been.'

'No.' He stroked her leg. 'I've told you. It's nothing. Forget it.'

'But—'

'How many times do I need to say it? Stevie wasn't the reason I was found out. He just got dragged into a big mess, that's all.'

'But I should have told you. No more secrets, promise.'

'Good. Now forget about it.' He smiled. 'That's an order.'

She kissed his head and huddled close into him with her feet on his lap.

'I just need time,' he said.

'Take all the time you need. I'm not going anywhere.'

'You'd better not.' He pinched her waist, then rested his

head against her chest. 'Things will get easier.' He sighed. 'They have to.'

Vivien didn't stay for supper. He guessed she thought that with his dad working late, he should spend some time alone with his mum. After a pleasant meal of spaghetti Bolognese and coffee cake, during which he was grateful his mum did not force conversation on him, he made his way upstairs to read. He'd just taken off his shoes and lain down on his bed when the doorbell rang.

'Jack,' his mum called out, then giggled. 'Visitors.' He pictured her shiny blonde hair swinging about as she shouted for him, then turning back to whoever had shown up and laughing as if everything was back to normal.

When he didn't answer, he heard her pad up the carpeted stairs. She entered his bedroom a second after she knocked.

'Darling, Sid and Barry Klein are here.'

'Oh, right.' Her hand patted his head as he struggled to pull himself up.

'Your old mum's driving you barmy, isn't she?'

He took her hand off his head and kissed it. 'Never.'

'Oh you're a terrible liar.'

'I'll follow you down.' He looked at the floor and yawned. 'Won't be a minute.'

At least he didn't have to pretend with the Kleins. He greeted them in his checked pyjama bottoms and white vest, four days' worth of stubble and no smile, and they didn't attempt to jolly him up. They didn't hug him or tell him he looked well or remind him how lucky he was to be alive.

He sat down on a dining-table chair, the only chair that he could get up from without help, while the Kleins sat in silence on the settee and drank their glasses of water.

'Good news,' Barry started to say. 'Steven Pearlman identified Mickey. We got the police involved and—'

'Jordan has been arrested and charged,' Sid finished.

Jack fumbled in his pyjama shirt pocket for a packet of cigarettes and lit one. He didn't know he'd been nervous about this until now.

'Charged with what?'

'Organising and training men for Spearhead,' said Barry, 'for the purpose—'

Sid cut him off again. 'Of displaying force in promoting their politics.'

Jack kept his eyes on Barry so Sid would get the message. He couldn't stand Sid's hang-up about being the boss and having the last word, the way he always talked over Barry.

'On the strength of your statement, the police got a warrant to search Colin Jordan's house,' said Barry. 'They took a van full of stuff away – knives, Nazi uniforms, pistols. You name it, they got it. Stripped Jordan's house bare, by all accounts. He's finished,' he added. 'For now, anyway.' He pointed a finger at Jack. 'And it's all because of you.'

Jack said nothing.

'I almost forgot,' said Barry. 'Mickey's been charged with grievous bodily harm.'

They were both smiling at him but he couldn't share in their relief. With his head turned away, he blew the last of the smoke out of the side of his mouth. He hoped they would stop scrutinising him once he turned back.

'Make sure you get to Carl Seaton.' Jack could remember Carl shouting at Mickey that it was enough, to stop kicking him. 'I think he'll talk. And he knows a lot.'

'Address?'

'I don't know. He's a painter and decorator. Lives in Hammersmith.'

'We'll find him.'

Jack hoped they were close to the end of what they had come to say so he could go upstairs, crouch low over the toilet and throw up.

'The thing I don't understand is why they were following you in the first place,' said Sid.

Jack lowered his eyes and coughed into his fist, then shrugged in what he hoped was a casual, offhand way. 'I don't know,' he lied.

When he felt Barry's heavy-lidded appraising look, he heard himself echo Vivien by way of distraction: 'But thank God for the dog.'

He pulled himself up, pressing hard on his stick, then limped over to open his dad's minibar. Shame his dad wasn't much of a drinker. He hardly touched the stuff. There was only one bottle of brandy, a drop of whisky and a half-empty container of glacé cherries.

'Brandy?' He shook the bottle in the air and heard them say no thanks.

'This will be all over the papers tomorrow,' said Barry.

Jack poured himself a large measure. He drank it straight, then shuddered. He carried on standing with his back to them, staring at the mirror behind the bottles, hating the person he saw there.

What the hell was wrong with him? This news meant an end to his fear. Jordan and Mickey would probably go to prison. He'd foiled other bombings. He might even have saved lives. He should be ecstatic, yet he felt numb. It was as if the old Jack had been amputated, every ounce of feeling cut away.

He poured himself another brandy, turned and raised his glass.

'Cheers,' he said, then watched a look pass between them as if he was someone they should worry about.

*

Jack was up long before the paper boy had got out of bed. Alone in the kitchen, he stared at the rain coming down in grey sheets, then opened the windows because he liked the tinny sound of it hitting the inside of a watering can on the patio.

He made himself a cup of tea and drank it slowly, waiting for his dad's copy of *The Times* to drop through the letter box.

After he'd picked it up off the mat, he spread it out on the table and turned the pages. What he was looking for would never have made the front page.

SWASTIKAS, PISTOLS AND HOME-MADE BOMBS: NATIONAL SOCIALIST MOVEMENT MEN CHARGED. When he landed on the column on page nine, he read quickly and without surprise. He didn't expect to be told anything new.

Jordan had been charged. The trial date was still to be set. There was an inventory of the Nazi propaganda the police had uncovered in his home and a brief mention of how NSM rallies were always met with organised protest from the Jewish community.

Even Jordan's reaction was unsurprising: 'I look forward to my day in court, when I can prove that Spearhead has worked within the framework of the Public Order Act. Contrary to what the police are alleging, I know nothing about proposed arson attacks on synagogues.'

Jack closed the paper and lit another cigarette. There was one more thing he had to do. In the dining room he opened up his dad's writing bureau, fished around for a notepad and pen, then sat down and wrote.

Dear Henry,
I don't know if you will get this letter but I wanted to write anyway.
You may have noticed that I no longer visit Uncle

Colin's house. I am not allowed to. This is because I am Jewish and lied about why I was supporting the party. This made your father and Uncle Colin very angry.

Henry, I know that Uncle Colin began to suspect who I really was because I said to you that Jewish people aren't maggots. Mickey told me that you repeated this to Uncle Colin and that's why they pretended to throw him out of the party, so he could follow me.

I hope that one day when you're old enough to make up your own mind about things, you'll remember all the times we played football (and the day we smashed the plant pot in the hallway with your fantastic goal!) and went looking for worms and slugs in the garden. And I hope that when you do remember the fun we had together, you'll realise that it didn't make any difference who I was.

But I'm not going to tell anyone else how Uncle Colin found out about me. It will be our secret. I'll keep it to myself for ever.

I am very fond of you, Henry. You were the best thing about being at Uncle Colin's, and if I ever have a son I hope he'll be just like you.

Yours, with affection,
Uncle Jack xx

28

'You said you'd come,' said Barry, and sighed.

'I've changed my mind.'

Jack knew he was behaving unfairly, like a big kid. It wasn't as if Barry had turned up unannounced. He'd telephoned the night before and talked Jack round. A day out, just the two of them, and he'd made such a big deal of it that Jack had found it hard to say no. But he should have stuck to his initial response and refused because being unpredictable was tough on everyone.

His mum thrust his walking stick at him. 'Out,' she said. 'Go on. Some fresh air will do you good.'

Her clipped voice implied that arguing back wouldn't get him anywhere, so he took the stick and traipsed down the driveway to Barry's car. On the passenger seat was a chocolate bar wrapper and a half-finished bag of crisps, but two minutes into their journey Barry smacked his lips and announced that he was hungry. 'Fancy a spot of lunch?'

When Jack shrugged, Barry said, 'Look, shall I just take you back?'

Yes. No. What he wanted to say was, 'Help me, please. I don't know what the hell is going on inside me.'

'What?' said Barry.

'I didn't say anything,' said Jack. 'All right. Let's get something to eat.'

Jack drummed his fingers on his thighs as the traffic moved, then halted again.

'Good piece in the *Jewish Chronicle*.' He was referring to Barry's letter in response to the Board of Deputies' attack on the 62 Group's activities. He'd been impressed by Barry's counterargument for confronting fascism, and the likes of Jordan, in a very direct, head-on way. 'Your writing killed it. You got a lot more column inches than the board's reply.'

'Yeah. That must have ruffled a few feathers.'

The board's reply had contained the usual claims that anti-Semitism couldn't be overcome through yobbish behaviour. That violence couldn't be met with violence. That the Jewish community should be seen to be law-abiding and try to change the views of politicians and journalists. But Jack had heard the same tired argument for years. Now it just went over his head.

'Your dad probably loved my piece too, right?' said Barry, smirking.

'Absolutely.' Jack smiled. 'He savoured every word.'

Bruce had ignored Barry's letter but read the board's response aloud over breakfast, even rereading bits that took his fancy, trying to needle a reaction out of Jack, who had buttered his toast and stared at his dad's reflected profile in the kitchen window. This from a man who had managed to avoid being conscripted during the war and had never joined his brother in a single protest at Ridley Road, even knowing the atrocities Robert had witnessed in Germany. All Bruce wanted was for the Jews to go around quietly and not make a fuss. Keep themselves to themselves.

As they sped along Whitechapel High Street, Jack bristled again, suspecting that they would be lunching at Bloom's. He was right. When Barry parked and beamed at him, Jack turned away, sighing. He couldn't fathom why this was one of Barry's favourite restaurants. The food was bland, the service sloppy. Why bother? London was no longer short of decent places to eat.

On the walk over there Jack had to keep yanking his elbow away from Barry's hands. He didn't need Barry's help. He could walk just fine, he just couldn't walk fast. His knee hadn't healed properly yet and he went at the pace he could manage.

Barry held the front door open as Jack felt another low mood come over him. He was about to tell Barry he'd changed his mind, he'd like to go home, but Barry quickly ushered him inside and tugged him in front a packed restaurant where cries of 'Surprise!' flew out towards them.

Men were standing by their chairs. Whistling. Clapping. Clapping him.

Chanting his name.

Stamping their feet.

Jack reached out to grab the end of the nearest table. Every bit of him was quivering. He glanced around. At first the men's faces blurred into one long shadow, but then he spotted someone he knew, then someone else. These were men from the 62 Group.

A glass of wine was thrust into his hand as he shifted from foot to foot, waiting for the noise to peter out. Instead it gained momentum. Now the sea of men was bobbing around, wolf-whistling, pounding fists on tables, tapping spoons against glasses. He took a mouthful of his drink. His face was burning and he was pressing so hard on his stick he thought it might snap in two.

By the time Sid walked into his line of vision, Jack was mopping his brow, desperate to go somewhere and turn his face to the wall. With a cigar pressed between his teeth, Sid raised his hand, restoring order in the room save for a few heckles from the far corner.

He hung his heavy arm over Jack's shoulders and pulled him close. 'Gentlemen.' He paused dramatically. 'I give you Jack Morris.'

Then, as he kissed Jack's crown and mussed up his hair, the roar went up all over again.

Barry led Jack round each table and introduced him to men who wanted to thank him personally and shake his hand. Some of them clung to him, eager to share their stories. The wife who'd been spat on pushing her pram down Mile End Road. Czech relatives who had perished in Theresienstadt. The grandfather who'd lost his sight in one eye after being glassed in the face during a fight with one of Mosley's lot.

Jack listened and thanked them for talking to him so openly, for their kind words and generosity, but he wondered how much they really knew about him. They might know he'd been an up-and-coming reporter at *The Times*, promoted twice in less than six months. They might even know that at first he'd been too arrogant, convinced he could nail Jordan without losing anything of himself. And they probably knew things hadn't gone to plan. That he'd messed up, broken rules, put the woman he loved in danger and was lucky to be alive. Jack kept shaking their hands while the voice in his head interrogated him about whether he really was worth celebrating. He still felt like such a fraud. Nothing like the hero they thought he was.

'Mr Morris.' Jack felt a tug on his arm. At his elbow was an impeccably dressed man with a velvet kappel pinned to his spray of white hair. 'I'm Rabbi Allen. Mr Klein invited me.'

Jack clasped his hand and shook it hard. Rabbi Allen was based at the shul he had daubed with swastikas.

'What an honour it is to be here, Mr Morris.'

'Jack, please. I did plan to write. I'm sorry for—'

'For nothing, Mr Morris,' he interrupted. 'For nothing.'

Rabbi Allen took both of Jack's hands in his. 'We may not be in the presence of the Torah, but let us thank God for his kindness in delivering you back to us. Are you familiar with the Birkat HaGomel?'

'No.' Jack shook his head.

'It's our prayer for surviving life-threatening situations. Something I imagine you've said in your own way many times.'

Together they prayed, and afterwards the rabbi smiled and touched Jack's shoulder again. 'I mustn't monopolise you. Others are keen for your company.'

'Thank you.'

'Be happy, Mr Morris. And always be grateful.'

'Yes, sir. Thank you.'

As the rabbi moved away, Jack stood alone amid the swirl of activity. He'd have liked to sit down and rest, but as he limped forward more hands groped for his as if he were somebody famous. He thanked everyone but it was beginning to make him feel uncomfortable and he wanted it to stop.

'How's it going?' asked Barry from behind.

'OK. A bit overwhelming.'

'I'll bet.'

'Sid just told me that you're officially leaving the Group today.'

'Yep.'

'So soon?'

'Well, I was only ever going to help Dad get things set up. I want to spend more time with Sandra and the kids.' He grinned. 'I cannot tell you how good that sounds right now.'

'They'll be sorry to see you leave.' Jack gestured around.

'Nah. It's Dad they'll miss, if he ever goes.'

'Give yourself some credit, Barry. Look at the progress the Group has made. That's all because of you.'

Barry ignored him. 'Have you met Lou? He's replacing

me.' He pointed across the room at a balding man who was dressed from top to toe in green and was deep in conversation with Jeremy.

'No, who is he?'

'Old friend of Dad's. A jeweller. Sharp as a tack. And he thinks the sun shines out of Sid's backside so everyone will be happy.'

They smiled at each other.

'All set for Manchester?' asked Barry.

'Just about.'

'How long will you be gone?'

'Not sure. A while. Until things settle.'

'Well, I know Dad's pleased you're going help him train up infiltrators.'

Jack thought of Phil. 'I want to stay involved.'

They looked at each other for a moment without speaking.

'Well, it's something to tell the grandchildren, eh?' said Barry.

They laughed, hugged, then drew apart because a buffet-style lunch was about to be served. Shoving the kitchen doors open with their hips, waiters came out clutching plates and yelling through pinched mouths for everyone to get out of the way, even when their paths were clear. Guests were laughing and bantering with them, the atmosphere was jovial and friendly, but Jack felt as if he were on the outside looking in.

At the table Barry guided him to, he was trying to decide what he thought of the plate of tongue, coleslaw and crisps someone had prepared for him when a man shouted his name and pointed towards the door. Vivien and his parents were being greeted by the Kleins.

Vivien came to him first, her eyes shining, her mouth pursed into a slightly coy smile.

'You knew about this,' he said.

'Yep.' She bent down. 'My hero.' She acknowledged his smile but her frown told him she saw something else; she'd guessed he was burdened by the scale of this celebration in his honour.

'People need to thank you,' she whispered. 'Let them.'

He nodded gratefully. He was lucky to have such a kind, adorable confidante. She reached inside the back of his shirt collar and lightly massaged his neck with her fingertips, then turned to receive a kiss from Jeremy. As Jack's glance shifted, he noticed his mum holding on to Sid's hand and laughing and his dad scanning the place nervously.

He got to his feet, squeezed Vivien aside and beckoned his father over. When his dad stuck out his hand as if he were in his consulting rooms on Wimpole Street, the formal greeting didn't surprise Jack but it irritated him. He reluctantly put out his hand.

'I still think what you did was foolish,' said Bruce, clasping it. 'I'll never change my mind about that.'

'I wouldn't expect you to,' said Jack.

'But you did what you thought was right.'

They stared at each other for a moment, then his dad reached over and wrapped his arms around Jack in a genuine embrace, the sort he'd always appeared uncomfortable giving, before he surprised Jack a second time by kissing him gently on his cheek.

'Now, Steven, it goes without saying. Mind your Ps and Qs.' Sid Klein was walking a little ahead of Stevie.

'Of course, sir,' said Stevie. 'I wouldn't dream of causing any trouble.'

'Good.' Sid held his glasses and rubbed the bridge of his nose between his fingers. 'Don't make me regret inviting you.'

'No, sir. I would never embarrass you. I'm very grateful that you let me come.'

'OK.' Sid reached forward and pulled a man out of a small gathering. 'Jack, this kid has come to see you. Steven Pearlman, Jack Morris.'

Kid? That wasn't the introduction Stevie was hoping for and it made him flush so quickly, he thought of running straight out. Worse still, at the mention of his name Vivien broke off her conversation, whipped round and now the pair of them were studying him.

For the first time since his preoccupation with Jack had begun, Stevie was up close enough to familiarise himself with his gaunt face and hollowed-out eyes. He was considering whether putting out his hand for Jack to shake was too presumptuous, given the circumstances, when Jack beat him to it.

'Jack Morris,' he said warmly as Stevie pumped his hand.

'Yes, sir.'

'Jack, please.'

'Hello, Vivien,' said Stevie.

She stood perfectly still, tight-lipped, a curt nod in his direction.

'Please, can I talk to you both? Somewhere private.'

Jack shrugged. 'Sure. Let's go outside. It's pretty busy in here.'

Huddled on the pavement close to the front window, Stevie asked Jack how he was.

'Pretty good.'

'You have no idea how happy I am to hear that,' said Stevie. 'Look, you know what a hash I made of things. I've never behaved so stupidly before. I'm truly sorry.'

'We know you are.' Jack reached forward and patted him on the shoulder. 'Don't go upsetting yourself.'

Stevie hadn't even realised his eyes were wet. He blinked and quickly ran his fingers over them.

'I see your plaster's come off,' said Vivien.

'Yeah.' He wriggled his hand. 'No damage, thank God. I've even started playing the drums again. And I'm going to practise ...'

He cut himself off again. 'Sorry.' His plans would be of no interest to them.

Jack cuffed his arm. 'Go easy on yourself. They got to you too. It's great you're doing well.' He smiled. 'Look, I think I'll get back. I haven't eaten a thing yet.'

'Me too,' said Vivien. 'I'm hungry.'

'Take a minute,' said Jack gently. 'I get the feeling Stevie might want to speak to you on your own.'

'You do?' Vivien asked Stevie.

'If you'll let me.'

'Mind how you go, Stevie,' said Jack, and he sounded so genuine, so thoroughly decent, Stevie felt a touch of awe. He wanted to be just like him.

'I got it all wrong with you,' said Stevie once he and Vivien were on their own. 'I got myself into a state. I don't know why. I guess I'll figure it out over time.'

'Stevie,' she said gently, 'what you felt for me wasn't real.'

'It felt real enough.'

'But you don't even really know me.'

She didn't sound that angry, just matter-of-fact, then she nodded comfortingly as if she saw him exactly for who he was: just a frightened boy trying hard to be a man.

'Goodbye, Stevie.'

As she made her way to the door, he stood straight, head up, chest out. 'Vivien,' he called out. She turned round. 'Good luck.'

'You too, Stevie,' she said. 'I mean it.'

He smiled weakly. He wanted to say this conversation

didn't wound him, that he was indifferent to her, but he wasn't. He was, however, relieved. He believed that by coming here he could finally put it all behind him.

He began his slow, steady walk away from Bloom's to catch his bus back home. Mum would be fretting, wanting to hear how he'd got on. Dad wouldn't say much, but he'd probably offer to shout him a beer at the pub before tea. Later, he'd get behind his drum kit again; tomorrow he'd search for work, and all the while he'd try to stop seeing Vivien's face everywhere he looked.

Jack was woken by Barry shaking his knee and telling him they had arrived. Groggily he moved in his seat. He must have fallen asleep within minutes of setting off from the restaurant. His suit felt warm and crumpled, his throat scratchy. He rubbed his eyes open and yawned. Then he glanced around and frowned. Barry was meant to be driving him straight home. 'Where are we?'

Barry was staring up through the windscreen, then back at a slip of paper in his hand. He looked a little confused, then said, 'This is right. It's over there.'

'Barry? What are we doing here?'

His question was lost on Barry, who was already out of the car. Hurrying around to the passenger seat, he helped Jack out, then walked ahead at a brisk pace, occasionally looking down at the paper in his hand until he stood in front of a squat, dark building where a couple of drunk-looking men sat playing cards on the steps.

'In here,' he said over his shoulder.

The smell of boiled green vegetables hit Jack first, followed by the faint sound of Adam Faith's 'Poor Me' and a snatch of a heated argument. When a baby cried out as they climbed the staircase to the first floor, it struck Jack that his body felt as heavy as it had done every time he'd climbed the stairs to his bedsit.

As Barry knocked on the door of Flat 7, Jack had to remind himself that this was not where he lived, that his days in that terrible bedsit were behind him and he'd never have to go back. He just didn't really believe it yet.

The door opened and Jack gasped when he saw the Jewish man he'd knocked unconscious at the rally. Staring at the man's long face and the white kappel sliding towards his fringe, he thought his heart might explode.

'Barry Klein.' Barry shook his hand, then smiled down at a little girl with brown ringlets peeking out from behind the man's legs. 'We spoke on the telephone.'

'Stefan Krakowski. Come in, gentlemen, please.'

Jack followed Barry down the hallway, past the coat stand in the corner and the shoes of different sizes pressed neatly against the wall. In a doorway at the end a timid-looking girl around Vivien's age pushed aside a curtain of coloured beads to peer out, then blushed and quickly disappeared.

In the living room two boys aged six or seven who were sprawled out on a checked rug playing snakes and ladders, stood up and moved their game to the other side of the room to allow Barry and Jack to sit down. Three children, thought Jack in amazement. Stefan couldn't be much older than twenty-five, a year or so older than him.

Jack sat forward. 'I didn't catch your surname.'

'Krakowski. Stefan Krakowski.'

Jack took out a cigarette. 'Do you mind?'

'Please.' Stefan sat down opposite them and called for his wife in a Slavic-sounding language. When she appeared with an ashtray, Jack saw that another child was on the way. He offered Stefan a cigarette but he shook his head.

'How are you, Stefan?'

'Very well.'

Barry glanced at Jack. 'See? I made a few calls. A nurse I know at the hospital told me he'd been brought in.' Barry shrugged. He had contacts all over.

Jack turned back to Stefan. 'Did ...' He faltered. 'Did I hurt you badly?'

'Not so much. A little concussion. It looked worse than it was.'

'I've thought about you a lot.' Jack's voice broke. 'I'm sorry. I didn't mean to hit you so hard.' Jack kept turning the brim of his trilby in his hands. He was shaking now and could hardly breathe. He was back at the rally, punching the man, then he was climbing back onto the platform and into the lorry. He remembered congratulating everyone but thinking only of the man lying on the ground.

'I was not hurt for long,' said Stefan, adding, 'anyway, I should thank you.'

'Why?' Jack stubbed out his cigarette and took a cup of tea from Stefan's wife. 'I put you in hospital.'

'My parents and I survived Auschwitz,' said Stefan. 'You did what you had to do.'

The saucer shook so much in Jack's hands, he had to put the cup on a side table.

'And how are you, sir?' Stefan leaned towards him while Jack looked at the floor. He didn't trust himself to speak.

Stefan sat back and sipped his tea. 'Sometimes there are no words.'

They silently watched Stefan's wife place a sponge cake on the lace doily at the far end of the table near the fireplace, then return with a cake knife and a stack of plates. The boys had forgotten their game. Creeping close to the table, they had begun to whisper excitedly about the cake.

Jack was unbearably hot. As he loosened the top two buttons of his shirt, the pretty girl with ringlets edged towards him, and as she clutched her skirt hem in her fist like

293

Vivien had done that day in the guest house, he realised he was crying.

He held his arm across his face but he could hear the children being ushered gently out of the room, the door shutting, then Stefan patting his back and saying, 'You're among friends here, sir, you're among friends,' and then Jack was crying so hard he thought he might never be able to stop.

29

Alan had given Barb her ring and the rabbi was about to recite the Sheva B'rachot when a shower of tiny hailstones on the roof's glass square cast the room in a sombre grey and made the crystal slithers on the chandelier tremble. There was a collective titter, but as the rabbi carried on Vivien held Jack's hand and strained forward to glimpse Alan's serious, loving expression. He seemed nervous of getting anything wrong, whereas Barb seemed to find it funny that it had just hailed for the first time that year, and that the train of her dress had got caught in the door.

Vivien had never seen a more stunning bride, and she was thrilled to have played her part. It was hard staying focused in such a chaotic household where the doorbell rang constantly and the bridesmaids shrieked endlessly and in unison, but it had been worth it. She was proud of Barb's elegant hairdo, and the hairpiece was a special touch. And she loved Barb's simple ivory silk dress. She couldn't wait to get a closer look at the twelve pearl buttons that ran down the spine and the lace trim on the three-quarter-length sleeves.

The other girls from Oscar's were sitting together on the opposite side of the chuppah, so heavily absorbed in the service Vivien had barely exchanged glances with them. With the exception of Marcia, she guessed this might be their first time in shul. She looked around, taking in the beautiful old synagogue with the candelabra hanging from the ceiling and the glitter of lights, and tried to imagine their reaction. They would enjoy it, she felt. They would appreciate the splendour of the place, the warmth and humour of the rabbi. But they would never feel as moved as she was by a shul's solid presence. It embraced her every time, reminding her that it had been there for her all along.

Now both Alan and Barb were giggling. Alan raised his foot, then brought it down on the glass. It smashed, the ceremony was over and shouts of '*Mazel Tov*' filled the room.

'Oh, it's wonderful, isn't it?' The woman next to Vivien, with a cigarette-hoarse voice and heavily rouged cheeks, shook her head. 'It's always so wonderful.'

'It is,' said Vivien, stealing a glance at Jack. As Barb hugged each of her parents in turn, Vivien thought of how her own dad would have loved to have given her away in their shul back home. He would have spent months meticulously planning the day and behaved exactly like Barb's dad, who was making his way around the congregation, openly crying as he shook people's hands and accepted their blessings.

Once again Vivien longed for Dad to be there with her. Yet for the first time since his death, her longing for him felt different. Less overwhelming, as if it was starting to break away from the main part of her and she might be able to distance herself from it. She pictured him in the photo she loved, standing with the rabbi and the cantor, and she heard a voice in her head starting to say goodbye. She wanted to run after that longing, chase it back and hold it tight, but she didn't. She closed her eyes and quietly let go.

Some of the guests were already squiffy. At the reception in the small second-floor function room off Dalston Road, everyone had been handed a glass of champagne on arrival, but many had already moved on to the potent gin punch.

Vivien scanned Jack's face, automatically looking for tell-tale signs of exhaustion. She must have glanced up one too many times because he bent down and kissed her crown.

'I'm fine,' he whispered. 'Stop worrying.'

'I'm not.' She really wasn't; she'd just got used to fussing. And she probably did less of that every week because she could see him inching back towards his old self. He didn't fly off the handle unexpectedly or change his mind about everything. She could tease him. He was gentle with his mum. Occasionally she caught him glancing around nervously when they were out, and he insisted they went everywhere by taxi and not public transport, but for the most part whatever had engulfed him was leaving. He seemed renewed, full of vigour and thinking about their future.

Marcia whispered in Vivien's ear, 'What a dreamboat.' She patted down a curl on her cheek. 'And you don't look so shabby yourself.'

Vivien blushed and looked down at her scoop-neck pink satin dress, an unusual choice but one that Jack in particular appreciated.

'Maeve did you proud,' Marcia added, and pointed to Vivien's red-tinted flickup. 'Very chic.'

'Thank you,' smiled Vivien, but was pleased when Lydia appeared and dragged Marcia away, because Marcia could spend all night dissecting everyone's appearance.

Chrissie, whose green floaty dress was ever so slightly see-through, leaned in and nodded her approval, then said, 'He's so nice,' and sighed. Vivien blushed again and swirled the punch around her glass.

'Have you ever?' said Maeve. She and Deirdre had just returned clutching a fresh round of drinks. 'A man older than my grandad pinched my bum on the way to the bar.'

'We saw the menu,' said Deirdre. 'Tomato soup. Chicken, potato kugel and peas. Lokshen pudding.' She frowned. 'And something else, but I can't remember what.'

'And the cake!' Maeve handed Vivien her drink. 'The bloody cake is this high.' She used her arms to gesture a ridiculous height. 'Madame Floris did her proud. I don't know what sort of knife is gonna cut through that.'

'This is a smashing bit of cloth, Jack.' Maeve ran her hand down the arm of Jack's suit jacket. 'You'll have to tell Mick where you bought it when he gets back from the loo.'

'I got it in Rome.'

'Rome!' Maeve's eyebrows shot up. 'What I'd give to go to Rome. Not that I ever will. Mick doesn't believe in flying. I keep saying, what's there to believe in? It's not a religion.'

'You'll have to take Vivien there on the honeymoon,' said Chrissie sweetly.

'Good idea,' said Jack. 'She'd love it.'

'Show us again.' Lydia pulled on Vivien's left hand to coo admiringly at the diamond engagement ring Jack had presented to her the week before. Vivien wallowed in the fuss the girls made of her news. She'd never been so happy, so sure. Why bother being reserved about it?

'It's just beautiful,' Lydia said to Jack, sighing. 'So elegant.'

'Isn't it,' said Chrissie dreamily.

'How are we all?' Barb descended on them, wearing a huge sunny smile. The girls tripped over each other to compliment her dress and the beautiful, moving ceremony, and she kept thanking them in a voice that sounded genuinely elated.

'We're thrilled that you're well enough to be here,' she said to Jack.

'Thank you,' he said. 'It's great to be here. We're having a lot of fun.'

'Where's Alan?' said Marcia. 'I've not congratulated him yet.'

Barb looked around, puzzled. 'I don't know. I should probably go find my –' she paused theatrically '– husband.' The girls clapped, Lydia whistled and swarms of people parted for Barb as she swept through them.

The station bar was warm and smelled of bacon and rain. While Vivien stood sipping her espresso at the end of the counter nearest the window, people kept coming in, shaking their umbrellas out of the door and commenting on the weather. She didn't engage with them as some of the other customers did. She felt quiet. She hadn't felt like this in the taxi – she'd been giggly and expectant, her head on Jack's shoulder, her hand on his thigh – but there was something sobering about being back at the station, staring out at the trains on the platforms. Last time she was here she had seen Barry instead of Jack.

The overhead lights flickered off, then back on, and everyone around her roared and cheered. She smiled. A room of strangers united by the weather.

As she fumbled in her bag for a tissue, her hand came upon the letter Jack had sent her dad, and she paused before reading it again. It was strange to picture herself all those months ago. Her slow, cautious walk off the train onto the platform; her first sleepless night in strange lodgings, dogged by fear; discovering the address for Jack was useless. She couldn't have guessed how her future would work out.

A man flung open the door and stamped the rain from his shoes. When he leaned down to remove a wet leaf, she pictured Dad wiping the soles of his shoes every time he came into the house. She sighed, bracing herself again for the coming days, when she would be packing up the remainder of his belongings. This was something she had to do before she and Jack could move forward into the future. But at least Jack was going with her. He would stop her burying herself in Dad's suits and crying as she folded down the arms on his shirts. He would gently tease photos and records and books from her clutch and help her decide which possessions to save and eventually bring back to London for their first home together.

Esther would also help. She'd promised to telephone Vivien daily, and when they were ready she would help them to make plans for an engagement party. Jack wasn't as happy with this – he worried his mother might be too much for Vivien – but she saw things differently. She could never have too many people around her, reminding her to reach forward, not back.

A toddler in a pink coat and wellington boots ran past the window on wobbly legs. A man charged along behind her, reached forward and caught her. He bent down on one knee, and from his severe expression Vivien could see he was telling her she mustn't run off like that.

Vivien had done that once. Run off in the park and hidden behind a blackberry bush. When Dad had found her, she was sure he'd scold her, but he just whispered her name lovingly and rocked her against him. She was remembering how good it felt to have his arms around her, keeping her safe, when the door opened and Jack walked in, still a little cautious without his stick.

'Done.' He slapped the tickets down on the bar top. 'We're on our way.'

In his grey suit with the colour back in his cheeks, he looked as handsome as he had done the first time they met.

'Whisky, please,' Jack asked the bartender. 'Anything else, sweetheart?'

She shook her head. It gave her such pleasure to hear the worry gone from his voice. And he looked so contented and free, his head held high. Jack Morris had returned. He wasn't someone else any more.

Jack drank his whisky in one go and pushed the empty glass away. He threw down some change, checked his watch, then put his big firm hand on the back of her neck and turned her face towards him for a kiss. Now she had someone else to run after her. They would keep each other safe. Together they would carve out new memories, make their own story.

'Ready?'

She nodded, and when she let him go he picked up both their suitcases and headed for the door. As she gathered up her coat and hat, the room fell into grainy darkness again and stayed that way. A few people clapped. The bartender began to light candles and line them up along the bar. There was more laughter, then someone ran their fingers over the piano keys and began singing in a sweet, gentle voice.

Jack pushed his shoulder against the door to keep it open for her. She smiled and went through it, tilting her face towards the bright, steady light.

Author's Note

Ridley Road is a work of fiction inspired by true events. I read numerous books and articles, consulted newspaper archives, watched footage and interviewed people.

However, I frequently distanced myself from the truth in order to serve the story. I used reported information about Colin Jordan and the National Socialist Movement (NSM) but altered various details and events. The anti-fascist organisation, the 62 Group, did form in response to the NSM rally in Trafalgar Square on 1 July 1962, but the members of the Group, along with every other character, are born from my imagination. Again, for the purposes of dramatic tension, I changed details regarding the Group's activities.

Ultimately, *Ridley Road*, and the world it depicts, is a story I carried around in my head for some time before it found its way on to the page.

Acknowledgements

While writing *Ridley Road* I drew on information from different sources, but I found these books and articles especially useful: 'The Jewish Community and the Fight Against Fascism: The Defence Debate 1946–1950' and 'The Fighting Sixties', two features by Steve Silver for *Searchlight* magazine; *Soho Night & Day*, with text by Frank Norman and photographs by Jeffrey Bernard; the chapter '1960s: The war on the streets' by Gerry Gable in *Searchlight*'s *From Cable Street to Oldham: 70 Years of Community Resistance*, and Gerry Gable's obituary of Colin Jordan in the *Guardian; The Fifties and Sixties: A Lifestyle Revolution* by Miriam Akhtar and Steve Humphries; and Morris Beckman's *The 43 Group*. I found David Herman's documentary *62* for If Not Us Films enlightening and I gleaned key details about Colin Jordan from *The Times* online archives. The staff at Hackney Archives and City of Westminster Archives Centre were always very helpful.

Huge thanks, as ever, to my fantastic agent Rowan Lawton and her colleagues at Furniss Lawton, and to my brilliant, insightful editor Kirsty Dunseath and her team at W&N, particularly Jennifer Kerslake and Sophie Buchan. They have all contributed more than I could have expected.

I could not have written this novel without help from researcher and journalist Steve Silver. His knowledge of the post-war anti-fascist movement is second to none and his tireless support, patience and friendship has been invaluable.

Like most writers, I'm exceptionally grateful to my readers for their beady eyes and constructive criticism: Kefi Chadwick, Alex Cooke, Beverley Etkin and Rachel Grant.

I am also thankful to Geoffrey and Carol Bell, Patricia O'Brien, Alan Dein, Carlton Dixon, Monty Goldman, Barrie Greene at Back In The Day Walks, Gilad Hayeem, Daniel Hersheson, Clint Hough at sixtiescity.net, Rob Kraitt, Matthew McAllester, Beth Miller, Ed Platt, Alvin and Jennifer Portman, and Annie Weinstein for sharing their anecdotes or answering my many questions.

Thanks to Julie Bargh and Felicity Criddle for providing wisdom along the way.

I am grateful to my sisters Sara and Claire for their support, and I'm particularly indebted to my parents, Stanley and Isabel, for their big-hearted unconditional love and constant encouragement.

A huge cheer for my wonderful son Samuel, born between drafts two and three, who continues to give me so much joy.

And finally, Jonny; a first class reader and writer whose excellent critiques played an essential part in shaping this novel. Most of all, I want to thank him for his love and for always making me laugh.

Ridley Road

READING GROUP NOTES

In Conversation with Jo Bloom

What inspired you to write *Ridley Road*?

A few years ago, at a funeral, I met an elderly man from east London. He had been an active anti-fascist all his life, and when he mentioned the 62 Group, a Jewish organisation which formed in 1962 to confront a resurgence of fascism in London, I knew I had to find a way to tell the Group's story. How, less than twenty years after the end of the Second World War, British fascism had reared up again. Only now it was opposed by members of the 62 Group, who took matters into their own hands and spent the Sixties and beyond fighting fascism on the streets.

How much research did you have to do for the novel, and did you find it difficult to balance truth and imagination?

I did a lot of research, but I was lucky to be guided by my friend and researcher Steve Silver. Steve had been an editor at Searchlight, the anti-fascist organisation, and had worked closely with members of the 62 Group. He provided me with a lot of background information, and we had regular discussions about plot points, because it mattered to me that I kept true to the spirit of the 62 Group and wrote a credible tale. Ultimately, though, I always kept in mind that I was writing fiction. The research had to serve my imagined world.

London is described so evocatively throughout the novel; at times I felt that I was wandering the streets with Vivien. How well did you know London before writing *Ridley Road*? Did you spend time visiting different parts of the city to get a feel for the people who lived and worked there?

I grew up in London, which helped, but I also visited photo archives and watched lots of footage and films about London – particularly Soho and Hackney – from around that period. Things have changed so much that it was essential for me to immerse myself in lots of visuals to try and capture a feel for the time.

What do you enjoy most about the writing process?

I love editing. I find writing the first draft particularly torturous, but once I have something to wrestle with, I feel a lot more excited. It's thrilling to see a story take shape.

Sadly, it seems that far-right attitudes still exist today and anti-Semitic incidents appear to be on the rise. What reaction have you had to your novel from within the Jewish community?

A lot of readers in the Jewish community have said that the story at the heart of *Ridley Road* is as relevant now as it was then. This is obviously sad to recognise, but I am proud to have shed light on a relatively unknown slice of Jewish history.

If you could live in another era, would it be the Sixties?

Absolutely! *Mad Men* has cemented my passion for Sixties style, so I'm ready whenever you want to send me off in the time machine …

Do you ever think about what the future holds for Vivien and Jack? Do they live happily ever after?

I'd like to think so. I vaguely imagine that Jack writes non-fiction books or has gone into politics, Vivien has opened up her own salon and they have had lots of children who also make bold decisions with their lives . . .

Who are your favourite writers and who influences your writing?

I consistently return to Alice Munro's stories, but I also love William Trevor, Colm Tóibín, Elizabeth Strout, Sarah Waters, Raymond Carver, Andre Dubus and Richard Yates.

What are you working on now?

My next novel. It's set in London in the mid-to-late Fifties and focuses on two main characters, Aud and Harry, who are in their early twenties. I love research, so it's been fun to learn about another decade. But doing research is easier than writing, so I need to watch that I don't use it as a means of procrastination.

Discussion Points

- Discuss the balance between love and duty in the novel.

- Vivien has just lost her father when she decides to head to London to find Jack. Do you think she's running away from her grief?

- What do you find most exciting about Jo Bloom's depiction of London in the 1960s?

- Do you see *Ridley Road* as a coming-of-age novel? How naive is Vivien when she first arrives in London? How does she change?

- How far were you aware of Colin Jordan and the rise of fascism in post-war London before reading the book? Had you heard of the 62 Group or the 43 Group? Has your experience of reading *Ridley Road* changed your ideas about ethnic, racial and religious differences?

- What role does friendship play in the novel?

- Is Jack a good man? Do you think there's a moral distinction between keeping secrets and telling lies? How could he have handled his relationship with Vivien differently?

- Examine how Jo Bloom creates tension and suspense in the novel.

- Can you sympathise with how Stevie acted? Do you think Vivien treats him fairly?

- Discuss Jack's relationship with little Henry. Do you think his letter of farewell will make any difference to the boy's views and behaviour as he grows up? Is *Ridley Road* a hopeful book?

- How well can you know someone really? Do you think it's possible to share everything, or will there always be secrets, even between lovers?

Sounds of the Sixties:
Jo Bloom's *Ridley Road* Playlist

- Helen Shapiro 'Walkin' Back to Happiness'
- Billy Fury 'Halfway to Paradise'
- Stan Getz and Charlie Byrd 'Desafinado'
- Ray Charles 'I Can't Stop Loving You'
- Johnny Kidd & the Pirates 'Shakin' All Over'
- Marty Wilde 'Jezebel'
- Elvis Presley 'Surrender'
- Adam Faith 'Poor Me'
- Acker Bilk 'Stranger on the Shore'
- Juliette Gréco 'Jean de la Providence de Dieu'
- Roy Orbison 'Dream Baby'
- Neil Sedaka 'Breaking Up Is Hard to Do'
- Cliff Richard 'We Say Yeah'

Further Reading

An Education by Lynn Barber

The Country Girls by Edna O'Brien

Brooklyn by Colm Tóibín

Fallout by Sadie Jones

Jubilee by Shelley Harris

Call the Midwife by Jennifer Worth

The Hand That First Held Mine by Maggie O'Farrell

For literary discussion, author insight,
book news, exclusive content,
recipes and giveaways, visit the
Weidenfeld & Nicolson blog and
sign up for the newsletter at:

www.wnblog.co.uk

For breaking news, reviews and exclusive competitions
Follow us 🐦 @wnbooks